MARIËTTE WHITCOMB

DECEPTION

ISBN Paperback: 978-1-990988-61-5
ISBN eBook: 978-1-990988-62-2

This novel I dedicate firstly to every person who has been too ashamed to admit they had been sexually assaulted. Shame is never yours to carry, you survived. May you see yourself as a survivor and not a victim. That mental switch is important for your healing and recovery.

Secondly, this novel is dedicated to everyone who has struggled with infertility, and suffered the loss of a child. No one will ever understand your pain or longing. You're not alone.

One

Again, I found myself on an aeroplane. This time not scarred, broken or unbeknownst heading towards the abyss. I turned my head and stared at the man sitting next to me. This man I will protect not only to my dying breath but with my entire life. It's the least I can do after he had saved my life three times, in the literal sense.

In a single year our love, our life, had taught me that I can be – me. The real me. I can fight the war against the depravities of this world the socially acceptable way. Now, we spent our lives in the light, no longer hiding behind masks. With each other, we never needed masks, although it had brought us together and created an unbreakable bond. Forged in darkness, we are stronger together. No one knows me like he does. People suspected; he sees what I am capable of, just as I know his truth.

We had both come a long way since the first night we laid eyes on each other in a dark, decrepit parking structure.

Aidan removed his earphones and turned to face me. "Do you see anything you like?"

"Can you blame me for admiring the view?" He was a sight to behold even after hours spent on an aeroplane. Our first international vacation.

"You're not seated next to the window." He reached for my hand.

"Not the view I'm talking about." My eyes followed the movement of my hand being lifted to his mouth; the warmth of his lips still made me catch my breath. His eyes held mine, and I kissed the boyish grin from his face.

"Have you figured out where we are heading?"

Aidan had asked me if I trusted him two months before

1

the day of our departure. I said yes. I trust no one more than I trust him. He asked for my passport and gave it back to me at the airport.

"No, but I have my suspicions," I lied. Our flight connected in Singapore, we could have been heading anywhere.

"Patience, my love. Only a short layover and then we are off to our final destination."

"Can you please not say that while we are thousands of kilometres above solid earth?" I rubbed my palms on my thighs.

"What? Final destination? Your fear of flying is ridiculous, you do realise that?"

"I'm *not* afraid of flying." Afraid is not a strong enough word.

"Finley Duncan Williams, why do you keep rubbing your hands on your pants? Why do you grab my arm every time we hit slight turbulence? Why have you drunk three Walkers already?"

"Because the only Walker I want is unattainable. I'm not confessing to having a fear of flying, but do you know what would help me relax?"

"Watching a movie? Or do you want to badger me again with questions about where we are going?"

"Aidan, I love you more than I ever thought it possible to love anyone or anything and I will do anything and everything to make you happy."

"Here we go." He changed position to face me, resting his hand on my thigh after patting it three times.

"If you love me, really love me, you will help me become part of the mile-high club." Even at that altitude, porn-star Finley made an appearance. I never knew she existed, not until I met Aidan Walker. His ridiculous no-sex-sex-rule had driven me insane for a year. *The longest year of my life.*

"Aidan, it's not like we haven't done it. Come, help me forget I have no control if this plane goes down."

"Flying is the safest form of travel."

"Not the answer I was looking for, Doctor Walker."

"Woman, you." He reached for my face, running his thumb over my bottom lip as he brought my mouth to his. The kiss was abruptly ended by the overzealous stewardess asking if we wanted chicken or beef. *No option to devour Aidan?*

She handed us our meals, and I checked the time to destination for the umpteenth time since we departed Marcel, our home city. I was not giving up that easily, so I staggered my way back into the earlier conversation.

"Is that a no then? You don't love me enough to help me tick a box on my bucket list?" I pushed my bottom lip out and looked at him with my best puppy eyes. With no mirror on hand, I hoped it looked the way I intended and not like a sleep-deprived hooligan.

"What are you trying to do with your face?" Aidan roared with laughter while other passengers turned to look at us.

"This is my begging face." Maybe I should've practised *the face* in the onboard lavatory.

"You don't beg, you punch or shoot 'til you get what you want. Why can't you try to be patient? Yes, we made love, once, almost a year ago. I told you then it was mind-blowing, like we knew it would be, but I want to wait until we're married. Patience, Duncan."

"I warned you about calling me Duncan. Don't make me stab you with this knife." I waved the plastic utensil the stewardess had placed in front of me in his face.

"Oh woman, I know all your moves. It's great we train together as we not only get to spend time together, but it also means I'm familiar with *all* your moves. You can never fight me and win." Aidan was the master of Krav Maga; we often sparred, and he is as formidable as he is brilliant.

I ate my meal in silence and wondered what the cuisine would be like where we were heading. The stewardess cleared our plates, and I ordered another whiskey. Turbulence is not my friend. Aidan shook his head and reminded me I have him to be my most loved Walker.

He always will be, but I do love a good whiskey. "Where are we going?"

"Nice try."

"Give me a hint."

"Alright, Miss Williams, the adventure you're about to embark on, well, technically you're already on it, will be the best of your life. I promise your life will never be the same."

"That's not a hint smart ass. And for the record, the best adventure started a year ago." His stubble tickled my anxious hands, and I pulled his mouth to mine. Kissing him made my heart race more than bumps in the air.

Aidan, 1 – turbulence, 0.

He was right; it would forever be the best holiday, adventure, two weeks of my life.

Little did we know we were heading towards a bottomless pit. It had been there, waiting, since before we had met.

We checked in for our flight in Singapore. Only once we reached the boarding gate did I see where we were going – Hanoi, Vietnam. My excitement was audible to most of the other travellers in the departure terminal.

Vietnam had always been on the Finley bucket list and Aidan had remembered; I had only told him once, the night we met. His eidetic memory helps, but it also reminded me of how much he loved me; he listened when I spoke. What more could a woman want? Well, this one wanted many things but nothing more than this man. The one whose secret I will protect no matter the cost.

Vietnamese cold coffee, noodles, egg coffee, cyclos, more noodles and scooters everywhere – that's what I will remember of Hanoi. Aidan and I spent hours walking the streets of this enigmatic city, absorbing the culture, noises and smells.

To my surprise, this was the place where I felt the most beautiful, not because of how Aidan treated me or the things he said daily, but because to Vietnamese people a light complexion is beautiful, desirable even. I bought Lizzie a Hello

Kitty facemask, the same mask many of the women wear while driving or walking to protect their faces against the harshness of the sun.

I now knew we were in Vietnam, but still had no idea what our daily itinerary would be. Aidan kept it a secret, only informing me over breakfast, and my second cold coffee, what the day held.

After six days in Hanoi he asked me to pack because we were leaving for our next destination and would travel via helicopter. This is not the safest form of travel, and even less so when it's a helicopter that has been in service since a very unpopular war. I told him as much, but he told me it would be worth it, still not saying where the bird would take us.

"Welcome in Halong Bay," the pilot said as the bird settled on beloved soil. I do not enjoy flying. Aidan had held my hand throughout the flight, but my stomach still struggled to digest breakfast. How can a decorated soldier and previous warrior of darkness be afraid of flying? I had questioned my sanity the full forty-five minutes we were in the air.

"*Cam on.*" I thanked the pilot as we got out of the relic which should've been in a museum rather than still taking to the air.

Aidan had booked the Captain's View Terrace Suite for our two-night cruise through one of the most awe-inspiring places in the world. The colour of the water reminded me of Lizzie's eyes.

"You have out done yourself, Doctor Walker." Emerald water surrounded us as the boat departed.

For as long as I could remember I had wanted to see the limestone islands; the green water, the beauty which to this day leaves me breathless. In all my life, all my travels, I never saw anything as majestic as that place. It's a place of magic, mysticism, and you almost expect to see a descending dragon, as the name suggests.

"I have another surprise for you."

"Nothing will top this. Ever."

"You never know, I might have a few more in store for you during this trip. You need to hurry; you have a spa treatment in half an hour."

"Are you joining me?" I hoped as I wrapped my arms around him, breathing in his scent. My stomach no longer unstable from the flight, but fluttering as he took my face in his hands and dipped his mouth to mine. *Magic.*

"Is that a yes?" My eyes still closed.

"No, this is just for you. Maybe I will join you tomorrow, but today is all about you. Happy birthday, Finley." He hadn't forgotten. I had been wondering since he woke me with his lips on my neck.

"Will you still love me when I'm old and no longer beautiful?"

"You are old." My fist to his shoulder told him what I thought of his answer. "Monkey muffins, you will always be beautiful. Every time I see you, you still take my breath away."

"Monkey muffins? Is this the one you want to try out today?"

"No other nickname is fitting. I can't call you what the media used to." He smiled, danger flashed in his eyes.

"Then let's not do nicknames. I find it adolescent, and Aidan is the most beautiful name, so why call you anything else?"

"You need to hurry; the spa is next to reception. I'll wait here for you. I'll unpack and shower. We can go for a drink on the sundeck when you get back." He pulled me against him and kissed me as if he would never kiss me again.

I forced my lips from his. "I don't have to go for a massage now. Did you take the coin from the dresser when we left Hanoi?"

His laughter filled every space in the cabin, and my being. "Go, Finley, I will be waiting for you. Enjoy, my love." He pushed me towards the door.

"My love? That's a nickname." I winked, reaching for the doorknob.

"No, it's not, you are my love, my life, my future. Hush now and go."

We had both come so far, shutting the gates on darkness. If I had known what waited for us in Marcel, I would have made him stay in Vietnam forever. Our dreams and worst fears were about to collide, and we never saw it coming. Life does not give you a heads-up, only sucker punches.

Two

"Miss, this for you. Please open." The spa therapist handed me a gift bag. I would have opened it in our cabin had I not noticed the tremble of her hand as she held it towards me. During the massage, her hands had been strong and steady. *What's wrong here?*

"*Cam on.*" I took the bag and pulled out a small jewellery box. My hands started shaking as I opened it, my heart raced all over the ship. The note inside the small box; I ran back to the cabin.

The cabin door slammed against the wall, my hands still unsteady. "Aidan?"

He walked in from the deck, mischief in his blue eyes. "Yes?"

"Ask me." My heart still raced.

He took the box from my hand, dimples playing under his light stubble, and bent down on one knee. "Finley, I won't-say-your-full-name, Williams, will you be my orca?"

"Try again, Doctor Walker."

"Finley, will you be my wife?" He slipped the ring on my ring finger and it was perfect, the ring, the fit, the moment, the setting, the way he asked, him. I pulled him to his feet and wrapped my arms around his neck. "Try again, Miss Williams."

"Aidan, no-middle-name, Walker, I want nothing more than to be your wife. Yes!" I kissed my fiancé until my chin burned from his stubble, just as it had the first time we kissed. Halong Bay turned out to be better than I ever dreamed it would.

My fiancé and I kayaked on calm waters, swam at Titov Island, dined under the stars, and did Tai Chi as the sun rose over limestone pillars rising out of calm green water.

The next stop on our itinerary had still not been shared

with the soon-to-be Mrs Williams-Walker.

To reach our next and last destination, we had to travel by taxi from Halong Bay to Haiphong, and yet another flight, this time to Danang. Aidan promised it was not in the ancient metal bird, and to my surprise I was excited to get onto the red and yellow aeroplane. Not an airbus, but at least not ancient; the more engines the better, no rotors.

Aidan hadn't lied when he said we would stay in the most beautiful resort in the world. It had received this accolade a few years earlier by a travel and tourism organisation. If I could have stayed there for the rest of my life I would have. The lush vegetation, the monkeys, the unspoiled private beach.

"Aidan, come look at this bathroom. If you think we had fun at The Marcella, this will blow your mind." The shower took me a while to find; the head was built into the ceiling next to the bath, and the full-length window provided glorious views over the bay.

"I might just join you for every shower, or just stand here and watch you." He washed his hands smiling at my reflection in the mirror.

"Sure, like you have ever been able to allow me to shower in peace."

"If it's peace you want it's peace you will have."

"Don't you dare, you know why I fell in love with you."

"Because you met me in a bar where people hooked up for one-night stands?"

"Do you forget why I was there?" I had not thought of the reason I was in Alias for almost a year, but I told Aidan the truth about what had led me to that place, every detail, and still he stayed with me. The police had still not arrested anyone for the murder of that vile thing, the man who had raped my sister. It led to Aidan and I meeting when I went to cancel my sister and I's memberships, the best thing to ever come out of that place.

"Are you ready for dinner?" Aidan pressed his lips to my

forehead as if he knew I was remembering.

"Can we not stay here? It's hot and humid outside and we need to make sure this shower works." It was a heat I had experienced nowhere else, and not just the climate. Marcel has a subtropical climate, but when the humidity gets too much I escape to my lake house.

"No, we are going for dinner down at the bar on the beach and early to bed."

"Yes please." I bit my lower lip.

"We are not married yet, patience my orca."

"You have put a ring on it, and we vowed to keep each other safe a year ago. The commitment we made is binding, just like marriage." Negotiator Fin was no match for hostage-taker Aidan. I pushed him down on the bed, his skin appearing darker on the white linen. The sun loved him; loved me too after a day of tinting me lobster red.

"Yes and no. Our promise is definitely not something most people ever make, but I promise you we won't be engaged long. I don't believe in long engagements."

I never asked him about his first wife, knowing what losing her and their son did to him. We both came to the relationship with baggage, but the baggage was left on the deck of my lake house when we had committed to putting our hunting days behind us and focused on our future.

The following morning, I found Aidan in our private pool. It wasn't even 0700 hours yet and it was already scorching; perhaps the sight of his wet body made it hotter...the man is gorgeous and brilliant, which makes him even more attractive. The only person I have ever met with an IQ higher than my sister's.

"Beautiful view." I took off my clothes and got into the pool with him. "Are you up for a game of Marco Polo?"

He wrapped his arms around me and gave me my good morning kiss. "Maybe later, we need to go for breakfast; I need a cold coffee. I hope we can sit outside. Ever since I found this place on the internet, I've wanted to sit in one of the Non-La hat-inspired booths."

Two cold coffees did nothing to cool either of us, but the view was well worth the sweat running down my back. The rest of the morning we spent at the beach, and after lunch Aidan received a phone call. The first since we had left for Vietnam. No one knew where we were; they just knew we were going away, and that Aidan had kept the destination a surprise.

"Who was that?" I reached for his hand when he returned.

"The hospital, the doctor standing in for me had a question about one of my patients." I didn't believe him. "We need to head back to our suite, this heat is getting to me. Maybe we can take a nap while we wait for the sun to set. Tomorrow we are going to Hoi An."

"That's a first."

"What is?"

"This whole trip you only told me what you have planned the morning of, not the day before. What's up?"

"Nothing, just wanted to talk to you about Hoi An. I believe it will be the highlight of the trip."

"Better than getting engaged?" I held my hand up to show him the rock he had marked me with. Well, it's better than being marked with pee, and much prettier. I might not be made of sugar and spice, but I still appreciate something nice. *Nice? Understatement of the century.*

"Do you like it?" He pressed his lips to my rock-bearing hand.

"I love it almost as much as I love you, and this adventure."

He smiled and pushed the sunglasses from his eyes, quickly returning them after a few squints. "My parents bought this diamond years ago for my future wife."

I yanked my hand from his. "This was your first wife's ring?" I reached to pull it off my finger.

"No. Finley, do you really think I would do that?" He took both my hands as we sat facing each other on the sun loungers, hell sand burning the soles of our feet.

"They never wanted her to have it, *refused* would be a better word. My parents never thought she was the right woman for me, but the first time they met you my father pulled me aside and said he would give me the diamond as soon as I'm ready to propose. Both my father and mother knew from the moment they saw you that we would spend our lives together."

"I really did not want to have to throw it in the ocean."

"Why would you throw something that costs as much as your SUV in the ocean?"

"What? Is it that expensive?"

"It's a blue diamond, do you have any idea how rare they are? Ironic."

"What's ironic?" I saw the diamond in a whole new light.

"The diamond is the same colour as your eyes, and the chances of us finding each other were just as rare." He pulled me to my feet and told me we had to get back to the suite.

We didn't take a nap, but we used the coin. Afterwards, we lay on the oversized bed and spoke about where we would live after getting married. Maybe it was time for us to move into a new place and start anew. Aidan left to shower, and I kept touching the diamond. *Precious.*

"Fin, you need to go shower. After you're done, look in the closet, there is something for you. Put it on and meet me at the beach in an hour. I have already arranged for the driver to be here and instructed him on where to take you." Aidan slapped my bum as he walked past me into the walk-in closet.

"What?"

"Do you trust me?" His boyish grin still made my legs jelly. With the boulder on my hand, I would have tipped left.

"Don't ask dumb questions, you know I trust you more than anyone in this world. Well, a tad more than I trust Lizzie."

"Shower. Get dressed, and come to the beach. I will meet you down there. But you need to go shower now. You can't be late."

I obeyed, and by the time I finished showering – very difficult to do when your hands don't want to follow cues from your brain – Aidan had left. In the closet hung a clothing bag I had not seen before. A note pinned to the bag read 'Wear me'. I removed the bag from the closet, placed it on the bed, and pulled the zipper down.

A floor-length, off-white satin dress came out of the bag. It was backless, and identical to the black dress I had worn to Ashley and Kyle's wedding. The dress Aidan had loved. A million thoughts created a mosh pit in my mind until only one was left standing. My lungs drew air in, but didn't want to let go.

I don't think I have ever dressed, blow-dried my hair, or did my make-up so fast. The dress fit as if it had been made for me. As I stood looking at mirror Fin, heart drumming to a heavy metal rhythm, there was a knock on the door.

The driver met me at the door and refused to say where we were heading, I asked more than once. After my third attempt he simply shook his head.

We rounded the last corner and there she stood. I bit my tongue so as not to scream her name, and my chariot, a golf cart, slowed down. I considered leaping from the back and taking over from the driver. Her being there added to the fairy tale.

I thanked the driver and rushed to my sister who clutched a bouquet. "Lizzie, what are you doing here?"

"Hello, Finley, lovely to see you, too." She kissed my cheek.

"Hello, Lizzie, what are you doing here?" Every part of me trembled as she handed me the bouquet of orchids. My favourite flowers.

"Let's go, you don't want to be late."

If only I could have seen her eyes, then I would have known what awaited me on the beach. In the reflection of her sunglasses I only saw myself. Lizzie took my hand and led me towards the beach. Behind us the sun was setting over the mountain – Monkey Mountain.

"Okay, but you need to tell..." Mid-sentence it struck me.

"Wait here for the music to start, I will wait for you there. Unless you want me to walk with you."

I shook my head.

Our song filled my ears, the corners of my once darkened soul. I drew a deep breath and smiled a smile my face had never been capable of before as I made my way towards my fiancé. "Aidan?"

"I told you, you wouldn't have to wait long." He came closer for a kiss, but pulled back, resuming his position and asked the stranger to begin.

The only part I can remember was when the heavily accented man said Aidan can kiss his wife, which he did.

Three

"Are you going to tell me what happened when you got back to your suite?" Lizzie took a sip of cold coffee, smiled, and returned the glass to the table.

Aidan and Eli dished food on the other end of the restaurant. I had expected Lizzie to ask the first time we were alone; she never understood our decision to wait.

"I will not befoul my marital bed by telling you what happened between my husband and myself last night." Wow! It was worth the wait and then some.

"Come on Fin, just tell me if it was worth waiting?"

"What do you think? We love each other, and Liz look at him. I swear he's the most beautiful, intelligent, and awe-inspiring man in the world." I took a sip of my newfound favourite coffee, and then another, hoping the men would return before she could ask more questions. No such luck.

"I still find it strange with your body count. You took what you wanted, when you wanted, and never took names or numbers. If I remember correctly, you need five hands to tally your score."

Not about to tell her the carcass count was closer to ten hands, but she didn't know about the life I had given up a year before. To my sister, I simply got around at university, she didn't know about the time I spent in the abyss.

"Lizzie, we aren't children anymore, and with Aidan I realised there is more to a relationship than just sex. And it's not like we didn't fool around, you know about the coin flipping."

She opened her mouth but kept the thought to herself. "Have you decided where you are going to live?" Lizzie asked instead, spreading butter over her croissant.

"We'll stay at my place until we find a home, we both want a property with beach access, but in the current market it's scarcer than blue diamonds."

"Have you spoken to Uncle Tom? Does he know you got married?"

"No. I'm also not going to tell him unless I see him."

Our relationship had never been the same after he threatened and tried to punch Aidan. I hated not being close to my godfather anymore, but he had forced my hand. I will always choose Aidan.

"We should throw you a party when we are back in Marcel. Ashley is going to be upset she wasn't here for the wedding."

"Eloping without even knowing it is exactly what I always wanted, but we will have to get married once we are back for legal reasons."

"How did Aidan take it when you told him about Williams-hyphen-Walker?"

Why were the men taking so long? I reached for my coffee and took a couple of sips. *Brain freeze.*

"You didn't tell him, did you?" Lizzie's laughter reached Aidan and Eli and they turned to look at us. I smiled and waved.

"No, we haven't had time to talk."

Lizzie nodded and leaned back in her chair. "You're making up for lost time."

The men rejoined us, and as Aidan sat down he whispered something to me. I gave my husband my good morning kiss. Didn't matter that the restaurant was full of people, we were married and on our honeymoon. With my sister and her fiancé. Less awkward than one would think.

"Are the next few days our honeymoon?" I asked.

"Do you really think I would invite Liz and Eli to join us on our honeymoon?" Aidan shook his head and took the knife from my hand, bringing my hand to his mouth. "We are going on our honeymoon in a few weeks, why do you think I had your passport for so long?"

Eli smiled. "After what you two have been through since your parents died and everything else that has happened, we wanted you to spend some time together. We have heard so much about what you two got up to when you travelled that we thought it would do you good. And we wanted to see both of you drunk and hope to be the hotties you bag." Eli and Aidan both started laughing.

I love Lizzie, but when she's intoxicated she has a tendency to either turn into a horny teenage girl or brag about our youth. There were many tales from our youth I hoped to keep in the past.

"Thank you both. And thank you for your help with the wedding arrangements." I stood and walked to Lizzie and Eli, giving them each a hug.

"What are we doing today?" Eli's Israeli accent less heavy than when we had first met.

Aidan finished chewing and drank all of his coffee, wiping the condensation from the glass on his napkin and placing the napkin next to his food-stained plate. He knew I hated it when he took long to answer, but I let him be this morning. Too in love and happy to care that he tried to play on my nerves.

"We are going to Hoi An and we are going to have the best dinner ever. Dress comfortably, we are going to walk a lot and stay in Hoi An until after dinner." I loved how in charge he was. "Please excuse myself and my wife, we need to change and will meet you at reception in an hour. I will arrange a taxi for us."

I squeezed his hand and Aidan tried not to smile as he said, "Make that an hour and a half. Come, wife."

I did as my husband commanded.

Hoi An – lanterns, Japanese Red Bridge, yet more noodles, and rows of streets with tiny shops. More scooters. Crossing the Red Bridge felt like walking into another world. There were lanterns overhead which made colourful streaks on the streets and old buildings at night. We only saw the true beauty during our Vespa foodie tour that night for dinner. We were driven from one restaurant to the next, eating delicious signature dishes and drinking Bia Hoi, a local beer. All four of us were tipsy and laughing so hard that a few of us nearly fell from the back of the Vespas as the drivers manoeuvred through people down the streets. It rained; we were soaked, we were happy. We did the tour twice while we were in Danang and it was even more fun the second time, or maybe we just drank more. We could have stayed there forever. *Could've, would've, should've.*

Aidan and I left two days before Eli and Lizzie. Only when we landed in Singapore did I switch my mobile phone on, something to do to kill the time while we waited for our flight to Marcel.

I had five missed calls, three from Tom and two from Ashley. Numerous text messages kept coming through. I didn't have the emotional energy to read them. Not in the mood to speak to Tom, I phoned Ashley.

"Finley, where are you?" Hope made noises in the background. Incoherent speech but not bad for an almost two-year-old.

"Hello, Ashley. What's going on? Is Hope okay?"

"Where are you? I've been trying to get hold of you for the past two days."

"Aidan and I were in Vietnam. We're in Singapore now waiting for our flight to Marcel. I need to tell you something."

"Fin, we found Ari. He's in hospital."

"What do you mean you *found* him?" I didn't know he was missing, or that anyone was looking for him. We had not spoken since the day he left to wage his own war against a ring of human traffickers. Well, he had sent me a message and the video link which led me to the thing that did what it did to my Lizzie.

"He's not in good shape. Something happened to him, but he has no recollection. He has been asking for you since he woke up earlier today. Fin, you need to get to the hospital as soon as you land. You might be our best chance of finding out what happened, and who did this to him."

"Ashley—" Hope started crying in the background.

"I need to take care of my daughter, just call me when you land. I will meet you at Marcel General." She hung up before I could tell her.

Aidan pulled me into his arms, my hands unsteady against his chest. "What's going on?"

"I don't know, Ashley just said they found Ari. I need to phone Eli." Aidan and I had never discussed Ari or the fact that we had once been involved.

"Phone Eli. I will talk to the airline and see if I can get them tickets for today or the earliest flight tomorrow, even if they have to fly via Hong Kong."

"Thank you."

We should've stayed in Singapore.

Four

Aidan was able to book Eli and Lizzie on a flight via Hong Kong; they arrived seven hours after our flight landed in Marcel. During our flight from Singapore, I told him about Ari, how we met when he had been my Krav Maga instructor which led to Eli coming into Lizzie and my lives. I admitted to Aidan that Ari and my relationship had been intimate and that it had been brief as he had left because of his own work. Aidan asked if I had loved Ari. I explained what he had meant to me at a time when my body could only remember the horrors done to it during the war, and that it was good for me to reclaim power over that part of my body.

Kyle met us at the airport and took me to Marcel General. After he dropped me off, he took Aidan home to get us a vehicle. We were home.

The dream forever over.

Ashley waited for me in the foyer and took me straight to Ari's room on the second floor. My hand reached for the door handle, trying to make sense of what she told me and gain composure to face him.

"Finley D. Williams, what is that on your hand?"

I looked at my ring and stepped back, dropping my hand to my side. "That's what I wanted to tell you. Aidan and I got engaged and married while we were in Vietnam."

I fought hard not to show her how ecstatic I felt. To tell the person who has been my best friend for more than half of my life my greatest news was all I wanted to do, but under the circumstances, it didn't feel appropriate.

"I'm so happy for you!" She wrapped her arms around me. "My father won't be."

"Let's have lunch tomorrow, then we can talk about my

two-day engagement and wedding; now doesn't feel right. Any last words before I go in?"

"I have my suspicions about what happened and why he isn't remembering. I want to hear your professional opinion." Not yet professional as I had another year before I would receive my Doctorates in Psychology. Doctor Finley D. Williams-Walker – profiler. Not a bad name for a rapper.

Again, I reached for the door handle, this time with my right hand, pushed the door open and stepped into the room.

"Ari, can you hear me?" Black hair stuck out from underneath the bandage, his beard longer than when I had last seen him.

"Ley, you're here. I missed you." His smile no longer intoxicating, but seeing him so vulnerable, laying in a hospital bed, the sight pulled at my heart. Big, dark, and strong he still was, but his eyes held something else.

"How are you feeling?" I built up to the questions Ashley needed me to ask. I took a seat to his right.

"Better now that you're here." He pressed the incline button on the bed's remote, the blanket fell down exposing the torso which once made me weak. I waited for him to get comfortable.

"What did the doctor say?" *Slow and steady.*

"Apart from the knock I took to the back of my head, I should be fine and out of here soon."

"Ashley told me she has been appointed as your psychiatrist." I held a glass of water and helped him position the straw between his lips; a mouth I no longer wanted to feel on mine.

"Yes, the doctor said I have amnesia and Ashley is trying to help me remember."

"What's the last thing you recall before waking up here?" Patience is not a synonym for Finley.

"I was held captive somewhere. I don't think I was alone."

"Your captor was there with you the whole time?"

"No, but I remember having this idea that there was at least one other man."

"Can you remember anything about where you were being held?"

"No, just a room."

"Anything specific about the room?"

"It had a double bed with grey bedding, I think there was free weights stacked in the corner, and an adjoining bathroom. Only a shower, sink, and toilet."

"A window?" I asked, trying to create a layout of the room in my mind.

"Yes, I think so. I can't remember looking out of it." His Israeli accent still heavy.

"Do you know how long you were gone?"

"Anderson said six months."

"How would Tom know?"

"I stayed with him when I got back to Marcel." For the first time since I held the straw to his mouth, his eyes met mine. "A year ago."

"What did you do for six months staying with Tom? Did Eli know you were back?" My stomach turned on itself, not because he hadn't come back to me as he had promised he would. *Why the secrecy?*

"Eli didn't know, does he know I'm here?"

"He should be here in about four-and-a-half-hours, their flight is still expected to arrive on time." I crossed my arms over my chest. "Why didn't you at least tell your best friend you were back?" Confusion pushed my internal organs around.

"Because...I saw you." His eyes left mine.

"What do you mean you *saw* me?"

"At your lake house. Ley, I came back for *you*." He rubbed his hands over his face, pulling too much air into his lungs. "I saw you."

"Yes, you said that, but I still don't understand what you mean. Ari, tell me." The hand closest to him reached for his.

He exhaled. "I saw you with him on the couch. It rained, but I heard you laugh, it was the most beautiful sound I have ever heard so I walked around to the deck. And then I saw what you were doing."

My heart stopped; my mind scrambled for a reply. Ari had witnessed the first time Aidan and I had made love. The only time before we got married. "I'm sorry, Ari." The best sentence my brain could construct without blood.

"Ley, I came back for you. I never stopped loving you." He pulled my hand to his mouth, but midway he stopped and stared. Ari shook his head then tilted it to the right, exhaling hard.

"You're engaged?" His eyes met mine; darker than I had ever seen them before.

"I'm married."

He released my hand and looked towards the window. The blue sky had turned grey. "Please go now, I need rest."

"Do you want me to visit you again?"

"Anderson believes you're our best chance at finding whoever did this to me. So, I guess I have to."

"He hasn't asked for my help. And I'm still busy with my Doctorates, I can't give that up now. If Captain Taylor has requested my assistance, they need to discuss it with me and my professor."

"You two are not on the best of terms." Ari looked through me. "Can't blame him."

"You have no idea what you're talking about." My fists drew into themselves and I pushed to my feet.

Ari grabbed my arm. "He won't stop until he has proof. He knows, I guess I should say your *husband*, is a killer."

I slapped his hand away and stared back at him, gritting my teeth.

"There she is. Hello, I haven't seen *you* in a long time." His smile reminded me of evil stepmothers and witches in fairy tales.

"Ari, you listen to me," I said, poking a finger at the air between us. "Aidan isn't the Marcel Sniper and I will annihilate anyone who tries to come between me and my *husband*. I have told Tom as much and it seems I need to say it to you too."

"Believe what you want, he won't stop until he has proof and you know him. Tom *always* gets his man."

"He will have to come through me first." I left Ari's room. If not for the automatic closing mechanism of the door it would have slammed shut.

I pressed my back against the wall, closed my eyes, fighting for composure, and I willed my hands to unclench. *What the hell just happened?*

As adrenaline levels started returning to normal, a hand touched my face. I grabbed hold of an arm even before my eyes opened.

"That bad?" Aidan asked.

"We need to talk. Not here. Please take me home."

Aidan pulled me into his arms and whispered every reassurance I needed to hear.

"I love you more each day. Do you remember my vows?" I asked, and lifted my head until my eyes found his perfect mouth.

"I really can't remember much, not with the way you looked in that dress. I could only think of what I could finally do to you. It was a *very* long year."

I laughed and pressed my lips to his. "I can't remember much either, maybe we will remember more when we get married here. But I'm not repeating the same vows, not in front of people who want to...let's go, we need to talk about what happened in there." I gestured with my head to the left.

"Your wish is my command, Mrs Walker." He took my hand, and we started toward the stairs.

"About that." Aidan stopped walking. "As you know I was named after my father, the whole him-not-having-sired-a-son drama. Well, he made me sign an agreement when I was twenty-one in which I agreed to hyphenate my surname when I get married. Never thought it would happen at twenty-one, so I signed. But I know how much it meant to him. I'm sorry."

"So, you will be Mrs Williams-Walker. I don't care about your surname. You're mine." He started walking again.

I stopped and took possession of both his hands when he turned to look at me. "Aidan, I am yours, no one will ever come between us. I love you, and I will fight to the death to protect you. Just as you protect me."

"What happened?" He reached for my face and I leaned into his palm, pressing my lips against his wrist.

"Not here."

"Game face on, Wife. Tom walked in the same time I did. No, I didn't talk to him."

I'm not good at playing team sports; my game face is not friendly. We found Ashley in the foyer, no sign of the bloodhound.

"Congratulations on your wedding, Aidan. I'm a bit peeved we weren't invited." Ashley hugged him, her eyes darted, searching for the bloodhound.

"I'm sorry, Ash, it just happened. Okay, it didn't just happen, but under the circumstances I didn't want personal vendettas overshadowing our day. Finley deserves better after everything she went through. By eloping there wasn't the constant reminder of her parents not being there."

Aidan was right, I never thought about my parents until we were on the flight back. Time helps, it doesn't heal.

"The reason you're the perfect match – you understand her better than even I do."

The hair on the back of my neck stirred and my back stiffened. *Bloodhound.*

"Glad you could pull yourself away from your own lives to be here." Not the first time he had said something childish in the preceding year.

"Hello, good to see you, too. We were on our way back when I saw the missed calls and messages."

"Have you seen Ari?" He asked me but directed at Aidan. Nothing rattles Aidan's cage.

"Yes, I want to discuss my assessment with Ashley, in private. You need to explain to me why he was in Marcel, staying with you, for six months before he disappeared and not even Eli knew. He told me the reason I wasn't informed, but it's despicable that neither of you informed his best friend."

"That's between Ari and Eli, not something you need to concern yourself with."

"Not a good way to get on my good side if you want to ask for my help with this case." Hatred poured out of my mouth, directed at my once beloved godfather and confidant.

"He told you?" Disbelief in his eyes. Not sure if it was at the harshness of my words or the anger in my stare.

"Yes. But I don't think it will be a good idea. Not because of our history – yes, Aidan knows – but because I'm not yet qualified and my thesis is far from being done."

"I've already spoken to Professor Scott, and he thought it was a wonderful idea that you assist, he said you can include this as a case study in your thesis. It will give you real life experience at the same time."

I didn't need more experience with the monsters of this world. I had survived three serial killers and made almost ten hands full of the worst monsters commit suicide. I had tortured them all, paedophiles, rapists, and killers, to breaking point, but they made their final decision.

"You went behind my back to my professor and asked for his consent even before you asked me? What happened to the honourable man I used to love?"

He looked at Aidan and flicked his chin towards him.

"I'm done. I won't help you. Not because I don't feel terrible for what happened to Ari, but because you still won't let this thing with Aidan go. This is the reason you will not receive an invitation to our wedding." My rage darkened to match the darkness outside. A storm was upon us.

"You're engaged?"

"We got married in Vietnam." I held up my ring to his face.

Aidan took my hand, and we headed towards the entrance. I stopped walking, and when I turned back, I saw Ashley wiping her eyes. "I will see you tomorrow for lunch and then I will tell you what I suspect."

"I have suspicions too, but until we have spoken and you have confirmed my suspicions let's keep it to ourselves."

"Who am I going to tell? The only person I could share these things with is standing next to you and he chose to remove himself from my life and my future career. I love you, Ashley, I'm sorry this is affecting you." I resumed walking, gripping my husband's hand.

I heard Ashley beg the bloodhound to give up his frivolous man hunt.

Aidan had parked in his designated parking spot in the basement, saving us from an epic drenching. I needed a shower; as comfortable as first-class flying is, there still isn't a shower. Airlines really should look into this, and snake repellent, just in case. Even in business class, one had slithered in. This one had smacked my bum as I made my way to the lavatory, which should really be called a pee-coffin. He required medical attention on landing for a fractured hand. Aidan was so proud of me. With our military backgrounds, we can take care of ourselves, but our true strength lies in our unity.

"I have something for you." His boyish grin made me forget about the conversations in the hospital.

"And I have something for you, but seeing as this is where you work, you need to wait until we get home." I pressed my lips to his neck, his smell reminding me of our wedding night.

"You might prefer my gift." He held it out to me, and I took both.

"You know me, my life."

"My life? Thought we aren't doing nicknames."

"It's not a nickname, you are my life." I holstered my SIG to my belt and wrapped the strap of the Glock Gen 4's holster around my ankle. My husband watched me with a smile.

I pulled his mouth to mine. Chin sore, I pulled away from him and kissed his nose.

"What happened with Ari?" he asked, driving out of the basement garage.

"I haven't seen him in two years, people change."

"What does that mean?" Aidan shot me a glance, returning his eyes to the water-streaked windshield.

"He knows about Tom's vendetta against you and I have a strange feeling he knows more than he lets on. But the strange thing is, he says his doctor diagnosed him with amnesia, but he remembers more than he should. And why would Tom want me to help find Ari's captor? My thesis is on serial killers, not abductions or prolonged captivity."

"You need to help, Finley."

"I don't *need* to." I watched rain drops streak past on the window next to me.

"This might be the perfect situation for you and the bloodhound to work out your differences and get back to the way you used to be. It might even get him off my back."

"I want you on your back."

"I'm being serious, woman." He ran his hand through my hair, rubbing my neck.

"I know, so am I."

"Will you help?"

"If you think it might help, I will."

"You must make your own decision and not follow my advice; it's your choice, you don't have to, but it intrigues you. The darkness is once again playing in your eyes."

"I don't like it when that side of me comes out. It only surfaced because Ari provoked me."

"I thought he loved you, once?"

"He did, but like I said, two years is a long time. I don't know what happened to him for the year he was away working undercover. Or what happened the six months he was in Marcel before he disappeared for close to six months. He came looking for me at the lake house and saw us." I rolled my head on the headrest and focused on Aidan's beautiful profile. "He saw us the first time we made love."

"Well, that explains the mystery of the hooded man on the camera footage."

"I guess it does."

"What's bothering you?" Aidan placed his hand over mine where it rested on his thigh.

"I need to discuss it with Ashley." I didn't know how to tell Aidan what I suspected had happened to Ari. "But I saw something in his eyes I have seen before, not in his though."

"Discuss it with Ashley, and if you want to talk to me about it, you know where to find me."

In my bed. The thought made me giddy. "How are you so understanding?" I pulled his hand to my mouth, pressing it multiple times to my lips.

"You're emphatic; I see the burden you carry."

"After how our conversation ended, I feel anything but empathy towards him."

"Promise me this won't pull you back in." Aidan squeezed my hand.

"I promise. Not with Ari, and not into the abyss. My days of hunting predators on the dark web is over. We both promised to never go back to what we were."

"I'm not worried about Ari. I'm worried about your need to protect and your lust for vengeance."

"Ari can protect and avenge himself, he's not my concern. I love that you're not jealous. How is it possible you get sexier every day?"

"Sexier than I was on the flight between Danang and Singapore?"

"Yes. Thank you for helping me tick *that* box."

Aidan pulled into the parking garage and we made our way up to the penthouse. The following day he would put his place on the market and we would stay at my penthouse until we found our first home.

Five

Ashley and I needed to discuss the Ari situation in private. On my way to her office I picked up our favourite lunch. As I drove through the wrought-iron gates of Tabula Rasa, Tabby Manor, as the guests referred to it, the longing for my mother struck me. She had started it and left Tabula Rasa to me to chair after she and my father had died in a car crash. Jetlag was getting the better of me, and Aidan and I had resolved to spending the morning in bed and to getting back into bed the second I got home. It might have been newlywed sleep deprivation and not jetlag that made me feel as if someone had eaten my brain.

"Hello, Mrs Walker." Ashley has an uncanny ability to know the precise moment I pulled through the gate and always met me outside.

"I hope you're in the mood for pizza?" I asked as I pulled two large boxes from the back seat of my SUV. Jetlag left me ravenous.

"Let's eat in my office, we can talk in private there." I followed Ashley to her office, and we both ate two slices without saying a word.

"What is your assessment of Ari?" I returned to my chair after tossing the paper napkins in the wastebasket.

"I suspect he's repressing certain memories, but one is vivid and it's the one he wants repressed the most. The doctor diagnosing amnesia is not accurate. He's a neurologist, not a psychiatrist, and this is just my observation of what he exhibits."

"I will just come out and say it – Ari was raped." No bushes in her office to beat around.

"I concur. He pushed himself into the bed when I was with him yesterday morning when a nurse came in. The surprising thing – it was a female nurse."

"Too many women have raped men or other women through object rape, this is not strange, but his reaction helps in compiling a profile of his attacker. Anything specific about the woman that struck you as different to others who may have entered his room? Did he show the same reaction to any other nurses? He didn't act strange around me." He did, but I kept the rest of that conversation to myself.

"Also not around me, but he knows us. The only thing that struck me as different was that she had long, beautiful red hair."

"So, we are looking for a red-headed woman. That could be anyone. What shade of red?"

"Auburn."

I wanted to buy a wig and scare him after the way he spoke to me. Maybe Tom's childish behaviour had rubbed off on me. I have been known to get vindictive when someone tries to back me into a corner. Nobody puts Finley in a corner. But Ari was a victim and no matter how angry he made me, his words might have come from a place of pain. We had loved each other once.

"Ash, did you talk to him about your observation? His reaction to the nurse."

"No, it didn't seem appropriate to blatantly ask him. I wanted your opinion first."

"Now you have it. The Black-ops specialist, Krav Maga instructor, and human weapon is the victim of rape. And you know men aren't as forth coming about this as women are. Stigmatisation doesn't help at all, and a strong man like Ari won't admit to it."

"He knows what you and I both went through, perhaps we can use our, let me call it experiences, to get him to talk."

"Can I wear a red wig?" It slipped out.

"Finley, that would be cruel. How can you say such a thing?" I told her. "Still, you can't do that to him, revenge is not sweet."

Oh, but it is, red velvet sweet. As cruel as I can be towards predators, I could never hurt a victim.

"We could show him a slideshow of various images to help trigger his memories and sprinkle a few photos of red-headed women in the mix." Food always comes to mind when I contemplate torture. *Stop it.* "He's already connected to the heart rate monitor, he might not even notice what we are doing. Do you want to go now?"

"I first want to talk to you about how this will affect you. Ari meant a lot to you."

"*Meant* is the operative word."

"And Aidan is okay with you working on this?"

"He proposed it, said it might mend my relationship with your father."

"I'm sorry for the way he's acting, I know this is hurting you. Your anger towards him is not unfounded. I told him after you left to stop this. His relationship with you is more important than whatever issues he has with Aidan. When they adopted me, I was jealous of the relationship you two had; he never spoke to me about his work."

"You know why he didn't talk to you about his work. He didn't want to remind you of what you went through to get to them, and us." Sold by her mother to a paedophile ring at the age of ten, Ashley had the courage to run at sixteen and she kept running until she stumbled into Tom who was in the area looking for a murder suspect, long before he became a state prosecutor.

Ashley nodded, then shrugged. "We found our own father-daughter things to do. But this thing needs to end between you two, it has been going on for a year."

"This will end when he stops trying to pin murders on Aidan that he didn't commit." *I will protect him until my dying breath, no one will ever understand his reasons.*

"He will, I tore into him yesterday and didn't stop until he was in tears."

"I would have paid good money to see that. Maybe a camera

caught it; doubt there will be audio."

Ashley laughed until she struggled for breath.

"Give me your laptop and hit me up with a few ideas for images to add to the slideshow. If you don't have any commitments we can go to the hospital this afternoon. I'm desperate to get back to my husband."

"Aidan is not the Marcel Sniper. That man loves you, and even though he was a sniper while he was enlisted, that doesn't mean he killed innocent people here."

Not innocent people. "Thank you, it means a lot to both of us."

Ashley handed me her laptop, and I started with the slideshow to jog Ari's memory. I might have put a few too many images of auburn headed women in. No one threatens my Aidan and gets away with it. Perhaps I wanted it to be over as soon as possible; find the culprit and return to my normal life – not that my life has ever been normal.

"Do you know anything more about this case?" I asked.

"Ask my father to give you the case file and talk you through it. Something doesn't add up, but I only read through it for information to help me with Ari's memory loss."

I sent Tom a text message asking him to meet me at The Marcella later that afternoon with the file.

Ashley knocked on the door of Ari's room and I followed her in. Eli stood next to Ari's bed.

"Hello, brother." I walked over and wrapped my arms around Eli's waist. He and Lizzie weren't married yet, but he was my friend and Aidan's, and Eli had carried me out of that barn.

"Hello, sister. Please thank Aidan for booking the tickets for us and upgrading it to first class. At least Lizzie could sleep." I know why he hadn't slept; I hadn't been able to either. As Eli pulled away from me, I saw the questions in his eyes.

"Were you also in Vietnam?" Ari asked Eli.

"Yes, Lizzie and I helped plan the surprise wedding." Eli gave me another side hug.

"Let me get this straight, because my head is still foggy." Ari pushed himself upright in bed. "You had no idea you were getting married and the next moment you were?" His laughter not joyful.

"If you knew Aidan, or anything about our relationship, it wouldn't surprise you in the least. A lot has happened since you left, Ari; none of us are the people we were back then." I forced my eyes not to reflect my true emotions, instead keeping my focus on helping him. "And neither are you."

Ari looked away from me. In that moment I knew he knew that I knew what had happened to him.

"Eli, can I talk to you outside for a minute?" I took his hand and started towards the door.

"I will catch up with you later," he said to Ari.

We walked a few doors down the passage before I turned to Eli. He placed his hands on my shoulders. "What happened to him?"

"Do you really want me to tell you? Because I think you already know. He hasn't said anything yet, but both Ashley and I picked up on it, we have both seen that look in our own and each other's eyes, and..." I didn't have to remind him of what had happened to Lizzie.

"He says he has amnesia. Are you not maybe looking for things that aren't there?"

"No, trust me I'm not. Ashley and I will conduct a test with him now to try and jog his memory. Let me see what we can establish today, and I will tell you tomorrow, if you're up for a training session? The past twenty-four hours have been rough on both of us and it will do you good to try to floor me." He always did, which made training with him so much better.

Eli never held back the way Aidan did. I shuddered to think what Aidan could do to me if he wasn't more controlled, not that he would ever hurt me. I saw what he did to Eli and the bruises his fists had left; even with Eli, he remained in control of himself.

I returned to Ari's room and found Ashley helping him get

comfortable. He smiled as I took the same seat I had the day before. *Sneer or smile?*

Ashley excused herself to talk with Ari's doctor.

"Finley, I'm sorry about yesterday. You're right. I have no reason to have said the things I did. From what Ashley has told me, while you were talking to Eli, Aidan is a good man and he loves you. The day I left I told you I wanted you to be happy. I just never thought you would find someone with whom you can share what we once had." *Sneer or smile?*

"I'm not saying this to hurt you, but first, thank you for apologising, but you need to understand what Aidan and I have is different to what you and I had. What you and I shared, yes, it was special, but we were destined to crash and burn. You were part of the conversations we had all those hours after training together. Do you remember the darkness that surrounded us and what I did?"

"I remember." He nodded and reached for my hand, stopped mid-air, and settled it on his lap.

"Ari, I loved you, but you left. I had to continue down my path until I could no longer stomach the darkness. Did Tom tell you what happened to me?"

"Yes, he did. I'm so sorry you had to go through that. If they found you a second later..." He dropped his gaze, staring at his hands.

"Aidan saved my life. I flatlined twice after they brought me into the ER. And more than that, he and I first met when I was ready to give up the darkness and live a life of fighting the evil in this world the right way. He's a decorated soldier. I'm sure Tom told you Aidan is one of the best snipers in this country, make that the world. He killed more people in the line of duty than he can remember, but he chose life and became a doctor. How can I not want to be with him and live a life with him? You and I together, we would always remain warriors because that's what you are, and it's the life you chose. I never wanted back in, but do you remember the Angel Taker who killed fifteen little girls?"

He nodded. "I can't forget."

"So, you remember what pushed me down that path?"

"Yes, I do. But Ley, I came back for you. I want to be with you."

"I'm sorry you feel that way. I'm married and I love Aidan, I love what we have together. You need to accept that. Again, I'm not saying this to hurt you, but even if we weren't married, it wouldn't change anything between you and me."

"Can I meet him?" His eyes met mine.

"Why do you want to meet him?" *Sneer or smile?*

"Because I want to tell him to his face that if he ever hurts you, he will have to answer to me."

"Don't be childish about this, please. I have enough to deal with, with Tom's constant attacks on Aidan. And I need to help find whoever did this to you. I can't work with you if you have an endgame. You need to make peace with the fact that I have moved on. What would help us move past what you said yesterday is if you tell me what it is that has Tom so convinced Aidan's a killer?"

"Why don't you refer to him as Uncle Tom anymore?"

"He's no longer the man I knew as my Uncle Tom. I don't like the person he has become. So, if there is anything you can tell me I would appreciate it if you did."

"All I know, he believes without a doubt that Aidan is the Marcel Sniper and he's dead set on proving it."

My nails pushed into the flesh surrounding my knees. "Ari, he knows I killed the man who raped Lizzie. Tom suspects, perhaps even knows, I was the one the media referred to as The Hangman."

It still bothers me that neither the police nor the media ever suspected a woman to be responsible. "He was the one who asked me to get involved in the search for the Scarecrow. It's because of him that I was tortured and died twice because of what they put me through. If he knows all this about me, why is he so hell bent on trying to keep Aidan away from me? For the millionth time – Aidan isn't the Marcel Sniper."

His eyes flicked up to the right. "Maybe he just thinks you would be better off with someone else." *Liar!*

I was just about to push Ari on the matter when Ashley walked in.

"Have the two of you resolved your issues?"

"Yes," we both said. I wasn't done, not by a long shot. *What does Ari know?*

Ashley removed her laptop and handed it to me. While I waited for it to start up and open the PowerPoint presentation, well rather slides, she explained to Ari what we would do and what the aim of the exercise was. He agreed to it, reminding us both that he didn't remember much. Ashley and I stole a glance. "Are you sure you're up for this?" Ashley asked while closing the curtains. Better to eliminate outside distractions.

"Yes."

I was unsure if I still wanted to torture him with images of auburn-haired women. I'm vindictive, but I suspected that if I wanted to get to the truth I had to get on his good side.

I cued the slideshow and Ashley and I both sat back from Ari's peripheral vision, allowing us to monitor his reactions without him feeling watched. But he understood what we were trying to do. The heart rate monitor came in very handy as it's difficult to gauge someone's reaction if you're not seeing them face to face, but this was not an interrogation.

We showed him various images – happy faces, sad faces, funny memes, war scenes and several other images to create a baseline reaction, and also to see if we could get information that could lead to his captor. *Captress?*

The following images increased his heart rate: black sedan, a bedroom with grey bedding, auburn hair, chain, women with auburn hair, and the strangest reaction to me was one which showed BDSM. One I included on a whim.

During the time we spent together, he never showed any interest in the lifestyle. Then again, we weren't involved long enough to get to know everything about each other.

***

Dazed, I walked into The Marcella. Confused by Ari's reaction, trying to make sense of it when confusion clashed with anguish and anger. A rumble erupted inside me; I rooted for no specific winner. The man, no longer my darling uncle, waited for me at a side table in the restaurant, away from unwanted ears and humidity. I took a seat across from him and ordered a Walker, the drinking kind. No Vietnamese cold coffee in Marcel.

"Did you bring the file?" I asked. No point in faking politeness.

"Yes." He retrieved it from his briefcase, placing it on the table in front of me. The file thicker than I expected for one victim's abduction. One who claimed to remember nothing.

Tom cleared his throat, took a sip of his coffee, and held his hand out to me. I kept both my hands on top of the brown file. "Finley, I need your help with this case. I wouldn't ask if you weren't my last resort."

"Like you asked me to help with the Scarecrow case and look where that got me." He still hadn't apologised for putting my life in danger. The horrendous torture I had endured still haunted my sleep at times. Absent minded, my thumb ran along the scar tissue on my left wrist. No longer visible, covered by a tribal inspired tattoo of an orca, I never forgot the searing pain of the spike being hammered through my wrist. Still grateful my shooting hand is my right.

"I realise I have never apologised for putting you in danger, but I had no way of knowing they would abduct you. Just like you, I never suspected there to be more than one killer."

I shook my head, fighting the urge to tell him to shove his coffee where the sun doesn't shine. How dare he use the fact that I didn't suspect a second killer against me? Profilers with years of experience didn't profile team killers. "I will take the file and read through it, because, honestly, I'm intrigued by its size." My hands wrapped around the file and I pushed my chair back.

"I'm sorry."

I waited more than a year to hear those words and felt

nothing. "Too little, too late." I got to my feet.

"Finley, what do you want me to say? I'm sorry I asked for your help. I'm sorry you were held for three weeks and almost died because I was desperate to put an end to the killings."

"*Almost* died? I did die. Twice. Oh, and who saved my life? That's right – Aidan. Your goddaughter is saved by this remarkable man and now you badger him, taunt him, because you suspect he's something he isn't. In your mind, how does that add up?"

"I realise my conduct is unprofessional and wrong as your godfather. I'm sorry, can we move past this and try to work on our relationship? Get back to how things were?" His eyes remained locked on mine.

"We can never go back. You have done and said too many things this past year. For the Scarecrows I might still forgive you, but as long as you hound Aidan, you're no longer a part of my life. On top of all of this, you forget the sniper saved my life when Tony Andretti came after me. If not for *him*, you and I would not be having this conversation. To this day you haven't shared the ballistics report with me, but it's because it was the Marcel Sniper who saved me. Why can't you just let it go?"

"If I promise to stop trying to prove Aidan is the Marcel Sniper, could we then rebuild our relationship?"

"Maybe, but you need to accept him as my husband. Why did you not tell either Eli or myself Ari was back?"

"Ari didn't want me to. It's not my place to tell you, but he came back for you. The day he went to the lake house and saw you, well, he wanted to ask you to marry him."

I sat down, hard.

"Why would he come back after being away for a year and think we can just jump into marriage?" Something didn't add up.

"He still loves you, Finley. He might have been a means to an end for you, but you mean everything to him."

"Ari was never a means to an end for me, the relationship

served a purpose at that time, but you know as well as I do it wouldn't have lasted. And you told me the day Ari and I saved Riley you were concerned about the fact that we knew each other and were seeing each other."

"Ari is a good man, Finley. He asked for my blessing."

A thin thread snapped. "So, that's what this is all about? You're upset because Aidan didn't ask for your blessing? Why would he with the way you have treated both of us this past year? I'm your goddaughter. I'm a grown woman in my thirties and don't *need* your permission to get married." I never say my age out loud.

"Are you going to help with this case?" He changed the subject. I allowed it.

"Yes, because Ari is hurt, and from the look of this file and what he mentioned yesterday he might not be the only one. Do you have forensic reports in the file?"

"No, still waiting for the results."

"Was DNA testing done on his underwear?"

"Why would they need to?"

I swallowed the last of my Walker, sighed and said to the palm tree next to me, "Ari was raped."

Tom sat motionless until he rubbed his mouth with his right hand. "What makes you say that? There were no signs of sexual trauma or blood on his pants; the forensic techs gathered as much evidence as they could."

"Ashley and I both suspect a woman raped him. Phone the lab and ask them to run a test for vaginal secretion on his underwear, also test for lubricants or spermicide." They had, the test results were inconclusive.

"That changes everything. Up until now we considered our suspect to be male."

"What do you mean?" For the first time I missed the notion and her confusing guidance. At least it was something.

"Three men had vanished by the time Ari returned to Marcel, and I asked for his help. Captain Taylor approved it. Ari became David Ezra. Six months before Ari disappeared, another man vanished. Ari, rather David, was the fifth."

"What do you mean vanished?"

"Everything is in the file but to summarise, from the evidence we could gather, including the evidence from Ari, one minute the men were home and the next they weren't."

"This David Ezra persona you created for Ari, are the full details of the cover in the file?"

Tom nodded.

"I will review it and will contact you once I'm done." I stood.

"Finley, I will try my best to be accommodating towards Aidan and make peace with your decision. I would love to attend your wedding."

Tom never mentioned the Marcel Sniper again.

Six

Absolute chaos awaited me in the penthouse. The type that ensues when two people move in together. Most of Aidan's belongings would go into storage, but somehow we still needed to make this work. Perhaps it's a good thing you're so blinded by the honeymoon phase when you move in together, you don't mind sharing your space with another human being, one who would now see everything. We had slept over at each other's homes during the year we dated, but if your stomach is upset, you go home, making up some excuse of forgetting the correct shoes when you end up wearing the ones you had on. Bathroom business should be private, but now Aidan and I were about to get to know each other. *Really* get to know each other. It didn't matter that he's a gynaecologist; his wife's stuff is still his wife's.

I scanned the mountain of boxes, wondering what he needed the most while we would stay there. One thing was sure, we had to find a home, and fast. A place without the ghosts of other people.

Aidan had left to collect the last of his things, and on the way back he would pick up dinner. Grocery shopping is the last thing on your mind when you return from your wedding slash some-kind-of-moon. I still had a wedding to plan; Aidan had already booked our official honeymoon. *When are we leaving? Is Ari into BDSM? Did Tom mean what he said?*

Too many thoughts, questions, and the heat of the day pressed on my shoulders. I poured myself a Walker and walked out onto the deck. Moisture clung to my face; I struggled to take deep breaths. Not the humidity of Danang, but the unseasonable heat wave was still unwelcome.

The yellow light making streaks in the pool's blue water

called to me and I obeyed, getting in wearing nothing but my birthday suit.

"Mrs Walker, are you home?"

"I'm in the pool."

Aidan walked out and stood towering over me. In the light cast by the pool's light, I saw the want in his eyes.

"Get in, but this time I'm not turning around." He jumped in fully clothed.

"You're cheating husband and you know how I feel about cheating."

"What are you going to do about it, Mrs Walker?"

I showed him.

Aidan drew me close against him and kissed me with a long, luscious kiss, less hungry than before. "If that's your form of punishment you can expect me to be very naughty."

"Are you into BDSM?" It wasn't our first date, so not unacceptable post-coital conversation.

"What?" Aidan bit back laughter, biting his top lip while he waited for me to continue.

"BDSM. Bondage, discipline, dominance and submission, and sadism and masochism." I tried to free myself from his arms; this was about to get real and I didn't want to spill my secret, not even Lizzie knew. The movement of his chest against mine always obliterated my willpower. It was possible I could still shock him. Then again, he saw me getting rid of the first id, torch a car and the rest I had told him. *Will he be shocked?* I had no intention of risking it.

"I'm familiar with the acronym and what it entails. What makes you think I would be interested? Are you not happy with our week-old sex life?" He pulled me closer, knowing full well how much I hate being cornered when I wanted to have a serious conversation.

"Can you please let me go? I need to have a serious conversation with you, and I need a man's opinion on this."

"Only if you kiss me, and promise me there is no secret

room in there." He tilted his head towards the wooden sliding doors leading into the penthouse.

"No, Aidan, I don't have a playroom." He released his hold, and I rushed out of the pool running towards the bedroom for towels, leaving a wet trail in my wake. *Don't tell him Fin. Don't tell your husband.*

I handed Aidan a towel and could taste curiosity on his lips. He stepped back, a hint of a smile on his face. "So, my wife is not as vanilla as I thought?" He smacked my bum, and I pushed him into the pool. Laughter bellowed out of him the instant he breached the water's surface.

"Maybe I am now." I regretted it the second I said it. In an attempt to divert his attention, I opened my towel and wrapped it around him as he again got out of the pool.

"This body of yours makes me forget my name, but you're not getting off the hook that easily. Pun intended." He smacked my bum – well, tried to, as there wasn't much room for a proper swing within the constraints of the towel. "Not-so-vanilla-Fin, do you forget you were the one who said we were never to have any secrets? You better start talking, or I will pin you down and tickle, no wait, smack your delectable ass until you talk. But then again it seems you might enjoy that." Laughter roared out of him and if it didn't mean getting wet myself, I would have again pushed him into the pool.

There is no place for secrets in a marriage, not if you want it to last, and the last thing I wanted was for Aidan to find out. Not that it was possible, no one had seen my face. *Except one.*

"Doctor Aidan Walker, my husband, the love of my life, do you promise to love me no matter what? Even if I did something questionable many years ago for a very valid reason?"

"Do I need a drink for this conversation?" His eyebrows reached for his hairline.

"It couldn't hurt, no pun intended. Let's get dressed, eat, drink many alcoholic drinks, and then continue this discussion. I cleared out the closet for you and we can move your boxes into the spare bedroom. Tomorrow morning we can unpack and make this your home. *Our* home."

"Good job on changing the subject, but I agree. We need food and a lot of alcohol. I'm a little worried about the fact that you haven't told me this specific tale yet."

We dressed, ate, and after the third double liquid Walker, we found ourselves on the couch overlooking the ocean. Silver streaks played on dark ripples. The air-conditioner was set to 21 degrees Celsius, but I felt hot and uncomfortable. I had opened my mouth and there was no turning back. Perhaps if I distracted Aidan with my female prowess he would forget this conversation. *Eidetic memory, he forgets nothing. Dammit!*

Aidan took the empty glass from my hand and placed it on the side table. *Vanilla Fin, time to tell Aidan about your dark chocolate past.* My head buzzed with liquid Walker courage to face my delectable, fleshy Walker. Those muscles, that smile, those eyes, his sexy voice. *Focus, tipsy Finley!*

"Promise you will let me finish and no matter what I tell you, you will still love me?" I drew my bottom lip between my teeth and gave him the bedroom eyes he could not resist. He was immune to my attempt at puppy eyes. I can't blame him, I had burst out laughing when I practised it in the mirror.

"I can promise to let you finish."

"Aidan."

He laughed and pulled me into his arms, kissing my mouth, cheeks, eyes, and neck before pushing me back to resume my original position.

"When I was twenty-two and still a student at UM—"

He interrupted. "This sounds like the beginning of a porn movie."

I stood, he grabbed my arm and pulled me back down. "You promised to let me finish."

He shrugged and pursed his lips, unable to hide the laughter in his eyes. I needed another liquid Walker. Or the whole bottle.

"As I was saying, Lizzie and I went to Wild Bay during our summer holiday and took my father's 1970 Dodge Charger without his permission. He had it customised, and I was dying to try the nitro fuel injector out. No way in hell would he have allowed us to take it, so we *borrowed* it, while he and my mother were on one of their overseas holidays."

Aidan's finger traced the back of my neck.

"One night while we were down there, Lizzie got wasted and on the drive home, started vomiting in the car. I opened the window and tried to push her head out but in all the madness I took my eyes off the road and scraped the entire passenger side of the car against a guard-rail. The next day we drove back and paid to have the car fixed. The guy was my father's mechanic, so we threw in a few extra thousand for him to keep quiet. To two students it cost a small fortune as we had to use the money we had saved for our own overseas holiday. We planned to go skiing in the French Alps two months later and we both had to save money for it – those were my parents' terms. So we needed to get money, and a lot of it, before they asked questions about why we cancelled our trip or needed to borrow money from them. We had told them we had the money before they left."

Aidan's fingers moved their play to my shoulder and collar bone. "Can you stop distracting me? That was the easy part of the story."

He placed his teasing hand under his chin, elbow on the back of the couch. There was no position in which he didn't look breathtaking.

"So how did you get the money?" He covered his mouth with the back of his hand, but couldn't hide the jerking movements of his chest.

I needed another drink to lubricate my tongue just enough for the truth to be uttered. In a single move, which would have made Eli proud, I jumped from the couch and headed for the kitchen, returning with the bottle. With unsteady hands I poured us more courage; well, whiskey for Aidan.

"We learned about sexual fetishism and the likes during my third semester of that year. The lecturer explained in great detail what BDSM entails and the difference between it and sexual sadism and masochism disorders. Ashley and I often joked that it would be easy money being a dominatrix. It isn't the same as prostitution as sex isn't always involved." I downed the content of the tumbler; Aidan's eyes widened. "It was the logical option to get my hands on as much money as possible in the little time we had."

"What did Lizzie do?" Aidan kept his mouth hidden behind his hand.

"Lizzie waitressed at The Marcella, but I made enough for her shortfall."

"What did you do?"

I pinched my nose between my closed eyes with my thumb and index finger, inhaled through my nose, exhaled through my mouth, and faced my husband. "I was a dominatrix."

Aidan gave a single nod. "Did you have sex with the men?"

"Once." Stupid lubricating alcohol.

"Once?" Aidan's eyes narrowed.

"Okay, so I was Lady Remi."

Amusement filled his eyes. "Like the Remington rifle?"

"Yes." I smiled.

Aidan shook his head, no longer trying to hide his. "That's my wife. Continue."

"No one ever saw my face. They were blindfolded, and I introduced new members at the dungeon to the lifestyle. So it was never more than spanking, introductory bondage, talking, those kinds of things. Sex wasn't allowed; part of the rules. One client refused a session with anyone else and paid five thousand extra just to have the blindfold removed. I wore a wig and masks, either a leather cat or a black lace one. Back then I didn't have this tattoo."

I traced the orca on my wrist. "Or any of the other scars you know too well. So he wouldn't recognise me if he saw me on the street. But I knew who he was. One night after his session he pulled me into his arms and begged me to meet him at a hotel. One night and one night only, he offered to pay me more than I needed for both myself and Lizzie."

"So you had sex for money?" The word formed in his eyes as he pursed his lips.

"No. I had sex because I wanted to have sex with him. The money was a bonus."

"Call it what you want Finley, but I call it prostitution."

Aidan was right, I never thought of it that way before because the man in question was dark, dangerous, and gorgeous. Each time he entered the room I got butterflies in my stomach, and the fact that a CEO of a Fortune 500 company wanted to be a submissive when he was dominant in his everyday life captivated me. Some of the other clients were also intriguing from a psychological perspective, but from the moment I laid my eyes on him I was attracted to him.

I'm not proud of what I have done, but I own my past; it moulded me into who I am. "You're right. I never thought about it before because I was attracted to him. He was older, accomplished, that whole cliché, but in the world of kink, I was his master. It was exhilarating to hold power over a man like him."

"Who is he?"

"I can't tell you."

"Meaning I know him or know of him?"

"Yes. I'm sorry, Aidan, I was young, stupid and desperate. I made a mistake but learned a lot about humans in general and who knows, I might use that knowledge now."

"We are not doing it. You and I are both dominants. It won't work." Laughter burst out of him.

"Not between us. We don't need to spice anything up and seeing you punch Eli or sparring with me is more than enough of a turn on for me."

"You're one strange, intriguing woman, Mrs Walker. Never a dull moment with you."

"Does it mean you don't judge me?"

"No, I'm judging you for the night with the mystery man, but I won't hold it against you, we all make mistakes when we're young. You could have sold drugs or made a sex tape to make money. You chose the easier option, although I guess it was hard for your clients."

I burst out laughing. Aidan and I are a perfect match.

"Tell me, my black forest wife, do you still have any of the outfits?"

"No. But I'm not opposed to handcuffs, blindfolds, and role play."

"Good, neither am I." He pulled me into his arms and lifted my chin with his fingertips until my mouth met his.

Aidan Walker is the most understanding, non-judgemental man, and he is mine.

Seven

We sat across from each other at the kitchen island. I stared at my husband, grateful that he hadn't run after I had yanked the last proverbial skeleton from my closet and threw it at his feet.

Aidan caught me staring at him as he drained the contents of his mug. "What did you mean last night when you mentioned you might use the knowledge you gained during your Domme days?"

"Why do you know the terminology?" I poured him more coffee and returned to my seat. I told him about the experiment Ashley and I had conducted on Ari the previous day and the strange reaction he had to a bondage scene.

"Did you guys ever?"

"No. Aidan, I told you we were involved, never went on an actual date, and back then things were not normal for either of us with what I was about to embark on. The subject never came up."

"Doesn't mean Ari is not a kinkster."

"Seriously, why do you know the terminology?"

"You would be surprised how many people end up in the ER because of edge play gone wrong, or not knowing how to do what they want to do without hurting themselves or their partner."

"Can we please put this subject in the vault?" The discussions or memories we no longer wanted to be aired we locked in an imaginary vault.

"Yes. Why haven't you looked at the file yet?" Aidan pointed with his fork towards the brown folder.

"Because today is all about you and us transforming this place into our home." I leaned over the table, cautious of the Eggs Benedict my husband had made for breakfast, and gave him my good morning kiss. "We also need to plan our wedding today. I don't want to wait to make our marriage legal."

"You have two weeks, Mrs Walker. We leave on our honeymoon tomorrow in two weeks."

"Are you serious? How must I plan a wedding in two weeks?" I covered my face with my hands.

"Think about it, where do you want to get married? Who do you want to invite? Do you want a big wedding where ninety percent of the guests are people we don't even have contact with?" He walked around the island and wrapped his arms around me. His smell brought calm, as it always does.

"At the lake house, next Saturday just before sunset, your parents and brothers, Lizzie, Eli, Ashley, Kyle, Hope, and maybe Tom. I will contact Lizzie's stylist; he's flamboyant, but he does good work."

"See, all sorted. I doubt Nathan will come, he's still finalising his divorce, and some business matters." Nathan Walker, the brother I had not yet met in person, only via Skype during Aidan and his weekly bro-chats.

"Catering, decor, and a dress. We can stay in my house, *our* house. Your parents and brothers can stay in your house Ashley and her family can stay at Tom's place, and Liz and Eli stay with us."

"That works for me. I take it you and Tom have made peace?"

"I won't call it peace, but we seemed to have reached a ceasefire. If he does anything, and I mean anything, he's not attending our wedding."

"I will unpack, and you look at wedding ideas. We can discuss it later."

"You want to help with the arrangements?" I turned to face him.

"It's my wedding, too. But first we shower, no coin." He picked me up, threw me over his shoulder, and carried me towards the bedroom.

The file could wait another day, or so I thought.

Eight

The following morning, Aidan left for work, and I had made it out of bed just in time to make him breakfast. Domestic life is not for the sleep-deprived, newlywed who now had access to what had been off limits for a whole year. The previous day we had spent as planned: unpacking, creating our home, and planning our wedding. I sighed with a smile, finished my coffee, and pulled the file closer. My mobile phone rang from the bedroom and I ran towards it, hoping it was Aidan with another of his whispered messages.

"Good morning, Tom," I greeted my long-lost uncle.

"Finley, I'm on my way to pick you up. Meet me downstairs in twenty minutes."

I glanced down at my robe, ran my fingers through my bed-hair. "What happened?"

"We found another victim."

"Alive?" I ran for the shower.

"No."

Twenty minutes later, I rushed through the lobby, greeting the doorman as he held the door for me. Tom's car stood idling out front. I barely made it in before he pulled away, flooring the accelerator.

"Why are you in such a hurry?" My hand reached for the seatbelt.

"Because the body is still warm. You might pick up on something, and I told them to leave the scene undisturbed until you get there."

"I haven't had a chance to review the file yet." I watched as buildings and cars streamed past.

"Finley, this case is important. Why the hell have you not looked at it?" He gripped the steering wheel with both hands.

"I was busy. Aidan moved in, and it's not like one day will make a difference." But one day makes all the difference, ask anyone filing a missing person's report. I knew this but chose my husband, our life. The version of me I had been two years ago wouldn't have. That's the Finley Tom wanted on this case, but I refused to get sucked back into the abyss. I paid with my life, and some nights I still pay with my sleep for the time I had spent hunting predators.

"Are you in this or not? If I'm wasting my time bringing you in just say so and that will be the end of it." His knuckles turned white on the steering wheel.

"I'm in, on my terms. I have read almost half of what you compiled on each of the suspected victims. Ari, David Ezra's information, I left for last as I have an idea of what happened to him. Fill me in while you try to kill us." His arm blocked the speedometer, but I estimated we were doing close to 160 kilometres per hour, heading north, out of the city.

"Joggers found the body of a male victim next to a rural road leading from the highway to the estuary."

Why is it more often than not some unlucky person going for a run or cycle who ends up making a ghastly discovery? I wonder if they ever jog or cycle outside a gym after making such a life-altering discovery? I did, but I ran from my own demons and the ones I kept in my wine cellar.

"Are you listening?" He gave me a scolding look.

"Yes. So this one wasn't buried?"

"No."

"But Ari was?"

He nodded.

"Ari was found wandering next to this same highway." He again nodded as I massaged my temples, a headache approached like an armada. "I'm thinking out loud. You forgot how I do this."

"I'm sorry, Fin, continue."

He offered me a takeaway coffee, at least remembering I drink my coffee with milk but no sugar. I took a sip, burnt my tongue, bit back a curse word, and continued. "Why did you not bury this one? Did you bury the other four?" I asked as if the offender was there in the car with us. I have done this my entire monster-hunting life. "The file made no mention of any searches for the other four men. Have any teams been mobilised to search for disturbances in the ground in the vicinity of where Ari was found?"

"No. Ari was found on Thursday and we didn't know where to start."

"Bullshit. You should've started from where he was found, retraced his steps. How far is this body from where Ari was found?"

"We are short-staffed like most other police departments across the country. Close to ten kilometres."

"Phone Captain Taylor now and tell him to get people out here. There are four graves out there somewhere and the sooner you find them the better."

Ari had been buried in a shallow grave from what Ashley had told me, thus he had been able to pull himself out after his captor left. *Captress.* If he or she works alone, it would explain the shallow graves; the offender might lack the stamina to dig a proper grave or doesn't consider the possibility of his or her victims being found. There are numerous properties around the estuary. I remember my parents looked at a place on the north side before deciding on the lake house. Tom shook his head when I told him we might be looking for a woman.

"Why are you not tossing them into the estuary? You can weigh them down; your secret would be safe if you dumped them in the deeper parts. You're not familiar with the tides or you don't have access to a boat. Do you prefer being able to go back and sit at their graves? Dominate them even in death. Or do you miss them, long for them?"

"Are you sure we are looking for a woman?"

"Without a doubt. I need to review the whole file, but I didn't see any records of the men's diaries. The positions they held; they would have had electronic diaries."

"We didn't make printouts, there was nothing unusual in them. Why do you ask?"

"Five men, who we are aware of, who never crossed paths that you know of, all disappeared within months of each other. There has to be a commonality that we are not seeing. She didn't pick them at random, she chooses her victims for a very specific reason. Successful, handsome men with dark features who take pride in their bodies. Men who reached the top of their respective fields. She keeps them, rapes them, and then discards of them after six months by my estimate. Would help if you found the others and we could know for a fact whether they are dead and how long she keeps them for. I suspect she doesn't discard of one before she has a replacement. Ari mentioned another man being there."

I missed the notion; her unclear guidance still gave some direction and I no longer allowed the darkness to envelope me in order to understand the psyche of serial offenders. But I would have to find a way of understanding her if I wanted to find her. I could walk the streets of Marcel and stop every person who made my palms itch, call it my spidey-sense for psychopaths and violent criminals. My hands itch enough just when I go grocery shopping. That reminded me I needed to cook dinner for my husband. *Domestic Fin – Unsub.*

"Alpha males!"

Tom jerked the car back into the correct lane. "What the hell, Finley?"

"She chooses alpha males, dominant males. Does that make her a submissive or a switch? I doubt a submissive can get them to play with her, the way she needs them to. And she wouldn't discard of her Dom."

"What the hell are you talking about?"

"On Saturday, Ashley and I showed Ari various images, and before you ask, we explained to him what we were trying to accomplish. He was still connected to the heart rate monitor which made it easier for us to track his response. One image showed a dominatrix and his heart rate increased. I don't know if he's into the BDSM lifestyle, but it struck me as odd. Can you drop me at the hospital after we finish up here? I want to ask him a few more questions. Ashley needs to be there as his psychiatrist."

"He's being released today."

"Will he be staying with you? Surely he can't live on his own, not yet."

"No, he will stay with Eli and Lizzie until he's back on his feet."

My ex living with my sister and her fiancé, sleeping in the bed in which we did what we had. *These are the days of Finley's life. No sand. No hourglass.*

The body lay undisturbed, except for the swarm of blowflies zoning in on the exposed soft tissue. Clothed in dress shoes, denim pants, and a black shirt, his facial orifices were the targets of the blowflies. The sound of passing cars, and cicadas screaming at the warm air, drowned out the noise of eager wings. There were no visible signs of trauma on the body and no tyre treads or shoe impressions in the vicinity of the body. *Body dump, but how?*

Even in death, this man remained handsome with his chiselled dark features, if you could look past the insect activity. No indentation on his ring finger – not married. I gathered as much information as I could and made notes on my smart phone; I even took a few photos with Captain Taylor's permission.

Why were his eyes closed? How did he die?

Tom drove me home, and I left for Lizzie's to see my ex-lover. Bold move to stay with my sister.

Lizzie met me at the front door, closing it behind her as she stepped out onto the porch. "I should've told you, but I had no idea. Not until this morning when Eli phoned me to ask if it was okay for Ari to come stay here. I couldn't say no. They were partners, they're still friends."

"It's fine, Liz. He might recover his memories faster if he's surrounded by people he cares for, and you and Eli can keep an eye on him. Before we go in, I need to ask you, will you be my bridesmaid next week Saturday?"

"Yes!" Lizzie grabbed me and jumped with me in her arms. I gave in and jumped with her. She had already been my maid of honour and witness to my first wedding, but what the hell, even I can enjoy girly things at times, and being married to Aidan made me feel like a woman. One who no longer hid anything from him.

"Fin, are you insane? How are you going to plan the perfect wedding in less than two weeks and still deal with this case?"

"That's why you're my maid of honour. We can make your personal assistant our wedding bitch. That reminds me, I need to get Favio's number from you."

"He will not believe *you* are getting married. If there is one person who can pull a look together for you in such a short amount of time, it's him."

"I'm going to give him strict guidelines for the dress. I already found a few photos of dresses I like on the internet last night."

"Are you inviting Ari?"

Ah, the eternal question – to have exes at your wedding or not? There's only one answer.

"No. It will be too weird, and I don't think it's conducive to his recovery."

"If that's what you need to tell yourself."

"Would you have gone to Robert's wedding had he invited you, or better yet, will you invite him to yours?"

"No, but that's different. He left me on our wedding day. You and Ari had a fling, albeit an intense and passionate one."

"Aidan knows enough but please don't mention intense or passionate in front of my husband."

Well, after what I had told him the previous night, it might not even register I had been intimate with this man before him. I wasn't going to risk a Lizzie version coming out because her sentence would include 'bumping and uglies'. She's the second most intelligent person I have ever known but when under the influence of alcohol, she has the mouth of a dirty, scallywag of a pirate. She could make sailors blush; I've seen it with my own eyes.

"Ari went to go shower and unpack, he should be down any minute if you want to wait for him inside."

As if I wanted to wait in the scorching heat with no Vietnamese cold coffee to cool me down. *We should've stayed in Vietnam.* I wondered where Aidan and I were going for our honeymoon as I stepped into Lizzie's home. Ari stood at the top of the stairs.

He remained motionless with only a towel wrapped around his waist. Two years ago I might have rushed up the stairs and pushed him into any room, but I had woken up to the sight of my husband wearing nothing but a towel and there is only one view more seductive than that and it also entails Aidan.

I greeted him and followed Lizzie to the kitchen.

"He's so not over you. That's such a varsity-boy stunt," Lizzie whispered, pursing her lips, fighting hard to control her true response to Ari's stunt.

My laughter echoed through the entire house, possibly shaking the red bricks down to the foundation. Married Fin don't care about no semi-naked man if he ain't hers. Cue the gangster rap.

"This is the very reason I won't invite him to the wedding. He needs to move on. It has been two years for crying out loud." I marched towards the alcohol cabinet but stopped at the kettle. Caffeine would have to do.

"He clearly hasn't, and staying here with us will not help either."

"I won't visit you as often; rather come to my house."

Ari walked in and I handed him a mug of coffee. "We need to talk. Ashley should be here soon. A man's body was found this morning, next to the road close to the estuary. We suspect he might have been abducted by the same person who abducted you, but he has only been missing for three days. He disappeared the day you were found."

Lizzie excused herself to open for whoever rang the doorbell, not without sticking her tongue out at me behind Ari's back. The childishness of thirty-something-year-old sisters. *May we never grow up, adult like pros, but never lose our mischief.*

"Do you have a photo of him?" Ari placed his mug next to mine on the kitchen counter, standing so close I could hear air entering and exiting his lungs.

"I do." I reached for the phone in my back pocket, aware of the proximity between us, and took a step to my left. Ashley walked in and I knew what she was thinking. Almost twenty years of friendship had its perks or downfalls when it came to our ability to detect each other's emotions.

"Good afternoon to both of you. Ari, will you please wait for us on the porch? I need to run something by Fin."

I wanted to grab onto Ari's arm; I didn't want to hear what she was about to say. I would agree with her and she knew it. Ari took his and my coffees, and walked out of the kitchen.

"Finley, if it becomes an issue in this investigation that you two have a history, you can excuse yourself. I can relay information to you, and you could still compile a profile." Not what I expected but I tend to forget she's not as childish as Lizzie is at times.

"There's no problem, but I'm aware of the fact that Ari isn't doing too well with me being married. That reminds me, will you be co-matron of honour at my wedding next week Saturday?"

"Yes, of course, don't ask dumb questions. Also, don't change the subject. I don't think you and Ari should spend any time together, and it might be a good thing for him to meet Aidan. The sooner he realises there is no chance of the two of you to get back together the better."

I held up the rock on my hand; I would have pulled a muscle if I weren't in better shape. "Does it get any clearer than this?"

"Is he invited to your wedding?" Her brows furrowed.

"No. The second rule of weddings is never invite an ex."

Mischief played across my mouth.

"You can't make up your own rules for weddings, but it's a good one, and I will allow it. But only if you tell me what the first one is."

"I don't know, but in my head, it didn't sound like a first rule. Maybe the first rule should be *show up to your own wedding not wearing underwear.*" I shrugged, palms up. "This is only my second wedding and the first one I get to plan."

"Married life agrees with you. Risqué Fin hasn't reared her head in a long time."

"She has, but only around Aidan." I sent him a text message before I joined Ari and Ashley on the patio.

Later that afternoon I had planned to train with Eli and I still needed to do grocery shopping to cook for my husband, our first home cooked meal since tying one of two knots. Ari's little, well, big, towel stunt made me lose the little patience I have in general rather than my inhibitions, as I'm sure he had hoped. I took a seat across from them and pulled my legs underneath me. The gentle caress of the wind on my neck didn't calm my resolve to be out of there in less than an hour.

"Ari, are you into BDSM?" Ashley and Ari's eyes reflected nothing but confusion. "Yes, you heard me."

"Finley." Ashley shook her head.

"Why do you think that? As you remember, I'm a gentle and *thorough* lover."

Thorough was an unnecessary addition to a sentence with enough point in it.

Emotionless, I returned his stare.

"Do you remember on Saturday when U showed you the images? Your heart rate increased dramatically when we showed you a photo of a dominatrix. Why is that, Ari? Do you partake in kink play? Ari, are you a kinkster?" I sounded like an interrogator.

Ashley tried to push out her eyes in my direction.

"No, I have never done anything more than blindfolds and cuffs."

That wasn't with me. I fought to forget his hunger, the way his body moved.

You're married, Finley, to a man a million times more everything than him. Focus woman. Without realising, I touched my ring, sliding it up and down my finger. He smiled. I stopped.

"Then why did you react to the image?" I flicked my eyes down to my wrist.

"If you want to be anywhere else, please go. Ashley, and I can continue."

I forgot he was better at this than I am. "So, you recall nothing? What's the last thing you remember before you were abducted?"

"You didn't read the file?" He crossed his arms over his chest.

"No, I haven't had time to read the whole file, and I would rather hear your recollection as you might remember a crucial detail you didn't recall when your statement was taken." *Nice save.*

"Too busy setting up house with the doctor?"

Ashley turned to face him, and I recognised the friend who had my back many times when we were students at UM.

"Ari, Finley is married to a wonderful man who loves her and she him. You need to accept the fact that you left, and she moved on, just like you told her to do. Keep your focus on finding whoever took you and raped you." Freudian slip perhaps, but I knew she was as frustrated with his behaviour as I was.

Ari pushed to his feet, shaking his head and repeated a single word, "No."

Ashley met my eyes and nodded. We waited for him to steady himself and make sense of what she had said. I kept glancing at my wristwatch; it took him five minutes to sit back down. In between his pacing, I sent Lizzie a text message asking her to bring alcohol; maybe a beer would calm him or at the least get him to sit down. It worked.

He spoke in Hebrew, shaking his head, not knowing I

followed what he said. "Ari, men are raped. By men and by women. It happens. Just as it happened to Ashley and to me, it happened to you."

"How did you know?"

"That you were raped or what you said?"

"Both." He finished his beer and put the bottle down next to him harder than necessary. Ashley closed her eyes at the sound.

"You had the same look in your eyes both of us had." I looked at Ashley and smiled. "Do you remember anything about a woman forcing herself on you, or doing things to you?"

He dropped his head into his hands, elbows on his knees.

"What happened, Ari? If you tell us, we can help you, and we can also get a better understanding of who we are looking for. This is difficult, I know, but the sooner you deal with it the better."

"She didn't rape me. I had sex with her."

Denial, but at least we were getting somewhere.

"Did you go to where she held you out of your own free will?" I realised what Ashley was implying and left her to steer the conversation.

"No."

"Would you have slept with her if you met her in a bar?"

"I don't know."

"Did you initiate the sex?"

"No."

"Did you become aroused without any assistance from her whatsoever?"

"No."

"Were you free to move around during?"

"No."

Ashley reached for his hand. "Ari, do you realise what this means?"

He yanked his hand from hers and stormed off, cussing in Hebrew between laboured breaths. Ashley and I both wiped at the tears we had controlled in front of him.

***

Neither Eli nor I had held back during our training session. I didn't want to explain my busted lip to Aidan, but he was bound to see Eli the following day, when Eli's left eye-socket would turn a purple-blue.

While I prepared dinner I wondered why Ari decided to move in with my sister, instead of moving back in with Tom. Ari had, after all, stayed with him for six months, without even Eli being informed of his return to Marcel.

Aidan walked into the penthouse as I dished dinner. "What the hell happened to your lip?"

I have my spidey-sense, Aidan has hawk-vision. "I happened to my lip." Attempting a smile, I only made it bleed again.

"Who did this to you? Tell me." I loved it when he played protector.

I pressed ice to my lip; half my mouth attempted a passable smile. "You should see the other guy."

"Finley, I walk into our home and find my wife with a busted lip and you're making jokes."

"You will see the other guy tomorrow morning when you train with him."

"Eli did this to you?"

"Who else?" This was not the first time I came home with a trophy after a session with Eli.

"Okay, but how am I supposed to kiss you if your lip will bleed?"

"Think of another way you can show me how much you missed me today." I pulled his body against mine, matching the need in his eyes. I placed the ice cube on the kitchen counter; we paid it no attention as it melted next to us.

After dinner, I told Aidan what had happened earlier in the day, omitting the details of Ari wearing a towel. Aidan isn't the jealous type, but I knew better than to poke the dragon.

"Does he remember anything about, you know?"

Why do men not talk about it?

"He does, but he told himself he wanted it. He realises now

what happened to him was not consensual." Aidan pulled me closer. I watched the curtain dance in the wind, a white circle suspended in the darkness outside our biggest source of light.

"Have you compiled a profile yet?"

"No, still haven't found time to go through the file. I have asked the police to get hold of the victims' diaries for me. Men like them have every second of their day planned out, including time for meals, commuting, and training. Tom said they had officers review the entries, but I'm sure they missed something. How is it possible that none of them met before or frequented the same places? They weren't abducted from the street. Whoever she is, she knew their home addresses. I also told them they need to look for shallow graves around the area where the victim was discovered this morning and where Ari was found."

"Where is Ari?"

"Staying with Eli and Lizzie, he got discharged this morning. Why do you ask?"

"I went to his room on my way to my office after doing rounds and he wasn't there."

"Why do you want to see him?"

"It's about time we meet."

A tingle ran down my spine and burrowed its way into my stomach. I shook it off. They could become friends or friendly enough. Maybe if Ari saw us together, he would realise there was a person behind the boulder on my hand. Did Ari believe Tom, that Aidan is the sniper? Did Ari know the sniper saved my life from the man he maimed? Was he jealous of the fact that he's not my knight in combat armour? To be honest, Aidan wore a biker skull mask, but I will never forget the night he kissed me in the decrepit old building where the Marcel Sniper and the Hang*woman* first met. When we were who we no longer are.

"I think so, too."

"Has he hit on you?" Perhaps even Aidan wasn't immune to the green-eyed monster.

"Yes." No secrets – our rule. Secrets tear people apart.

"I don't blame him. If I lost you, no power on earth could keep me from you." He rolled me on to my back and brushed his lips against mine, conscious of the split skin, but the rest of me, fair game.

Nine

Aidan left for work, and that morning I woke early enough to give him the send-off a husband deserves. I poured myself a second cup of coffee. Now I would be fully awake. I took the file off the bookshelf. Leaving it on a counter reminded me of bringing darkness into our home. Perhaps it was time I cleared out the study and made it usable for both Aidan and me. My father no longer used it to formulate miracle drugs; we could use it to hunt and heal. Our new way of dealing with the darkness in this world.

The study had remained as my father had left it, nothing out of place. Medical and psychiatric journals lined the walls. My father would have loved Aidan like the son he never had. I came close, but oestrogen is not testosterone.

I made myself comfortable in my father's oversized chair; oversized to me, but a perfect chair for my father who had had Ari's height and build. My head rested on the back and I took in the emotions of being in another of my father's spaces I had refused to enter for so long. Time does not heal.

The file fell open as I found the last page I had read the day before. The whiteboard to my left would be used to map out my *death thinking*, the very board my father used for formulating medicine, which betters lives to this day.

Ari's lacerated skull stared at me; the back of his shirt stained a reddish-brown. I removed the doctor's report – blunt force trauma, flat object. *Shallow grave.* Had Ari been struck by a shovel and buried alive? I reached for my mobile phone.

"Anderson."

"Did you find a shallow grave which would explain the dirt found on Ari's clothes and body?"

"Finally looking through the file?" My palm tapped on the

dark oak desk. "What is that noise?"

"My patience running out. As you know I don't have enough as it is." I growled.

"Yes, they found a hole in the ground, but I don't think he was buried, rather covered with branches and leaves as we found some pushed to the side and in disarray."

"The report says there was dirt in his mouth and in his nose. Is it possible he was placed face down and then struck with the shovel, or was he struck with the shovel first?"

"How do you know about the shovel?"

"I didn't, just figured he was struck with a shovel as the doctor noted the trauma to the back of his head was cauased by a blunt, flat object. Dirt in his lungs and nose. Two and two go together. Any feedback from the forensic pathologist as to the manor of Jason Rogers' death?" The victim who had been found the previous day.

"No, should receive it later this morning. Will phone you as soon as I get it."

"Any other bodies recovered so far?"

"No, the search teams are out there again this morning. As soon as I hear something, you will be my first call."

"Do I need to work directly with Captain Taylor? I'm aware of the big gang related case you're working on. When is it going to trial?"

"You can contact him if you can't reach me, but he asked me to relay information to you so I can stay in the loop. If you talk to him, please send me an email with the details of your discussion and I will look at it as soon as I get a chance. Finley, how is Ari doing?"

"You need to ask Lizzie or Eli, I haven't spoken to him since yesterday. He needs time to come to terms with what happened. Ashley said she would visit him today. Will ask her to discuss his progress with you. I need the copies of the victims' diaries. Today."

"I need to go, talk to you later." He ended the call, and I stared at the whiteboard.

It was time to understand. I picked up the whiteboard marker and got to work.

Without realising, I switched on the overhead light and continued working through the file, making more notes on the board which had a few spots of white left on it.

"Honey, I'm home," Aidan called out into the darkness of the rest of our home.

"I'm in the office. Why are you home so early?" My back to the door, staring at words that didn't want to be understood.

"Fin, it's 2000 hours." His arms warm around me. Aidan brushed his lips against my neck. The words made sense.

"Kiss me again." He did, and I pulled out of his embrace. "Why would you abduct them at intervals of every six months? Ari's in great shape, you took care of him, didn't you? You didn't want to kill him. Why did you? Are you out hunting now because Jason Rogers died of a heart attack? You know where they lived, but you weren't aware of his congenital birth defect for which he required surgery. You took Griffin Stark two years ago, six months later Ashton Kent, six months later Leo Wayne, then three months later Eric Parker. And Ari, David Ezra, three months after Eric Parker, but David Ezra you kept for six months. How do you select the next one before you kill the one you have? Or do you keep more than one at the same time? Was Griffin Stark the trigger, was he the one you wanted?"

Aidan leaned against the door frame, leaving me to talk to air-conditioned air.

"It doesn't make sense. What happened between Leo Wayne and Eric Parker's abductions? Why keep the others for six months but not the two of them?"

"Maybe they didn't want to play along?"

I spun around almost losing my footing to face the commentator whose presence I had forgotten. "What do you mean?"

"If she keeps them and feeds them, she might be in love

with them in her own twisted way. But the two you mentioned didn't want to play her game, they might have tried to fight back or get away. Have the police found any more bodies?"

As I opened my mouth to answer, my phone rang. "I hope you're phoning with a very good explanation as to why I didn't receive the diary entries today."

"It's being emailed to you as we speak. Fin, they found six bodies."

"Six?" I steadied myself in Aidan's eyes.

"Four men and two women, we don't think the female victims are related to this case."

"Why not?"

"They were both hacked to death, not buried, and were found together. Couldn't have been out there for more than six days, the bodies are still bloated. Will know more once we receive the autopsy report."

"Hacked?" I asked. Aidan mouthed that he would start dinner, and I thanked him with a wink. Few things sexier than a man who can cook better than his wife.

"Axe was found next to the bodies."

"Let's assume for the time being that they are unrelated to our case. If the four men you found are our missing persons and Jason Rogers was in fact her last abduction, that means she's hunting for the next one. We need to know when the four men died and how."

"The autopsies will be done first thing tomorrow morning, do you want to attend? Include the process in your thesis."

"I doubt I need to include it, but I would like to be there. What time?"

"Be at the morgue at eight, I will meet you outside. Are you sure you're up to it?"

"I have seen my fair share of dead bodies." I shook my head at the man who still considered me in too many ways to be an innocent young girl.

"See you tomorrow, send my best to Aidan." *Sneer or smile?*

I switched off the light and closed the door, realising I

hadn't eaten, drank or done any other human bodily things the entire day. Aidan and I ate while we discussed our wedding arrangements. I didn't mention what Tom had said; still trying to figure out if he meant it.

Tom waited for me outside the morgue as I pulled into the parking lot at 0745 hours. Throughout the autopsies I stood motionless, breathing through my mouth. The stench unbearable. Few pieces of flesh remained on the body believed to be Eric Parker. The other three bodies were skeletonised, but not complete skeletons. Teeth marks suggested that jackals or stray dogs had removed parts we might never find. They would conduct DNA tests to confirm the four bodies were that of our missing men.

I left the morgue and headed to Lizzie's; I had to talk to Ari. He opened the front door as I pressed the doorbell for the second time. Without a word he stepped aside and let me in to my sister's house. I walked straight to the liquid Walker and poured myself a tumbler full, taking a beer from the fridge for him, not asking if he wanted a drink.

His eyes burned into me, but I didn't return his gaze, not until we sat outside.

"Enough with the bullshit, I know you remember everything." The memories of what I had seen earlier in the day forced the whiskey into my body.

"The doctor said I have amnesia, Ashley said I'm repressing memories." He forced vulnerability onto his face.

"And I'm telling you you're full of it. Tell me now or I walk from this case." I removed my sunglasses from my head and kneaded my temples.

"Do you want me to rub your neck? It always helped for your headaches."

"No. Tell me. Now."

"Ley, I don't remember."

"Don't call me *Ley*. Not now, not ever. I'm done, Ari. Done. Good luck finding whoever abducted you." I got to my feet, the whiskey rushed to my head, but I composed myself and headed for the front door.

Ari grabbed my arm and pulled me against him hard, the same hunger in his eyes which had made me weak a lifetime ago. I pushed him away, and he fell onto the chair behind him.

"When are you going to get it through your thick skull that I'm off limits to you? I'm *married*. No chance for a love triangle, Ari. I wanted to help catch whoever did this to you, but if you can't get over yourself and realise we will never be involved again, then I can't work on this anymore."

"I'm sorry, Ley."

"Don't call me Ley." My hands drew into themselves, my back stiffened, and my jaw locked. "Aidan wants to meet you, but it's the worst idea ever. He will take one look at you and realise you're trying to move onto his territory. Trust me, you don't want to get on his bad side. Why do you think we are together?" I didn't give him time to voice an opinion. "He's the only man I have ever met who I have reverence for. Aidan is strong, dedicated, and controlled. Maybe I will just say it – you don't match up to him. You might be an alpha male around other men, but the second you enter Aidan's domain, you, Ari, are a beta male."

I walked into the house and poured myself another glass, drank it in one swig, and turned to find Ari standing behind me. "Did I not make myself clear? We are over, you chose to leave."

"I regretted my decision even before I walked out your door."

"I came here to talk to you about the case, to tell you they found four bodies and we think it might be the missing men. The decomposition adds up to the timeframe of their disappearances; well, the next one's disappearance. Why are you lying to everyone about not remembering? Or am I the only one you're lying to? To what? Make me feel empathy for you, to worm your way back into my life, my bed?"

"I love you, I can't stop loving you. I tried to forget about you, but the second my undercover operation ended I rushed back to be with you. The day I *saw* you, I wanted to ask you to marry me. To put all the darkness behind us and spend our lives together. The life you now have with someone else. That's what I want. I want you."

"I will not apologise for finding happiness with someone else. You don't know what happened after you left. And you can't comprehend the bond between me and Aidan. I chose to end our relationship before it got serious and I should never have given us a second chance. I had been desperate to cling onto something, someone, as I felt myself slipping into the abyss. You watched the darkness swallow me and you left, you didn't have the balls to be the man I needed. Aidan is that man." I considered pouring myself more tranquiliser.

"Your biggest problem is your jealousy, not because I'm married, but because you were not the person to save me. You didn't kill the Angel Taker. The sniper did. And you believe Aidan is the Marcel Sniper because Tom told you he is, with no proof to back up his claim." The look in his eyes told me I had struck gold.

"I should've been with you. You were mine to protect, not some serial killer's."

Laughter erupted from me. "And you're not a killer? Ari, we are wasting time. I need to finish my thesis and you need to move on."

His body offered no resistance as I pushed past him and headed for the door. Anger kept me sober. My resolve started to crumble as I reached for the doorknob. Not because I wanted Ari, but because of my need to find *her* before she struck again. I'm a warrior and always will be, and it was time I stopped fighting it, again.

"If I promise to move on, to never again say I love you, never say how much I long to hear you laugh from joy or see your face when I wake up. If I do that, will you stay on the case? There is no one better than you to find Sophia. The name she gave me."

Soap opera plot – amnesia to win love back. I'm not gullible, and I'm not his to win.

"First you will tell me why you lied and then you will tell me everything that happened. If you lie to me, I will make sure you get deported back to Israel so fast you won't have time to say Yiddish. Don't push me."

"Please stop reminding me of your fire; it drew me to you from the moment we met. What happened to your lip? Did he do this to you?" He reached for my face and I stepped back as laughter shook the house once more.

"Aidan will never hurt me. Eli's infamous left hook."

"It explains his eye." He laughed. Situation diffused.

"Talk, I have a lot of work to do. Still need to go through their diaries."

Ari claimed he told me everything. Nothing helped in giving me a better idea of who Sophia is or how we could stop her.

Ten

Aidan lay on the lounger as I walked out onto the deck, my body still sore and sweaty from my earlier session with Eli.

"What happened?" he asked, eyes closed.

"What makes you think something happened?" I positioned myself over him, trailing my hands over his bare chest.

"You move soundlessly when you're happy, and when you're angry, the doorman can hear you."

I removed my moist shirt and sports bra, bent down, and brushed my lips against his.

"And this?" His mouth against mine, his fingers gripping my back.

"I want to have your baby."

He pushed me away and tilted his head. Moonlight sparked in his eyes. "We are not even married a month, are you sure it's not too soon? What happened today? Is this because you saw Ari again? Do you want to show him just how off limits you are to him?"

"No." I reached for my shirt, but Aidan grabbed my arms, pulling me against his chest and whispering into my ear. That was the last day I had to remember to drink any pill but prenatal vitamins and the extra folic acid my husband, the doctor, gave me.

I couldn't sleep, adrenaline still ran amok inside me. Being with Aidan sent all of me into a frenzy, and my oxytocin and endorphin levels were still returning to normal. The email with the missing – now found and laying in drawers inside the morgue – men's electronic diaries had been sent to my inbox while Aidan and I had enjoyed dinner. None of the men kept a hard copy of their daily activities; similar schedules for all six of them. Meetings, meals, and time set aside for exercise. I worked through each one's schedule up to a year before the first victim, Griffin Stark, had vanished.

In my sleep deprived, I'm-trying-for-a-baby-state, I didn't pick up on any anomaly consistent with all six of them.

Dawn brought clarity, and I reached for the pink highlighter I hoped to use as visual confirmation that I had found something. I highlighted the suspected anomaly and hit number four on my speed dial. If only I suffered from Tetraphobia.

"What time is it?" A sleepy voice answered.

"No idea, I haven't slept. I found something."

"Okay, I'm listening?" The voice more alert.

"This is consistent for all the men, some starting back a year before Stark disappeared, some closer to their own abductions. Each of the men, including Ari, had a two-hour block left blank, different days, but every week."

"What are you trying to say?"

"It was in the middle of their normal work day; they scheduled nothing for a two-hour period. They scheduled everything from their visits to the dentist, barber, women, but nothing for that two-hour period."

"Fin, the computer forensics guys didn't find any blank time slots. It's in the file."

"Yes, but this is where it gets strange. Why when they looked into it were there no unaccounted for time slots, but now there is? And they never checked Ari's or Rogers' schedules."

"What's your conclusion?"

"They all saw the same person. Someone hacked their computers or phones recently and cleared the information. It's possible they only saw the person for an hour, adding time to commute. Some of them did this for meetings not held at their offices. Who do you see for an hour every week?"

He groaned; I assumed he stood – his leg would never be the same. "A shrink."

"Not bad, old man."

"I'm not old."

"Tell that to your knee. I will phone Captain Taylor and ask that they track their mobile phone's movement on the specific days and see if it points to the same area. Once I have the information, we can look for psychologists or psychiatrists in the area." *A dominatrix?* I kept the thought to myself.

"Don't phone him now, I beg you. The man is impossible if woken up with something which could wait at least two hours. It's not even five A.M. yet."

"I didn't recall visits to a health professional in the file on Ari's cover. Was he seeing someone?"

"You should phone him and ask him yourself. I need coffee, talk to you later."

Ari could wait; I needed to spend half an hour in my husband's arms before he would get up and go heal the world. Aidan stirred as I climbed into bed next to him and snuggled into his arms. I drifted into sleep. He's my calm, my anchor. Darkness danced around me as I lay in his arms, protected by his love and our life. Committed to hunting monsters the right way, never letting go of each other and being drawn back into the realm of human predators.

Never like before.

After Aidan left for work, I phoned Ari. He asked me to meet him for a round of sparring later in the afternoon. Ari's reasoning – he was no longer hitting it, so now he could hit it. Victim and ex, he donned both personas with equal fervour.

I spent the day reviewing every bit of information in the file and tried to put myself in Sophia's head. Before I chose life, it was much easier, but now I fought for my sanity, knowing all too well what I'm capable of when I embrace the darkness.

Captain Taylor agreed to my request and reminded me they were understaffed; he still waited for the reports from the forensic pathologist and would share the information with me as soon as he received it.

On my way to meet Ari, I drove past the missing men's

homes to get a feel for how they lived and assess their security. There was something missing, but I would get Ari to talk, even if it meant I had to punch it out of him.

I looked forward to punching him in the face for all the things he had said since I had seen him in the hospital. He still had a slight concussion, so head shots were out, but kick him I did. He wasn't back to fighting form, not yet.

"Anything else you want to tell me about Sophia?" I licked the blood from my lip, same cut, different fist.

"No, nothing apart from what I told you before." His chest rose and fell, sweat glistening on his skin. He always preferred to spar without a shirt.

"Who did you see every week for an hour?"

"What? No one." This time I struck platinum.

"There you go again with your lies. I don't have time for this."

"Do you have somewhere you need to be?"

"As a matter of fact, I have an appointment in an hour." I had a dress fitting with Favio, but I wasn't sure if Ari knew I was getting married in a week.

"Is it for the wedding?" He knew.

"I'm asking the questions here. Stop avoiding the subject. Who did you see?"

"You always enjoyed being in charge." His smile no longer intoxicating. Now it activated a primal response – rage.

My nostrils flared and I stepped back, ready to walk away from the one-sided conversation.

"A psychiatrist, Doctor James."

"Did you see him as David Ezra or yourself?"

"I booked the appointments as David Ezra because that's who I was for a year. But *I* spoke to him."

"What did you discuss? If it wasn't pertinent to the case, I wouldn't ask." Curiosity, not the case, my motive.

"During the year I spent undercover, I witnessed things far worse than I had ever seen in my entire life. While I infiltrated, I was powerless to do anything to save them. If you think the things you saw on the dark web were bad, you don't understand what it's like to hear their screams and cries in the room next to you. All you can do is pray it will be over soon, and that you will live to avenge what was being done to them."

"Did you avenge them?"

"Yes."

His expression I understood all too well. "But?"

"No matter how many I killed, when we took them down, it didn't erase the things they had done to their victims."

"It never does. How many did you save?"

"Fifty-eight. The others died or were sold off before I had the name of the boss."

"Did you get him?"

"He died by my hands. This scar here," he showed me his arm, "this is where he bit into my arm before I slashed his throat."

"You did good, Ari." I hugged him. A hug shared by warriors.

"And then when I got back you were no longer waiting for me. The hope of being with you again was what kept me going. I carried so much anger and resentment in me, if I didn't talk about it, I would have done something I would've regretted. My current employer does not believe in psychological debriefing, so I kept my sessions private."

"Is Doctor James a woman?"

"No. He must be close to seventy, lost his wife a few years back and never had children."

My hand rubbed under my navel.

"Are you pregnant?"

"Why would you ask that?"

"You're rubbing your belly." He looked at his evidence.

"Just a muscle twitch, not pregnant." *Not yet.*

"What are you doing on Friday night?"

"Will be home with my husband."

"Not asking you out on a date, but it's time I meet Doctor Walker and find out for myself whether he's as good for and to you as everyone says he is." *Except Tom.*

"I don't think that's a good idea. Lizzie wants us to go out on Saturday night for my bachelorette party."

"Oh yes, I keep forgetting you got married without knowing you were going to." His left brow raised.

"We are getting married again next weekend. I need to go; I have a dress fitting with Lizzie's stylist."

"The guy who dressed you the night we bumped into each other at Rip Tide?"

"Favio, the one and only. I'm going to hear the word *bitch* more in the two hours I will be with him than I would in a lifetime."

"You will look breathtaking no matter what you wear. You make the dress, not the other way around." *Bad line, Ari.*

"I have to hit the shower. I will talk to Aidan about Friday night." I ran towards the shower, and my phone stopped ringing as soon as I opened the locker. I returned the three missed calls, all from the same number.

"The forensic pathologist's report is in your inbox. He confirmed all four bodies are our missing men. The cause of death for all four – bludgeoning, a similar object as what was used on Ari. But the skulls are shattered, indicating repeated blows."

"Why did she hit Ari only once?"

"Your guess is as good as mine."

"He's hiding something about this Sophia, and no matter how much I try to gouge the information out of him, he changes the subject."

"Keep at it, he will tell you. Hold on..." Hurried voices in the background. "Shit! Another man is missing, Logan Reid."

"If it's the one I'm thinking about, he went to high school with me."

"It's him, I remember his face, younger than the photo in my hand, from when I did a background check on him when the two of you dated."

We were eighteen, nothing more had happened than what

happened on instruction of Aidan's coin. Second base, no third, no home runs. "When did he go missing?"

"Last night, from his home. We can't find mobile phone reception activity in any area apart from his residential address. He didn't show up at work today, his personal assistant can't get hold of him, and his car is parked in the garage."

"It's consistent with what Ari said. Let me go talk to him, he's purposefully omitting or forgetting a crucial piece of information." I rushed out of the locker room and ran straight into Aidan's chest.

"What are you doing here?" I realised Tom was still on the line and ended the call.

"Training with Eli. What are you doing here? You train mornings."

"I sparred with Ari, trying to get more information out of him. Is he still here?"

"If you're referring to the Spartan god, yes he is."

"Is that a hint of green in my Norse god's eyes?"

"I'm not jealous, but I would have preferred a heads up before meeting the infamous Ari. What is his last name?"

"I've never asked. Aidan, can we press pause on this conversation until later? A man I attended high school with has gone missing and Ari hasn't told me everything, even after he swore he did. Where is he? I will beat the truth out of him."

"He suffered severe trauma to his occipital bone, hit him on the sternum," Doctor Walker said.

"Man, I love you." I pressed my mouth against his and ran toward Eli's voice.

"Ari!" He spun around and my fist connected right where my husband had instructed. I turned and basked in the approval in Aidan's eyes.

"What the hell, Finley?" Eli helped Ari to his feet.

"I will remove your teeth with my fists if you don't tell me the truth right now."

"What truth?" He grabbed his chest.

"You have evaded answering why you got into the car?

Because of your games, someone I know has been abducted. I swear, Ari, if you don't start talking now, I will hurt you more than anyone ever has." I drew my right arm back, hand in a fist.

Eli stepped between us. "Tell her whatever you haven't or I will stand back, and I won't even let Aidan save you."

"What does her husband have to do with this?"

"He's standing against the wall." I jerked my head back. "His first instinct would have been to save your life, but he knows when I'm this angry it's best to stay out of my way. Even Eli knows better."

Ari looked past me at the man standing behind me. Aidan gave a slow nod, and Ari started talking. "Okay, this is what I haven't told you and it's only because I have been running with this myself. The day of my abduction, a delivery was made to my house. Inside the package was a mobile phone, switched on, fully charged. Thirty minutes before the car arrived, a text message came through instructing me to shower and get dressed for the most memorable night of my life. I was intrigued, so I did. Exactly thirty minutes later, a car drove up to my house, but the driver didn't get out – he honked. I got into the car and there was a partition between the back and front seats. I blacked out shortly afterwards and woke up in the room I told you about."

"You didn't tell me or the police because it was one dumbass move." I shook my head.

"I know." He swallowed hard. "I needed to get out, and the agreement I signed with Doctor James stated he might use unconventional methods to deal with the reasons I went to see him." Ari focused his stare on the ground between us.

"It wasn't just as a debrief?"

"No. I don't want to discuss this here. Please, L..." He stopped in time to avoid a second fist to his chest.

"Okay, but where does this Sophia fit into all of this?"

"The first time I met her was in that room. I didn't lie when I told you that."

"No, but the fact that you didn't tell me the rest might cost Logan Reid his life. If she kills him, his blood will be on your hands. Your hands, Ari." My hands flattened on his chest and I pushed forward. He stumbled backwards but didn't lose his footing.

"Finley. Enough." Aidan walked closer, and the look in his eyes kept me in place. He extended his hand to Ari and Ari shook it. Eli formally introduced them as I excused myself and headed for the shower. Favio was going to kill me.

In record time, I showered and made myself look presentable enough to avoid another speech from Favio about my masculine and too-black style.

"Where are you going?" Aidan pulled me into his arms.

"Dress fitting with Favio."

"Please don't punch him. I can't keep up with looking after your victims. I need to get my training in," he whispered in my ear. I couldn't help but smile.

"Are you okay?" I asked Ari, holding Aidan's stare.

"Yes, thanks to Aidan."

I looked at Eli, he nodded.

"See you at home." I kissed my husband. "Ari, you can ask him about Friday night seeing as the two of you have now met."

As I made my way to the front door, I heard Aidan speak Hebrew for the first time. The man is as complex as a twenty-two by twenty-two Rubik's cube. Each square a different colour.

Favio stood outside the store, tapping his right foot with his hands pushed into his sides.

"Sorry I'm late, can't tell you my reason though. But I will make it up to you."

"Bitch, how you going to do that?"

"Pay you double?" I gave him puppy dog eyes, which would have made Aidan laugh.

"You know I love you, Mrs Walker."

He tolerated me because he loves money.

"There should be champagne inside. You could have waited for me in the comfort of an air-conditioned building, you know." I hooked into his arm and that was all the encouragement he needed; his sashay gave away his excitement to dress a woman he had once asked whether she wanted to be a dude.

"You're going to die when you see the dress I've picked for you."

For the first time, he knew what I wanted, and I couldn't wait to see Aidan's face when I walked down the aisle. A Justin Alexander design in off-white. I was, after all, getting married for the second time. The dress a charmeuse slim A-line gown with hand-beaded cap sleeves. A keyhole back in honour of my first wedding dress, and a belt to complement the detail of the sleeves.

"It's perfect, Favio. Thank you."

"Wow, bitch, wow." He stared at me as I admired my reflection.

My mother would have approved. I will never know whether she would have cried.

I rushed home to prepare dinner; domestic life is not for the fainthearted. You start thinking about the next evening's dinner before you've even finished the one in front of you. For the first time, my kitchen was being utilised. Aidan arrived just as I hid the dress in the spare bedroom.

"We are having dinner with Ari, Eli, and Lizzie at Lizzie's tomorrow night." He leaned against the door frame, a position he often took.

"I take it he approved of your Hebrew?"

"Yes, but he was more impressed by the fact that my maternal-grandfather is Jewish."

I closed the distance between us and settled myself across from him. "Is there anyone in this world immune to your charm?"

"Only one, but we won't speak of him."

The tone set for incoming emails on my phone sounded, but I kept my focus on Aidan's piercing blue eyes.

I didn't work that night as the lack of sleep the previous night had caught up with me. I dreamt of a woman crying, clutching her stomach. Aidan woke me up and calmed me down, only for me to drift back off into a tormented sleep. His arms couldn't keep me safe.

Eleven

Captain Taylor promised to have an officer dig into Doctor James' practise, and would share information with me as and when he received it. There were no other leads on Logan Reid's disappearance. Again, I read through the emails and the autopsy reports. All the men had been in good health when they died, no signs of malnourishment or torture.

"Why are you keeping them for so long? Companionship? Why take on the role of submissive with these men? Is that even what you're doing?" They couldn't all be submissive and allowing her to be dominant.

I reached for my phone. Ari answered without me hearing a ring tone.

"Why did you see Doctor James?"

"Good morning to you too."

"I don't have time for this, Ari. I'm stumped and I hate not understanding her."

"But you do, she has the same needs you do."

"I don't have needs." Well, I did, but I wasn't about to discuss my need for caffeine, sushi, hollow-point bullets, and my husband with my ex.

"All of us do. We need companionship, to love and be loved, sexual intimacy, and security."

"Did she spend time with you? Or did she only come into your room to do what she did?"

"Every other night she cooked a three-course meal, set a table, and we had dinner together. After which she would, as you put it, do what she did."

"Would you say that it was like a date to her?"

"Yes."

"Did she dress as if she was on a date?"

"She's a beautiful woman, that's why I don't understand why she needs to abduct and keep men hostage. Most men will fall over themselves when she walks into a room. She's tall, slender, strong, and has the most captivating green eyes. Her voice is husky and sexy."

"What did she share about herself during these dinners?"

"She always said how happy she was to have me there. Told me how much she loves me and that I made her feel desired, safe, and loved. Each time when she was done, she would tell me that she had never had a lover like me, that she had waited her whole life to feel as beautiful and feminine as I made her feel."

"Her only way to control you was the collar around your neck and the chains around your ankles and wrists?"

"Yes."

"This is going to be direct, but I need you to be honest. Did you pleasure her?"

"No, she always tied me to the bed. After months of being with her, I might have if she had given me a chance. Maybe I developed Stockholm syndrome." He sighed. "I'm not proud to admit it."

"It's understandable under the circumstances, considering how long she held you." I shook my head, but I understood his reasoning and the effects captivity can have on someone.

"Before you say anything, just listen to what I need to say. This is not about our history. Part of the reason I saw Doctor James was because I realised after I came back, and you were in a relationship, that I should never have left you. As much as I wanted to be with you, war and the hunt has been my life for so long that I didn't know how to choose anything above it. Yes, I needed to work through everything that happened during that year. But I also needed to learn how to be a normal man again, one capable of having a meaningful and lasting relationship. When I signed up for sessions, I thought the unconventional treatment methods might involve blind dates, things like that. Finley, I was excited to meet someone that night and where did it get me? I realise now, perhaps a normal life is something I'm not capable of."

I fought back tears, hearing the pain in his voice, and realising the courage it took for him to say this, to me of all people.

"Ari, I understand, better than you think. Perhaps you do understand the connection between Aidan and I; we were both where you are now. You need to keep seeing Ashley and work through everything you need to, and I do mean everything. When you're ready, start dating again. You deserve a full and happy life; you can't stay in the darkness forever. It has been killing you for years, started to long before we met."

"Do you think the other men also saw Doctor James? He's not involved in this."

"I'm waiting for Captain Taylor to get back to me with the information I requested. Can't Eli help us?"

"He's busy with another assignment. One he won't even discuss with me." He sighed again.

"Did she pleasure you?" I wanted to phrase my question more biologically but settled for the least crude sentence I could construct.

"Why?" Confusion and anger mixed in his voice.

"You said you enjoyed your dinner's together, the part where you weren't alone locked in that room. If she held you for six months, like she did with most of the others except, for Leo Wayne and Eric Park, why did she then decide to kill you?"

"I don't know why she thought it was time to get rid of me, but perhaps I had served my purpose."

"Ari, I need to ask again, did she pleasure you?" Closing my eyes, I cringed, knowing I had to ask him outright. "Did you ejaculate?"

"Why does it matter?"

"I'm not asking to make this more difficult for you, I'm asking you as a fellow survivor, as your friend. As the person who will find her and bring her to justice."

"Yes." His voice cracked; nails clawed at my heart.

"I have told no one this because I never wanted to admit it to myself, but one man, when I was being held prisoner during the war, he didn't hurt me like the others. When the door opened, I always hoped it would be him who walked in, because he was gentle. I didn't want to be there, being raped every day, but sometimes he simply sat with me, fed me, or helped me get dressed, or washed me. When he raped me, it didn't leave me hurting for days."

The mind has a strange way of protecting the body against horror. It took me years to deal with this realisation and no longer see myself as a hypocrite. Sometimes I wonder if his approach had been more psychological than that of the other men. It no longer mattered; he had taken his last breath the day of my rescue.

"It was still rape. It's the same as what you and Ashley told me."

"Yes, it was." The pain and guilt I had carried for so long threatened to rip through me. "I need to go."

Before Aidan and I left for dinner at Lizzie's, I told him everything. He held me until my tears were spent; guilt no longer had its claws in me. I could breathe. *No secrets, no judgement. Free at last.*

Aidan and I drove to Lizzie's separately, playing another of our games. He hated when we played at night, but I craved the adrenaline and danger. I needed to focus on nothing but the road and clear my mind of everything I had seen since we had returned from Vietnam. The moment I took the lead, I knew Aidan would be upset.

I parked in Lizzie's driveway and waited for what was to come. My hands shook as I removed my helmet, still sitting astride my Ducati Monster, hoping the sight might stir him enough to forget his anger. The sound of his motorcycle approaching had the same effect on me as his voice.

Aidan pulled up next to me, and I knew not even waiting

for him naked would do the trick. He yanked his helmet off, anger flashed in his eyes. "Are you insane?" he screamed over the low rumble of his MV Agusta Brutale 800 RR idling. Angry Aidan on that motorcycle, I had to fight for self-control and allow him to vent. "You ran a red light and that car nearly drove into you."

"But it didn't, I swerved left and I'm fine."

"I don't care what your reward is for winning. You don't drive like that in the city. You're not some bloody superhero. I swear if you ever do that again, I will sell that thing." He pointed at the motorcycle beneath me. "Stop looking at me like that."

Bedroom eyes focused on him; well, not bedroom eyes. I'm sure I had never looked at him with such raw want before. I bit my lower lip as I got off the Monster and walked over to him, bringing my face so close to his that the heat from his mouth teased my lips. "I'm sorry, Aidan."

He didn't move. "I can't lose you. Do you have any idea what it will do to me if you die? I'm serious, woman."

I had pushed him too far but waited for him to kiss me first. He did, and forced all of his rage onto my mouth. I never wanted him more.

"Are you two done or do I need to call the police and report a domestic disturbance?" Eli stood in the front door, Ari behind him.

"Done," Aidan said, but his eyes told me we would continue the kiss and what would follow later.

"You got a bike?" Ari asked as I walked past him.

"Yes. Wanted one for years."

"And you let her drive that thing knowing how she drives her car and SUV?" he asked Aidan.

"She got it before we met. Sort of." Aidan replied, and winked at me. The memory of the night he, the Marcel Sniper, watched me torch a car played through my mind.

Lizzie walked down the stairs, dark circles under her eyes. "No talk about war, abductions, serial killers, or any of that crap. Not tonight." She poured herself a glass of wine, filling it to the brim.

"Lizzie, what's wrong?" Doctor Walker walked over to assess a potential patient.

"You have never been in a room with the three of them, Aidan. How can I forget? You might enjoy it as you, too, played soldier."

Aidan took another step closer to her and pulled her into his arms. "War is not a game, Liz, and you will never refer to it as such ever again. You're tired, but if you aren't up to having company, I will be happy to take everyone out to dinner. You can get into bed and I will make you something to eat before we leave."

She held on to him. Eli and I turned to each other and shrugged.

"Lizzie, what's going on?" My hand reached for her arm.

"As you are aware, Jason Rogers is dead. I only found out this morning. The day he disappeared, we had a meeting that morning, and he had agreed to distribute the whole range of Williams Pharmaceutical products at the price I require to keep the overall costs low enough to stay competitive. None of the other distributors I contacted would even consider it. I'm screwed, Finley. Everything our parents worked for is going down the drain because I refuse to manufacture generic products, it was against everything Daddy stood for. And don't start with all the 'cheaper for the people' crap." Her green eyes moist as they met mine.

"Liz, let me make a call." Aidan walked past me, and I watched him until he was out of view on the patio, leaving me to offer her comfort when I had no idea what running the family business entailed.

Eli broke the deafening silence save for the sound of my heart still drumming in my ears from the ferocity of Aidan's earlier kiss. "What can I get you and Aidan to drink?"

"Walker please, mine neat, his on ice."

By the time Eli handed me my drink, Aidan had returned,

and he kissed the side of my head before walking to Lizzie.

"You have a meeting Monday morning at ten with the CEO of Duvall Distribution, at his office."

"How did you manage to get hold of him at this hour? He refused to meet with me when my PA contacted his."

"My father owns the company; Graham Hamilton is the appointed CEO."

For over a year I had tried to make sense of how my father-in-law accumulated his wealth, and as soon as I thought I knew what his empire consisted of, I learned of yet another tentacle.

"How do I thank you for setting this up?" She threw her arms around Aidan's neck.

"Promise you will take care of my wife tomorrow night and won't let her dance on any tables? She's not as young as she used to be." He palmed my bum just hard enough.

Lizzie turned to me, a devilish smile on her face, and drank the rest of the fluid in her glass, eyeing me over the rim. "I heard Griffin Stark is one of the victims. Wasn't he the guy at Dad's golf club you refused to make eye contact with? I swear you were the only woman in the world who never looked at him. How you could resist his broody darkness is beyond me."

I felt the questioning smile on Aidan's face, but I had to make sure. *Dumb, Finley.* He played with his tongue against his teeth, the biggest, baddest smile on his face. "He was my mentor in med school," the smile unwavering, "but I guess you knew him better." Aidan kept his eyes on mine.

I burst out laughing and somehow managed a comprehensible word. "Touché."

"What are we missing?" Lizzie poured herself another glass of wine, and I held my tumbler towards her for a refill.

"One more. You're not driving on that Monster of yours if you drink more than two."

"Yes, sir." I pressed my mouth against Aidan's and walked out onto the patio. Ari followed me.

"I get it."

"What?" I asked.

"Why you're so captivated with him. He swoops in and saves the day, and has you on a short leash. I never thought I would see the day strong, independent, fearless Finley Williams submits to a man."

"I don't submit to him. When you have a reason to live you kind of try to do whatever it takes to stay alive. He isn't wrong about me not needing to drink more than two drinks and get on my motorcycle. I'm reckless sober – you know how I get when I drink too much."

"I do."

"How are you doing?"

He didn't have time to answer as the others joined us.

"Seeing as the ladies are going out tomorrow night, how about we go out too? We can phone Kyle and ask him to join us, maybe Tom will look after Hope," Eli said.

"As long as you don't go to any strip clubs." I patted Aidan's thigh.

"Why? Don't want us to see you dance on a table? Or does it only happen when you need to win a wet t-shirt competition?" Aidan and Eli's laughter could have been heard by people living three blocks away.

"What did I miss?"

"We will tell you tomorrow night, Ari. It seems the Williams sisters have quite the arsenal of stories from their youth."

"Zip it, both of you. I will kneecap you both, and just because of your little comment, I think you need to phone Favio, Liz. Ask him if he's up to getting you, me, and Ashley ready for our night out on the town. Oh, and do ask him for a dress that will clash with my ring so I can leave it at home."

"You wouldn't dare, Mrs Walker." Aidan pulled me into his arms and tickled me. I laughed like I had the day at the lake house. I fought off Aidan's torturous hands and caught a glimpse of Ari's back as he walked into the house.

"Both of you, do me a favour. Wherever you go, make sure there are hot, single women, and help Ari meet someone."

"That's something women do, Fin, not men."

"He needs it, it can't be fun for him to be surrounded by the four of us. It will do him good to be in control." Their heads bopped in unison, reminding me of bobble heads.

Ari returned and held his mobile phone towards me. "Tom wants to talk to you."

My stomach twisted, but I took the phone. "Hello?"

"Can you meet me tomorrow morning at ten at my house? I have asked Ari, Captain Taylor, and the detectives working on the case to be here. We need to discuss the details. Every day is a day closer to Logan Reid's death, assuming he's still alive."

"I have plans tomorrow night. Can't leave your place later than 1500 hours."

"Then you better bring your A-game, Finley, because we have squat."

"If the forensic laboratory wasn't so understaffed and backlogged, we wouldn't be. Don't blame me for this."

"I'm not, but we need to catch a break soon."

"I know. I will see you tomorrow at morning." I lifted my eyes to Ari's. "Are you fetching Ari, or must I pick him up?"

"He's getting his new SUV on Monday, so I would appreciate it if you could pick him up."

"Will do."

I handed Ari his phone, and my eyes filled with compassion. "You don't have to be there. We need to talk about every aspect; I can talk them through it."

"Thank you, but I have to. For the known victims and Logan Reid."

"I will pick you up at 0930 hours."

"You don't have to."

"No point in arguing with her, Ari. And we are going out tomorrow night, you're coming with us," Aidan said.

At 0915 hours the following morning, I pulled into Lizzie's driveway. Aidan might not be the jealous type, but he had his ways to ensure I would think of nothing but him for the rest of the day. During the drive, I contemplated our decision to start a family. Since the night of Ashley and Kyle's wedding, I couldn't stop thinking about what it would be like to have children with him. Aidan had lost a child years before, and I knew he yearned to be a father. He loves Hope, and the moments they share are some of my favourite moments, simply being in the same room as him.

We might not have been married long, but I wasn't getting any younger. That night would be my last night to be young, not needing to worry about going home to a child who would want to play with a very hungover mother the next day.

Ari closed the front door behind him as I switched the ignition off, his shoulders hunched, and even with sunglasses covering his eyes I could tell he was exhausted.

"No sleep?" I asked as he got into the passenger seat.

"No sleep."

"Nightmares?"

"No."

"What then?"

"Dreams."

I turned to face him. Ari stared at the garage door in front of my G-Class. "I don't understand."

"I dreamt about her and woke up missing her."

"You don't miss her; you miss being with someone. That, my friend, is about to change." I touched his shoulder, felt the weight resting on it.

"What do you mean?"

"Tonight you're going out with Aidan, Eli, and Kyle, and you *will* enjoy it. And you're *not* coming home to this empty bed."

"I don't understand?"

"Do I need to spell it out for you? You're going to meet someone tonight and you will take that lucky woman home and have your way with her and she with you. Full consent."

"Are you encouraging me to have a one-night stand?"

"If you want to do it standing, that's up to you."

He laughed so hard the vehicle shook. "Thank you, Finley."

"For what?" I asked, and reversed out of the driveway, heading to a house I had not been to in over a year.

"For being you. A friend. Just being so understanding and knowing what I need."

"You were there for me when I needed someone, and you showed me what it was to reclaim power over an aspect of myself which had been ripped from me. The sooner you do it the better."

"I can see how much you love Aidan and I'm happy for you. I haven't made it easy for you, but I hope you realise that I appreciate what you did and are still doing for me. You're a good friend."

"So, we're friends? All the other crap is behind us?"

"Yes."

Time would tell if he meant it. I hoped he did.

"I need to tell you every detail, but please don't do that thing where your eyes change because you see me as a victim. What I'm about to tell you might give you a better understanding of her."

Ari turned to face me, and I listened, mindful of keeping my face devoid of any obvious emotion.

Before we reached Tom's front door I grabbed Ari's arm, and pulled him to face me. "You can leave any time you want to. I will leave the SUV's key on the table next to the front door, it should still be where it has been since before I can remember. And if they ask you any questions or if we discuss anything you don't want to weigh in on, just give me a signal and I will do the talking."

"Always someone's protector." Sadness filled his eyes.

"What's wrong?"

"Nothing. Let's get this over and done with, we both have big plans tonight."

"Yes, we do."

Tom opened before we reached the door and offered us coffee as we stepped inside and made ourselves comfortable at the dining room table. I placed the file and my laptop in front of me, careful to position the screen in such a way that Ari wouldn't see the notes I had made from our discussions as he took a seat to my right. The webcam covered by a Batman logo – a previous nocturnal occupational hazard. You never know who might be watching you, and I'm not referring to Big Brother.

Captain Taylor and the detectives joined us; the forensic pathologist had family responsibilities, but we had his reports.

Tom asked me to start, and I wished I had more to offer. It's a fine balance for me – living in the light, and fighting the unwavering pull of my inner darkness. If I was to become a profiler I needed to balance the scales. Darkness understands, but only light can bring it to justice.

I took the last sip of my coffee, hoping it contained something stronger as I had no idea what I would offer, and everyone counted on me as the qualified profilers were also stumped. "I will do a run through of the facts and will make notes on the whiteboard as I go. Please feel free to jump in at any time. We're all familiar with the victim profiles and autopsy reports. The four male bodies found this week were identified as our missing persons."

I shook my head, breathed deep, and continued. "Ari remembered a window in the room where he was held from which he could only see another building, perhaps a garage or part of the building in which he was held. Burglar bars on the interior and exterior sides of the window. Captain Taylor, we need to consider that the building may be in close proximity to the estuary, or at least in the vicinity. She won't risk travelling far with the men before she kills and buries them. Speak to whoever you need to and keep it discreet, she doesn't know Ari is alive. Our only advantage at this stage."

I rose and walked to the blank canvas which mocked my inability to understand this Sophia, if that was her name. "Has anyone been to the BDSM dungeons in Marcel? As far as I can recall, there are four, but there might be more as people are still not open about the lifestyle around here."

"Why are you thinking about dungeons?" Captain Taylor rested his arms on the table.

I looked at Ari, he nodded. "Ari estimates that the first week he spent with her, she wore an outfit worn by dommes or submissives, I'm still trying to understand her. Maybe she's a switch. She appears dominant in the beginning but as her captives show her they are not fighting her, she takes on the role of a submissive. She rewarded Ari for indulging in her fantasies." I hated talking about him as if he wasn't there, but he was our only living lead.

"How did she reward you?" Tom asked.

"She would allow me to take the shackles off of my wrists and ankles, but she wouldn't give me food if I didn't shackle myself again. Her way to control, but also gain trust."

"What kind of fantasies are we talking about?" a detective asked, I wasn't sure who.

I answered, trying to spare him. "She wanted to be spanked or punished, different tools or toys if you wish, on different days. The men have to tell her how naughty she has been, and that she's theirs now. Perhaps her way of getting over the previous man. In her own way I believe she falls in love with each of them and needs the next one to know he isn't the first, not to scare them, but to make her seem more desirable. As if they must compete with another man to have her."

"So, she seems to not be in control, but she is?" Tom asked.

"Yes, she sets the boundaries of their play and what she will have done to her. But if she wants it to end, the dominant must stop immediately. Most submissives have a safe word."

"What was her safe word?" Detective Shaw asked Ari, too many years on the job and too many victims visible on his face.

"She didn't have one. If she felt it went too far, she pressed a button and the collar around my neck tightened, telling me it was over."

"Why did you not take the opportunity to try and get away from her?" Detective McMann asked, younger than his partner, but his demeanour screamed authority. Perhaps ignorant and inexperienced more than authority.

"I was shackled, and she only came close enough for the whip, paddle or whatever to reach her. She always remained in control. I wouldn't have gotten far with the collar around my neck and the remote in her hand."

I regained control of the conversation. "She didn't continue with this, only as long as she needed to ascertain that the man she had taken would do as she asked. I think she presented herself as submissive from a psychological perspective more than for her own pleasure. The men she abducted, including David Ezra, are all what can be classified as alpha males."

"What does that mean?" The younger detective posed the question.

"Alpha male is a classification for men who are dominant over other men. Consider the victims." I pointed at the names on the board behind me. "They are all at the top of their respective fields, they exude power, dominance, and they get what they want no matter the cost. They are physically strong, attractive, and intelligent. That's it." I shook my head at my own stupidity.

"What did you see, Ley?" I let that one go.

"She's hunting for a mate."

"Why then kill these *perfect* men?" Tom sat back and folded his arms over his chest.

I shrugged. "Perhaps they no longer meet her requirements. From the way she spoke to Ari, she sounded in love with him, or the idea of him at least. Before she struck him with the shovel, she said she loved him and would miss him, but it wouldn't work, and 'thunk', shovel to skull. Sorry, Ari."

He shook his head but smiled.

"But, gentlemen, I still believe there is an element to this I don't understand." Vivid memories of the dream I had earlier in the week crashed through my mind. I shook it off; nothing more than a bad dream.

"Any feedback on the unofficial investigation into Doctor James?" Captain Taylor asked.

"He's clean; nothing we can find on him to indicate that he's involved in this, and we can't walk up to him and ask him outright."

"We can't, but Ari can. Or rather David Ezra can, as his patient." Perhaps the notion hadn't left me after all. "Are you up for a session?"

Ari nodded; vengeance swirled in his dark eyes.

"Detectives, can you ask your confidential informants about possible dungeons, and ask around about a Sophia while you're at it. She might go by another name there, but she's tall, has dark-auburn hair, green eyes, and she's a very beautiful woman. Someone might know her. Ari, have you sat with a sketch artist?"

"No, not yet."

"Why is it my job to think of everything? Seriously, people, start doing your jobs." My annoyance splashed across the table.

"Finley, we had serious budget cuts and we are understaffed."

"I understand your predicament, but when you were hunting Tony Andretti you managed to set up a task force."

"Don't forget the one set up for the Marcel Sniper."

My eyes burned into the top of his skull as Tom decided to stare at his fidgeting hands rather than meet the rage in mine.

"Yes, but that was pre-elections, and you know what happens after, no delivery on the empty promises made to gain voters."

"I don't care, find a way to make it work. Five men are dead, Ari almost didn't survive, and as we sit here Logan Reid is being held captive. We shouldn't assume we have six months to save him; she disposed of Leo Wayne and Eric Parker after only three months."

"Finley, I spoke to Professor Scott; you will get full credits for working on this case and receive your doctorates. You don't need to worry about writing your thesis as we understand how much time you're putting into this case."

I closed my eyes, nostrils flaring, and I slammed my fists onto the table. Not my proudest moment, but prouder than one which would follow later that night. "I *will* finish my thesis and I *will* work on this case. I don't want a special pass because of my involvement. Thank you, but I work for the things I want in life."

Tom's eyes beamed with pride; Ari's rivalled it.

"We need to get data on the men's mobile phone coverage on the days of those two-hour blanks in their diaries. Is there anything you can do to speed it up?"

"I will try my best, will ask the techies to work unpaid overtime. Will remind them we are hunting a serial killer."

"Thank you. Do you not think we should ask Eli to assist?"

Tom pushed his chair back, shaking his head. "No, Eli is working on something else and he can't split his attention."

"Would anyone like to add to this?"

No one offered anything more; eyes on me as if I held all the answers. I had nothing more to add myself.

Ari didn't utter a single word during the drive to Lizzie's. I sat perplexed at still not being able to understand her, this Sophia. I had either lost my empathy or it had been tortured out of me by the Scarecrows.

My mobile phone rang on the vehicle's Bluetooth system. My heart skipped a beat at the sight of his name. "Hello, Aidan."

"Hello, Wife. Where are you?"

"Driving back from Tom's."

"Phone me when you're in the basement parking, I have a surprise for you."

"Can I not pick you up outside? Then we can go with my G, I have a great playlist going and I'm not in the mood for your, I-want-to-shoot-someone, music."

"Woman, you said my death metal was growing on you. And no, where I'm taking you involves you being blindfolded."

Heat shot up from my neck and settled on my cheeks.

Ari cleared his throat. "Good morning, Aidan."

"Hello, Ari. Not the way it sounds. Fin, you should've told me you have company."

Aidan doesn't forget anything. He knew Ari was with me.

"I'm just going to drop Ari off and then I will head home. What's the surprise?"

Ari looked at me and shook his head.

"Just get home. I will give you a hint: it's my parents' surprise for you and not mine."

"Aren't they in Europe somewhere?"

"Yes. Get yourself over here. Don't speed. Ari I will see you later."

The redness ceased the attack on my face, but my fingers tapped on the steering wheel. I love my in-laws; they all accepted me as their own from the first day we met, and even Aidan's brothers took to me like a flame does to an accelerant. They love having a gun-wearing, people-hunting sister. This was the first time my new mom and dad had a surprise for me, and I nearly pushed Ari out of the door as I pulled into Lizzie's driveway.

"See you later, please try to get some sleep. It's going to be a late night."

In my rear-view mirror Ari stood in the driveway, watching me.

Twelve

Lizzie and I lived twenty minutes away from each other if traffic was bad. I made it home in ten. Before turning into the basement garage, I phoned Aidan. He had not yet given me my good morning kiss, an oversight he corrected before blindfolding me and helping me into his SUV. He denied it, but I knew he took several turns to try and disorientate me. After asking for a hint for the third time, he threatened to duct tape my mouth shut. Aidan is not the kind of man to make idle threats, so I bit my tongue and begged him to play my favourite song – he complied.

I read somewhere that a marriage is all about give and take. Whichever idiot said that doesn't understand the level of my curiosity. I have close to zero patience, and curiosity had already taken five of my nine lives. Aidan laughed as I sang, rather screamed, along, desperate to distract my mind and protect my last four lives.

He brought the SUV to a stop and left me alone for close to an eternity, sitting there, with the seatbelt still holding me in place. In reality it might have been seconds, but being blindfolded, not knowing where you are, it felt like hours. It's not for the fainthearted, clothed, or the impatient.

I listened; water crashed close by. Water crashing equals waves. We had to be close to the ocean. No real hint there, the entire city is next to the ocean. *Ugh.*

Aidan opened the passenger door, helped me out, and pressed my back against his SUV, pressing his mouth harder on mine. He removed the blindfold, my eyes strained against the harsh light.

"Welcome home, Mrs Walker."

When my eyes adjusted to the bright light, I flung my arms

around his neck. I might have screamed. Aidan lifted me off the ground and spun around with my lips against his neck.

My heart raced as my eyes took in the sight in front of me. All of it. "Why? How? When? Aidan?"

His laughter filled my soul; he took my hand and led me to the front door. I twirled through every room like the girly-girl I'm not. Too much to take in. *Perfect.*

I ran towards big sliding doors leading to a patio and a garden double the size of the one Lizzie and I used to play in as children. The garden ended by a wall, on the other side – the ocean. I stared at the dark blue water and ran my fingers over the orca tattoo. In this house there was no room for the abyss, only hope, love, and joy.

"Aidan, this house is way too big for the two of us."

"Who said anything about just the two of us living here?"

"Are your parents moving in with us?" *Nobody wants that.*

"No. Five bedrooms, one for you and me, one for guests, and the other three for our children."

"Three children?" My arms wrapped around his waist, and in his eyes I saw the same hope and love which leapt inside my heart. We had both come so far.

"Yes."

"I love you. Now show me our room so we can work on our family. Or the kitchen, what better place to put a bun in my oven." Not my best comment.

"Hold on, you haven't even heard the best part. There are two studies down the passage and next to it we have a state-of-the-art gym – my gift to you."

"You just don't want me to turn into an orca when I'm pregnant." I pressed my face against his chest, breathed in his scent, and tried to grasp the dream my life had turned into.

"I can't wait to see you pregnant, knowing my child is growing inside you."

"Then start working on it."

***

Favio was in an exuberant mood and flung the word *bitch* around like confetti. Ashley kept checking her phone no matter how many times Lizzie and I reassured her Hope was having a better time with her grandfather than she was with us. We had gathered at Lizzie's to get dressed for our night out on the town.

I had no idea what Lizzie had planned, but I knew I had to be scared. Killers don't scare me; anything my sister planned, which involved Favio and alcohol, did.

With Lizzie and Ashley dressed, Favio turned his attention to me. He had taken the liberty of choosing outfits for the three of us, and from previous experience I knew I would end up looking like a high-class hooker.

Favio held up both his hands. "Before you say anything, I did not choose this dress for you. You're too trigger-happy, and I like my body hole-free where it needs to be."

He took my dress out of its covering and held it out to me. There was no way I could carry a concealed weapon, not unless I wanted to tear the dress or hide it somewhere no gun, no matter how small, should ever be.

"Aidan!" His laughter flowed all the way from downstairs. For this he would pay.

"What's going on?" Lizzie stormed in from the adjoining bathroom.

Shaking my head, I turned to her. "I have no choice. I have to kill my husband."

Ashley rushed in behind Lizzie and fits of laughter and giggles overwhelmed them. I felt anything but amused.

"If this is how he wants to play, then I'm leaving my wedding ring at home tonight."

"You wouldn't." Long fingers with perfectly manicured nails covered Favio's mouth.

"Watch me. Favio, bring the black nail polish we need to make this look work. Lizzie, do you still have your riding crop?" A sinister smile filled her face.

I got dressed, ensuring Aidan would regret his little stunt, now and later. My wedding ring spent the night in Lizzie's floor safe.

Ashley and Lizzie made their way downstairs a few minutes after Favio left. I stood in front of the full-length mirror, tugging at the hem of the dress, but it refused to budge.

If Aidan wanted twenty-two-year-old Finley going out on the town to consume alcohol, then that's what he would get. I hoped wherever we were going there would be air-conditioning; the dress was hot, and not only in a sexy way.

I shook my head, breathed as deeply as the dress would allow, and grabbed the crop.

"No, no, no." Aidan rocked his head, his hands at his sides. "You can't wear that tonight." If he was a dog, he would have been drooling puddles at his feet.

"Doctor Walker, you chose this dress and these shoes. It would make me a very naughty wife not to wear your gifts." I twisted my right foot, showing off my defined leg muscles I knew drove him crazy, and continued down the stairs with slow, seductive steps. As I stood in front of him, I lifted the crop, leather trailed from his Adam's apple to his chin.

"We are going home right now, or upstairs. Dammit. I didn't think this through." He took in every part of me and I relished in the heat in his eyes. "Where is your wedding ring?"

"It clashes with my outfit. Black leather doesn't go with a blue diamond. And we wouldn't want people to think I'm married, now would we?" The crop trailed the length of his torso.

Eli and Ari walked in from the patio; glass shattered on tiles. Neither Aidan nor I broke eye contact at the sound.

"Have a good night, gentlemen. Doctor Walker, I will see you when I see you. Don't wait up." The crop smacked into his perfect butt cheek and I sashayed towards the front door, knowing what the sight did to him. I forced my feet to remain calm, but my face showed Ashley and Lizzie how much I enjoyed besting him.

Aidan muttered under his breath, then said, "You better

come home to me. Untouched, Finley Williams-Walker. You're mine."

I took my time to turn and face him, winking at Lizzie and Ashley as I did so. "You know I will do anything if the price is right." I bit my lower lip, winked, and left. *Beat that, Aidan Walker.*

He cursed as I closed the door behind me. This would be a night to remember.

I begged Lizzie to change our dinner reservation, but she refused. How could she miss out on seeing people's reactions when I walk in to a three Michelin star rated restaurant dressed like a high-class escort who moonlights as a dominatrix? It would have been funnier had I been drunk, but I reminded myself of what Aidan had to go through not knowing where I was but knowing full well the unwanted attention I would get gallivanting around the city dressed like this. Maybe it was the lesser of two evils compared to the two uptown ladies of the night accompanying me. *Favio should reconsider his day job.* I ordered my first drink as soon as we were seated in the restaurant. Lizzie still refused to disclose the evening's programme.

As I washed my hands in the ladies' room, I thought of Sophia and wondered how she dressed during the day and when she had dates with her captives. I made a mental note to ask Ari the next time I saw him. He had appeared startled by the sight of me before we left, the look in his eyes I had seen before – our last night together. I hoped Aidan and Eli remembered my instruction to get him, well, laid.

The rest of the evening we spent bar hopping, and I often found my hand rubbing the outline of the Glock in my purse. I hated not having it as part of my body. Our last stop for the evening had to, of course, be Rip Tide. Even in my intoxicated state I reminded Lizzie that Rip Tide is a misnomer. She was too drunk to care. Ashley kept checking her phone, but after two shots of Rip Tide's vile house-shot even she forgot we were no longer in our early twenties.

Lizzie glanced at her mobile phone and returned it to her purse. "Do you remember truth or dare?"

This would not end well for any of us – it never did.

"Yes, of course we remember, Liz." Slurred words from I think Ashley's mouth, could have been mine.

"Well, seeing as it's Fin's bachelorette party tonight, I think she should go first." She lifted her glass in my direction.

"Okay, Liz, truth or dare?"

"Truth." She never chose dare.

"Why are you and Eli not married yet?" Ashley moved closer. I had been dying to ask, but it seemed like a private matter to sober Finley.

"We live together, there's no rush." She finished what remained of her Cosmopolitan. "We have set a date, and I was going to ask you both to be my maids of honour, but it's Finley's night."

I didn't correct her. *Matrons of honour.*

"Okay, my turn. Ashley, truth or dare?"

"Dare."

"Ooh, let's make this interesting. I dare you to take off your wedding ring and get the number of the guy standing at the bar. He's been eyeing you since we walked in." Drunk Finley enjoyed drunk Lizzie's adolescent thinking.

"I can't do that, I'm married." Ashley downed the rest of her Daiquiri and lifted her arm. She might have been signalling the waiter, but it looked like she tried to swat a fly.

"You chose dare, and you never backed out at UM. Go." Lizzie's unfocused eyes tried to point in the bar's direction. Her head did a better job of it.

"Dudes, where's my car at?" In unison, we fell back into our chairs, our laughter rising above the music. *Old inside joke.*

"Okay, I will do it." Ashley got to her feet, steadied herself, and sauntered in the bar's direction. I'm not sure she got the number of the man Lizzie had intended but she came back with *a* number and my stomach sank. *Oh crap, my turn.*

Ashley took my hand. Horror and memories pushed

themselves out of the skeleton-filled closets of my youth. Plural. "Your turn," she said, in a tone reminding me of the night I had won a wet t-shirt competition, also on a dare. "Finny, do you remember *that* night in Wild Bay?"

"Which one?" An innocent smile tried to hide the fact that I knew full well where this was going.

"You know the one we never talk about. As you may recall, it was your birthday, so in honour of the tradition, we will give you double the odds. I will ask you a truth and Lizzie will give you a dare."

"This tradition of ours sucks. It's never in my favour." I lifted an empty glass to my mouth.

"No lying – we will know if you lie. Do you still have feelings for Ari?"

I knew it. "No."

"Are you sure? You guys share quite a history."

"Yes. I'm sure, and like you said, his-to-ry. A very brief one." The empty glass aimed again for my mouth. The waiter appeared with the next round, which I hoped would be our last. We were no longer in our early twenties. These thirty-something women can't handle their booze.

Lizzie checked her phone again and returned it just as quickly to her purse. "My turn. My dearest, darling sister, you know how much I love you."

Dread filled me. I considered crying to get out of whatever she had planned, but it hadn't worked in Wild Bay, and I doubted it would in Marcel.

"You're going to dance on the bar; the next song we chose for you and it's one of your favourites. Oh, and you must dance with the crop."

For the first time in years, I craved a cigarette, and even considered bumming one from the people at the table next to us. Lizzie shook her head. "Don't even think about smoking. You on the bar. Right now."

"How did you know?" Desperate attempt at stalling.

"You don't take your eyes off a cigarette and you breathe

deeper as if trying to inhale the second-hand smoke. Really, Fin, even I, who does not hold a degree in psychology, can figure that one out."

Ashley nodded, taking another sip of the drink in her hand. "Fin. Bar. Now."

Lizzie pulled me to my feet. "What the hell, you're only this young once." I should've realised it was a set-up when a ladder stood next to the bar. Drunk Fin appreciated not having to scamper onto the bar, ass out for all in the VIP section to see. I took a gulp of my frozen margarita, fixed my lipstick, and made my way to the bar. Confident steps, trying to remember how to dance. The song they chose activated muscle memory, and I danced as I had the night I won that stupid competition, but at least this time around I remained dry. As the song ended, I looked down and sobered up.

His boyish grin, the danger and want in his eyes, chased the alcohol gremlins into hiding. "I have never been prouder to call you my wife." He stretched his arms out to me and helped me down, taking possession of my mouth as my feet hit the floor. *Did they reach the floor?*

I gave in, knowing I had won the night's round of bagging the hottie. I wanted to bed the hottie, but we were in public. That would come later, if I didn't pass out first. "I'm sorry Aidan, they dared me. You know your wife never backs down from a dare."

"Whose idea do you think this was?"

"Yours?" My fists slammed into his pectoral muscles.

"I had to see for myself what you look like dancing on a bar."

"And?" My hands rubbed over the spots my fists had hurt.

"I have never wanted you more. And I'm more in love with you now than when you walked out of Lizzie's front door. More than anything, I have never enjoyed it more seeing how men look at you and knowing that you, Finley Williams-Walker, are mine."

"Just pee on me and get it over with."

"Excuse me?" Indignation filled his face.

"You don't have to mark me as yours, Aidan. I am yours. You, my love, are stuck with me. Forever."

As we made our way back to our table, I received a standing ovation from Aidan's co-conspirators. They would all pay. I like dishing out revenge.

"Where's Ari?" I hoped he was getting rid of his demons.

"Over at the bar, he's a man on a mission."

Ari stood next to the bar, talking to a gorgeous brunette. A woman can appreciate another woman's beauty. I smiled knowing what a night out of his head would do for his recovery.

As I turned to give Ashley a knowing smile, my focus fell on another woman; this one couldn't keep her eyes off Ari. He's a rugged and handsome man, but the way she looked at him made my muscles tense, and my hand reached for my purse.

"What's wrong?" Aidan asked.

"Do you see the woman in the green dress standing over there?" I gestured with my head.

"Yes, what about her?"

"She's tall, slender, has auburn hair, and she's a sight to behold."

Aidan placed his arm around my shoulder. "Do you want women when you're drunk?"

"No. That's the exact description Ari gave of the woman who held him hostage." The hair on my neck stirred but my palms did not itch. "That's her. That's Sophia."

As I stood, Ashley grabbed my arm. "Finley, you only have one chance at this. If it's not her, the woman Ari is talking to might get the wrong idea."

"Okay, I'm thinking." Difficult to do when your heart stops beating. I turned to Eli. "You fit the victim profile."

"Is that a compliment?" He flicked his arms out, palms up.

"Shut it and listen to me. Go over to Ari, start talking to him and the woman with him. You will know what to say to get him to turn around and look at the mystery woman. I will move to the door to block her exit in case it's Sophia."

"Okay." He made his way towards Ari, bobbing and weaving through the crowd of dancing people.

With my hand in my purse I headed for the door. The pressure with which I gripped the Glock's grip left an indentation in my palm. I tried my best not to glance in the direction of the red-haired women or Eli still making his way towards Ari.

People kept walking through the door, giving me bemused looks as they passed. I stole a glance as I pushed through the entering crowd and saw Ari turn.

I looked towards where he was looking but saw nothing. She had vanished.

I kept pushing through the late arrivals and continued down to the two levels of the club below, scanning each floor's gyrating bodies.

Nothing.

The bouncers at the door confirmed a woman matching her description had left seconds before. They agreed to ask the manager to give me their surveillance footage *if* I have a warrant. No problem, I have contacts in my speed dial who can help with that. As I took out my mobile phone to call Tom, the screen told me to wait until morning. The time – 0100 hours. No judge would grant a warrant based on my hunch.

I headed back upstairs, passing Ari and the woman he had been talking to. He smiled as our eyes met; neither of us said a word. Talking could wait, he needed this, and besides, Sophia, if it was her, had left.

"Did you find her?" Aidan asked.

"No, she left before I reached the main door. I will phone Tom later and tell him to get a warrant. There are cameras above the door and outside, maybe we can catch a glimpse of her face." I cursed.

Everyone stared at me.

"She knows David Ezra is alive. Ari's in danger."

"Don't you dare phone him, not now. Him going home with someone was your idea." Aidan placed his hand over mine.

"She could be waiting for him, I need to warn him."

Eli gave me a warring look. "No. The woman with him is a police officer, why do you think they hit it off so well? Tell him tomorrow, but for now, let him have some fun."

"Fine. One more drink and then I want you to take me home. My husband is out of town." I brought Aidan's hand to my mouth, the spark in my eyes hiding the clench in my gut.

We no longer had any advantage. Ari's in danger.

How long before Logan Reid dies?

Thirteen

Coffee. There is nothing like the smell of coffee when you've slept too few hours, your head heavy while your brain has taken over the pumping your heart used to be proud of doing.

Coffee. Remnants of unabsorbed alcohol burn into your stomach and you start to wonder whether you should just make yourself vomit or if your body would take offence.

I'm never drinking again. Why do my feet hurt? Where am I? Why am I naked?

"Good morning, Wife."

My eyes protested as I forced them open. I swear the sun had never shone brighter than on that specific morning. *Where are my sunglasses?* "Why are you talking so loud?"

"Not dominating your hangover this morning? Well, at least not like you did me when we got home last night."

"It was fun, wasn't it?" I stretched like a cat who had won a lifetime supply of cream. The smile which spread across my face matched.

"Sit, drink your coffee and these pills. In half an hour you will feel better, promise."

My body responded even though my being fought back. "Do you know what else helps for a hangover?" The sheet gave little resistance as I threw it towards the other side of the bed. *Why does my arm hurt?*

"I'm not touching you until you have showered and brushed your teeth, no matter how much you beg. It smells like a brewery exploded in here." Aidan opened the curtains and the sliding door.

Without a doubt the sun hated me – death rays pierced into the back of my eyeballs. "Excuse me, I wasn't the only one who came home slightly drunk last night."

"No, I might have been less than sober myself, but then again I'm not the one who danced on the bar. Have you seen the photos?"

"What photos?" I forced the handful of pills into my body. Aidan had made me Vietnamese cold coffee. *He loves me.*

"These." He retrieved his phone from the dresser. Across our bedroom floor lay the evidence of the effect I had had on him wearing the dress he had chosen for me. The dress hung on the dresser's mirror.

"No. Ouch, my head." I rubbed my bruised temples. *Who punched me? Did I hit my head?* Aidan held his phone out to me. "Who took these?"

"Who do you think?" Aidan grinned.

"I'm going to kill Lizzie. Where is my phone?"

"First drink your coffee. I wonder how Ari's night ended?"

"Give me my phone, I need to phone Tom, we need a warrant for the surveillance cameras. How could I have forgotten?"

"I sent a text message to him, from your phone. He replied saying he would let you know as soon as he has the footage."

The emotions storming through me killed the hangover. "You're amazing. I'm the luckiest woman in the world to be your wife." I got on my knees and pulled him closer by the waist of his pants while his hands rediscovered familiar places.

Aidan ran his fingers through my hair. "Shower. Now. Brush your teeth first."

My mobile phone rang as I took the last bite of the most delicious and greasy breakfast I had had in a long time. "Did you get the footage?" I asked.

"Yes. Can you meet me at Lizzie's? Ari needs to view it."

"I don't know if he's there."

"He will be, I spoke to him before I phoned you."

"I will be there in half an hour."

Aidan took my phone and placed it on the dining table. "I'm coming with you. Are you up for one of my ideas?"

"Always." His heat burned into my skin as I rubbed my

palms across his perfect abs, my fingers trailing perfect lines from his sides down to where his jeans obstructed my exploration.

"After you finish with Tom, you and I are going to have lunch in our new home. I will drop you off and pick you up. Maybe there will be another surprise waiting for you."

"Stop it, Aidan. How am I going to focus on catching a killer if I'm thinking of you the whole time?"

"You need to learn to compartmentalise, Fin. It's the same thing as last night. You got so caught up in the hunt that you forgot to be with us. She was long gone and still you wanted to go running around in those sexy high heels, chasing ghosts."

He was right, I needed to find the on and off switch which had up to that point remained hidden in my brain. "How do you do it? The things you see some days, all the emotions you feel every day."

"You need to have two personas, one being my Finley Walker. She's my wife, Lizzie's sister, friend to others, and soon to be mother of my child."

His lips trailed mine, and he bent down to press his mouth against my stomach. "Finley Williams-Walker, now she's a badass. She's the apex predator amongst predators. Finley Williams-Walker is the profiler. When you walk through the door of our home, you need to remember who *you* are. And when you leave, you put your hunting face on. The same goes for when you work in your study. Visualise barriers and don't cross them. I often have a bad day, but you need me to be me and not bring all the emotions home."

"But I want to share in every part of your life." I cupped his beautiful face in my hands.

"And you do. I share most of it with you, when we lie in bed at night talking about our day. But you need to know what to bring home and what to leave at the office." His thumb swept under my belly button.

"You do realise I'm not pregnant?"

"Not yet. But at the rate we are going it's only a matter of time. And we have six months before we need to go for check-ups."

I took his hand and pressed his palm to my mouth. *What was it about what he said that made my stomach twitch?* "What do you mean, six months?"

He took both my hands in his. "At your age, if a woman isn't pregnant after six months, she needs to see her gynaecologist for a full check-up to make sure there aren't any underlying problems. For women under thirty we give a year, if there aren't any other factors to consider."

"Aidan, you're the most brilliant man in the world. I love you, I love you, I love you!" I planted kisses all over his face and rushed to the bedroom to get dressed.

He waited for me at the door. "Are you going to tell me what that was all about?"

"I will tell you on the way. You just cracked the case wide open. Man, I love your brain."

Ari opened the front door as I approached Lizzie's porch. A smile filled his face, one I hadn't seen since I had been the reason for it.

"I take it last night went well." I patted his chest.

"Very well. You were right, you knew exactly what I needed. Thank you." He kissed my cheek and wrapped his arms around me, pulling me tight against him.

"I'm always right, Ari. You should know that by now."

He sighed, releasing his hold. "I take it your evening ended as planned. You should've seen Aidan. He beat himself up the whole time for sending you out, looking the way you did. For the record, it was the sexiest I've ever seen you. Even sexier than the black dress which drove me insane." Memory played in his eyes.

I remembered how he had looked at me back then, the things he had said. As we stood in the foyer, his eyes held the same intensity. I ignored the warning sirens going off in my mind. "Thank you. Did Eli tell you what happened last night?"

I made my way into the house, away from the fire.

"Why do you think it was Sophia?" he asked, and whispered, "I would never allow other men to see you like that."

My shoulders sagged and I tilted my head as I spun around. "Ari?" The fire in his eyes met the desperate attempts in mine to distinguish it. "I thought last night did you good?"

"It served its purpose, but it's not the same. You and I, we made love. One night will not change anything. Sex is sex. I want more. Do you remember our first time, all the passion, the raw emotion?"

"Don't do this. I thought we reached a point where we can be friends, only friends. For weeks we had spent hours together every single day, sharing things we couldn't share with people who hadn't spent time in combat. It's understandable that our times together would have been different compared to someone you only knew for a few hours. Are you going to see her again? Try to build a relationship with her and what you need will come."

"It won't. I need you."

I was way too tired for this. If not for the pills Aidan had given me, the hangover would have made me even less patient. "Ari, please don't do this. I told you I'm not interested in going back. I want Aidan, my husband, the end. You need to move on. As soon as you're ready, I think you need to move out of here and take an assignment somewhere far away from Marcel."

"I can't leave you again." The once brave warrior in front of me looked like a kitten being dumped next to the road.

Did I not make myself clear the last time we discussed this? Time for tough friendship. Love had left the equation years before. "Aidan and I are trying for a baby."

"You can't have a child with him."

"I can and I will."

"Ley, you can't have a child with a killer. Not with *him*."

My open hand struck the side of his face. If words did not make my decision clear, perhaps I could slap acceptance and closure into him. I turned my back on him and stormed towards the patio, passing Lizzie where she stood motionless at the foot of the staircase.

"Hello, Tom. I can't stay long." The look in his eyes told me he had overheard what had happened inside. I shook my head, exhaled, and sank into the chair closest to me. Lizzie and her neighbours would not approve if I emptied both my SIG and Glock into the trunk of the palm tree which called out to the frustration in me for release.

"Ari, you need to come see this!" Tom shouted into the house. Ari walked out and took a seat across from me, but I kept my eyes from him. He had gone too far.

Tom showed us the footage. I confirmed it was the woman I had seen, and Ari confirmed it was Sophia. We had a face. I wondered why I hadn't received a copy of the sketch artist's composite; Ari had said he would sit with one the previous day.

As soon as Aidan pulled into the driveway, I excused myself and left. The instant I closed the passenger side door, his hand reached for the door next to him. I grabbed his arm and shook my head.

"I'm going to kill him." His fists slammed into the steering wheel.

"You better hope no one heard you, and never say that in front of anyone else. Get in line because I'm considering it myself. Before you say anything, I won't visit Lizzie again until he has moved out, and I will make sure we never spend time together unless it's pertinent to the case for us to be in the same room, with other people present."

"I trust you with my life." Aidan cupped my face with shaking hands. "I'm not worried that he will come between us, nobody ever will. What infuriates me is that he doesn't respect you, or your decision, and that he makes you this angry. I saw the way he looked at you dancing on the bar and I realised he has no intention of ever giving up on you. Him going home with another woman was to make you happy, not for himself."

"I tried being his friend after what he went through. But he knows what I'm capable of when someone threatens the ones I love. He was the one who sent me the video link to show me what had happened to Lizzie, and he knows what I did as a result of that."

"Good." Aidan's thumb tugged on my bottom lip.

"Good?"

"Finley, I spent years in an active warzone. I worked in the ER of government hospitals where more often than not some gang-banger decided to finish the score when his victim had already been placed in my care. None of that ever scared me. I'm petrified of you."

"Petrified? Is that the word you want to use to describe how you feel about your wife?"

"How many people do you know who hunt predators, torture them, and then has the patience to wait for them to commit suicide? That, my love, is diabolical. And what you did to the man who raped Lizzie, well, my darling wife, there are no words to describe what you did."

"Macabre art?" My lips twisted into a smile. I have never lost a single night's sleep, or meal, over what I had done and looking back – he deserved far worse.

"I wouldn't call it art, but, Finley, Ari knows what happens to people who find themselves in your crosshairs. If I was him, I wouldn't push you."

"Neither should he push you, my love. You were the one who saved me from the Angel Taker. And your best kill was further than two kilometres; it wasn't documented, was it?"

"No."

Danger danced between us. I had never wanted him more. For as much as we cherished our life together, we embraced each other's abilities and capabilities. We were destined to be together for the rest of our lives, and our lives had started the day we met as two masked vigilantes in a decrepit parking structure.

"Let's go home to *our* home. I need to show you how much I love you." My tongue teased his lips.

"I know how much you love me. Do you know how much I love you?"

"I do."

"Save that for Saturday." Happiness filled the cabin of his SUV, and as he pulled out of Lizzie's driveway, I realised I never told Tom what Aidan had said after breakfast.

He answered seconds after I pressed the call button. "Did you forget something?"

"She's trying to fall pregnant."

"What are you talking about?"

I pushed my fingers through my hair. "Sophia's in her mid-thirties and trying to fall pregnant. That's why she chooses these alpha males, she wants the strongest genes for her child. In two years, she hasn't fallen pregnant, or she hasn't carried a baby to term. I will talk to Aidan and get back to you. Get a detective to dig into Leo Wayne and Eric Parker's medical histories, there might be another reason she killed them after only three months."

"*This* is why I wanted you on the case, you never cease to amaze me."

"Not me, this is all Aidan. Contact me as soon as you receive information about the two men's medical histories, there might be something there."

"Will do." He ended the call.

I turned to absorb every part of my brilliant and dangerous husband. *I am his.*

The Friday morning before our second wedding, I received a call. It started a chain reaction of events neither Aidan nor I could stop. The train barrelled towards a cliff, the bridge at the bottom of the ravine.

"Finley, phone my lawyer and get down to the police station."

"What's going on?" I clutched my phone so hard it would have cracked if not for the protective casing.

"I will explain later, just get down here."

Trembles rippled through me, waves of aftershock from what I had dreaded was going on unseen. I phoned Aidan's lawyer as I drove to the police station. Bats out of hell fly slower than I did in my SLS AMG.

I cursed with every step as my shackled husband was led into an interrogation room. "What the hell do you think you're doing?" I growled.

"You can't be here. Leave." My once-upon-a-time confidant said.

"Not until you tell me what's going on." Officers stared, I snarled back at them.

"Aidan tried to kill Ari." Tom tried to sidestep me, but I pushed him back against the door, much harder than he had pushed Aidan, the sound echoing through the building.

"Where's your proof? You will not utter a single word to him until his lawyer gets here. If you do, I will have you disbarred." He flinched at the proximity of my face.

Aidan's lawyer placed his hand on my shoulder and pulled me back. I spoke to him and explained the history. He promised to have Aidan out of there in minutes.

Ted Marshall is a man of his word – Aidan and I left minutes later, neither saying a word. I caught a glimpse of Ari as we headed towards the stairs. Aidan grabbed my arm and covered my mouth with his hand. The things I said would be construed as death threats; people just wouldn't realise I was making promises.

"What the hell is going on?" My hands shook violently as I held onto Aidan's face.

"I don't know, but I promise you I will find out." He pressed his mouth to my forehead until I found focus.

I pulled away from him with steady hands despite confusion battering me. "Okay, tell me what happened?"

"After doing my rounds, two officers were waiting for me in my office. They requested I escort them to the police station for questioning regarding an attempted murder. I said I would, but I had to first call my lawyer to meet me at the station and also talk to my receptionist as I had to reschedule patients. They only agreed because I wasn't under arrest. Not yet, they said."

I clawed at my arms in a desperate attempt to find clarity. "Why were you handcuffed if you weren't under arrest?"

"They had no reason to handcuff me, I believe they acted on Tom's instructions."

My nostrils flared and Aidan stroked my face with his fingertips. *Calm, focus.* "What happened in the interrogation room?"

"They asked where I was last night."

"What did you tell them?"

"The truth. I was about to leave our building to go for my evening run when I got a call to do an emergency C-section. With more than enough witnesses at the hospital, and the doorman who heard me take the call, they don't have a case. The proud new father has photos of me in theatre holding their baby."

"So why do they think you tried to kill Ari?"

"Tom said someone took a shot at Ari when he left after training with Eli. They recovered the bullet – a custom made .308."

"And of course with Tom thinking you're the Marcel Sniper, the logical conclusion is to pin this on you."

"He claims I have motive as you and Ari share a passionate past and your unresolved feelings are a threat to our marriage. Witnesses stated I was visibly jealous on Saturday night, even telling you to get off the bar and wrapping my jacket around you."

"You helped me off, and I asked for your jacket. What's going on?"

Aidan shrugged. "Someone is trying to set me up. If not for the emergency C-section, I wouldn't have had a solid alibi. My routine isn't that difficult to figure out."

"Aidan, did you tell them that if you wanted to kill Ari, he would be dead?"

"No, I'm not stupid."

I realised what I had said. "You hold the best damn kill record, why would you miss now?"

"Tom brought it up saying I might have wanted to scare Ari as I knew it would lead back to me."

"What did you say to that?"

"Nothing. I told him he was wasting my time and that if they had enough proof, he should arrest me or I'm walking. I reminded him I had filed several harassment charges against him, so he should tread with care. Finley, we need to talk, but not here. Let's go home, I need to show you something. And after we are done there you must please take me back to the hospital. My patients are waiting for me."

"You don't deserve to be in this mess, and I will get to the bottom of it. I will make them both regret whatever it is they're trying to do."

"No. You will leave this alone and let me handle it. This is not a request."

"Aidan, we are partners in life, marriage, all of it. Let me help."

"No. There are things from my past I haven't told you about and it's a side of me I don't want you to see. Trust me with this as you do with your life." His being grabbed hold of mine; there was no point in trying to fight him on it.

"We don't keep secrets, it's the foundation of our life." I rubbed my forehead against his chest.

"It has no bearing on us, but I will tell you when we have time. It's a long and complicated story, and it involves more people than just me."

I wrapped my arms around his waist. "Tom's not going to be at our wedding tomorrow, and I will remove myself from the Sophia case. I will take the file and my notes to Captain Taylor as soon as I drop you at the hospital. Aidan, I'm sorry."

"Don't say you're sorry, just trust me. I will sort this out. One way or another I will get to the bottom of it. And protect you and our child, no matter the cost."

To feel protected is a basic human need. Being protected by a man like Aidan can't be described in words. He told me to back off, let him handle it, but he should've known I wasn't going to. I would protect him until my dying breath.

We drove to our new house and Aidan showed me what he had referred to earlier. Now I understood why I loved *our* house more than I had ever loved any other I had called home. Perfect in every possible way.

My knuckles rapped below the brass name plaque on the door. "Captain Taylor?"

"Come in, we were expecting you." *We?*

As I opened the door, hatred boiled inside me, and if not for Captain Taylor sitting at his desk as a potential witness, I would have made what I had done before look like a child's birthday party. "I won't stay, here is the file and all of my notes. I will no longer be working on the Sophia case. Trust you will respect my decision." The brown file thudded onto his desk, papers stuck out, but I fought the perfectionist in me and left it in slight disarray.

"Finley, we need you on this case," Tom said to my back.

"Captain Taylor, as long as Tom's involved in this case, I won't be. I will explain the circumstances to Professor Scott, and I have enough information to complete my thesis."

"This is not my call to make, but I agree, we need you on this case. Please excuse me while I go talk to my superior officer. Perhaps there is a way around all of this." He left me to face the man whose throat I wanted to rip open with my bare hands.

"I brought him in for questioning, that's all."

My mind replayed what Aidan had said at our home. My stomach turned on itself.

"Finley, I was only doing my job. It's no secret Aidan hates Ari's guts. We have witnesses to corroborate this."

Still I said nothing, only grinding my teeth.

"When are you going to realise the man you married is a

cold-blooded killer, and he deserves to be in prison?"

Don't do it, Finley.

"Aidan tried to kill Ari. Are you so blinded by lust that you ignore the itching in your palms every time he touches you?"

The only thing my palms felt as I stood there were nails digging into them.

"Your entire life I have loved you as a daughter; you used to trust my judgement. What has gotten into you? Was it the events during the war? Or do you miss your parents so much that you will cling to this monster just to experience what you perceive to be love?"

My hand clenched around the 599 XT FOX Karambit in my pocket. Captain Taylor walked in and I released my grip, settling both my hands behind my back.

He took his seat and stared at both of us. "My superiors gave me clear instructions to remove Tom from this case, with immediate effect. Finley, if you're willing to see this through, we will forever be in your debt, considering the circumstances. You have a bright future ahead of you and what you bring to the table is invaluable."

Footsteps echoed through the building. Tom left without saying a word.

"Thank you, Captain."

"You don't need to see Ari either, all information will be relayed through me or the detectives."

"Do you know if Ari has seen Doctor James? I need to find out if he has anything to add to the investigation after his appointment?"

"I will email the report to you. He came by earlier to share the information, but under the circumstances, I didn't want to call you in. We should have information regarding the men's whereabouts on the days with the two-hour blanks in their diaries by mid-next week."

"Are you considering the possibility that Sophia tried to kill Ari? Assuming she can shoot a rifle. As you are aware, she now knows David Ezra is alive, and she saw him talking to another woman. I can only speculate as to what it did to her already fragile state."

"We are looking into it. I never instructed your husband be brought in for questioning. My superiors are well aware of the history between Tom and Doctor Walker and based on this they gave clear instruction to remove Tom from the case with immediate effect." There was a glint of something in Captain Taylor's eyes.

"Please remember I will not be reachable as of tomorrow until next week Sunday. The only disturbance I will allow is if you call to say Sophia has been arrested." I offered a passable smile as a sign of my gratitude for Tom being kicked off the case. I enjoy hunting hunters and didn't want to give up the hunt for Sophia, but for Aidan there is nothing I won't give up.

"Congratulations again on your wedding, Finley. Doctor Walker is a wonderful physician, and he's lucky to call you his wife. I met his father years ago. Ryan Walker is a formidable man, a force of nature. They are lucky to have you as part of their family, and you should be honoured to be a part of theirs. Enjoy your honeymoon, and I promise to not disturb you unless it's a case of life or death."

I had only once before heard my father-in-law described as a force of nature, by Aidan, when we had spoken earlier at our home. This had also been my conclusion the first time I had met Ryan Walker, but after what Aidan had told me, I had more respect for him and a greater understanding of why I had liked him from the day we met. After Aidan and I had spoken it also became clear to me that his past held much more than I could've imagined.

Fourteen

Our wedding day had been everything we had hoped it would be. Unlike other little girls, I had never dreamt of my wedding day. I believe if I had, it would have been exactly what my young heart could have dreamt. Aidan and I spent the evening dancing, eating, and madly in love surrounded by the people who cared most for us. Tom was nowhere in sight.

The following day we departed on our honeymoon. True to form, I had no idea where we were heading. Not once did I expect to honeymoon in Fiji. To call it paradise would be a gross understatement. We spent a week in a world far away from the events that had taken place since our return from Vietnam. My husband and I shared picnics on the beach, went horse riding, and the tranquil water called to us. *If only we had stayed in Fiji.*

Captain Taylor did not contact me, and I dreaded returning to Marcel. Not only to leave the intimacy Aidan and I had shared, but also because I still didn't know how to accurately profile Sophia. For the first time since I had started hunting predators, I found myself stifled. Perhaps because this time I had to do it in the confines of the law.

The week after our return to Marcel we spent packing and making arrangements to move into our home. The minutes didn't pass fast enough.

Aidan arranged with a moving company to transfer all our belongings, and we had dreamt during our honeymoon what we envisioned our home to look like. We had made a few online purchases, not wanting to face the reality swirling around us by leaving the penthouse. Inside our love bubble, life remained perfect. I realise I turned into a romantic, blubbering fool.

Living in the light brought out a side of me which shocked

me more than the ever-present darkness I had once embraced ever could.

A week after our return to Marcel I ran towards Aidan as he stepped through our front door. "I'm late."

"How can you be late if I'm the one who just walked in the door?" Aidan wrapped his arms around me. "I love what we have done to this place, it looks like ours now."

I pressed my lips to his chin and stared up at him. "Doctor Walker, if one of your patients said that to you, what would your response be?"

The way his face lit up was breathtaking. The sight will forever be engrained in my memory. Aidan spun me around and kissed my face, fell to his knees, and kissed my stomach. Tears streamed down his face as I pulled him up and into my arms.

"I love you, Mommy." He continued pressing his lips to my eyes, cheeks, nose, forehead, and mouth.

"And baby. We love you, Daddy." It was my turn to kiss his face. Stubble scratched my lips, but excitement blinded me from the sting.

"Tomorrow morning first thing you're going for a blood test." His brow furrowed. "You fell pregnant when we started trying. Now if that isn't destiny, I don't know what is."

The blood tests confirmed it – we were pregnant. Aidan and I decided to keep our happiest news to ourselves until after our first sonogram and after we heard our baby's heartbeat.

We never had the chance.

A week after the second blood test confirmed the pregnancy was progressing, I felt sick. The whole day I had a gut feeling something was wrong, and Aidan told me to stay in bed and rest. He checked in on me every chance he got.

I went to the bathroom expecting him to come home any minute. My stomach had cramped earlier, and I wondered if it was nothing more than normal pregnancy cramps – Doctor Google reassured me some of my symptoms were normal.

Aidan had forbidden me from self-diagnosing, but I couldn't resist; not listening to my qualified husband, I believed Mommy knows best.

As I sat down on the toilet, I breathed through another cramp, and felt something slip out of my body and into the water below. I jumped to my feet, bright red blood trailed down my legs and onto the pants around my ankles. I plunged my hands into the water and pulled what had fallen in out.

Downstairs, Aidan heard my soul being torn from my body.

"Put our baby back. Please, Aidan! Put our baby back inside me!" I held my hands out to him; tears filled his face.

I watched my husband's heart break, powerless to stop it.

In my hands, our baby, only an embryo. A white little bubble only a centimetre small, still attached to the dark purple uterine lining.

Our baby had died inside me, and I didn't even know. Aidan lost his second child and I could do nothing to save him from the pain. No matter how far developed a pregnancy is, the pain cuts into you and rips your being to shreds. Neither of us were ever the same after that night.

Aidan became withdrawn, and I resorted to my old coping mechanism – aggression. I often sat in front of my laptop contemplating downloading TOR, to resume hunting predators on the deep dark web, the abyss. My eyes would fall on my wedding ring and I slammed the screen shut. Release came from emptying magazine after magazine at the shooting range. I didn't want to train with Eli, knowing all too well the scars my rage and anguish would leave on his face and body.

A month after we lost our baby, Aidan walked into the house and without saying a word, made love to me, but it wasn't love I felt. His rage became mine; he didn't hurt me. Aidan's anguish thrust through me, and as I clung to him, I realised he, too, struggled against the darkness. We both fought back with all our might.

"What happened?" My fingers trailed along his naked body.

"I had to do a D&C today."

"I'm sorry. Don't you think you should just work in the ER for a while, if you can?"

"I can't." He rolled onto his side, the cold of the floor tiles not registering for either of us.

"We will get through this. Together. Aidan, we need to stop shutting each other out."

"I'm sorry. Funny how I have spoken to so many patients after they had suffered a loss and I don't even have the words to console my own wife." Brokenness darkened his eyes.

"I'm fighting the darkness with everything in me, Aidan. Every day I sit behind my laptop with the mask in my hand, but I don't put it on. Please help me, I don't want to be that person again." I dropped my forehead to his mouth. "I want our baby."

Aidan pulled me into his arms and together our bodies shook. We cried for the child we would never hold, never name, never know. Even though we couldn't do any of it, we still loved that child, *our* child.

It wasn't the last time either of us would mourn our child, but it was the first time we did it together.

"Fin, I'm fighting it too. Been fighting it ever since I found you on the bathroom floor. I couldn't do anything to take your pain away or save our baby, and it kills me. When we are ready, we can try again. You know that one in three pregnancies do not develop to term." He spared me that soul-destroying word.

I shook my head. "I'm not ready yet."

He got to his feet, pulled me up and into his arms, carrying me to the couch. As he sat, he didn't release his grip, cradling me in his warmth and strength. We both needed the raw intimacy like we needed to breathe and to love each other.

He placed his fingertips below my chin and eased my chin up till our eyes met. The hurt we both carried reached towards each other and grabbed hold.

"Fin, I think we need to go see Doctor Brown, the fertility specialist. Before you say anything, I respect that you want to wait and so do I. But we are no longer in our twenties and your body has been through hell more than once. Let's go for a check-up, do the tests, make sure we have the best chance to have a full-term pregnancy when we are ready to try again."

Aidan spared me all the medical terminology; in that moment he was the man who loves me, not the renowned gynaecologist.

Later, as I lay safe in my husband's arms, I dreamt of an auburn-haired woman clawing at her stomach. Her screams woke me.

I eased out of bed and made my way into our garden. On the other side of the wall, waves crashed in the moonlight. The crescent moon offered no answers, but I realised Sophia had to be hurting. Empathy rolled over me with each crash of the waves in front of me, empathy for the woman desperate for a child, not the killer.

Aidan and I left the house at the same time. He had early rounds with patients, and I had an early round with Eli.

Eli had already geared up by the time I walked in, but before we started punching each other, he pulled me into his arms. My first thought – he was trying to catch me off guard. "Finley, you're the closest I have to a sister. I know something is wrong with you. What's going on? Lizzie mentioned last night that you've been withdrawn lately. We haven't seen you in over a month." The warmth in his hazel eyes shattered my walls.

"A month ago, Aidan and I lost our baby. Now let's punch the snot out of each other."

"Hold on, let's talk first."

Gloved hands rested on my shoulders; not a good idea to touch me when I'm fighting for composure. I shoved him away. "Nothing to talk about, our baby died. Now punch me or I'm walking out of here." I dropped my backpack at my feet and pulled shocking pink gloves over my hands. One of Aidan's jokes.

Eli stared at something behind me. I pulled the last strap

tight with my teeth and turned around, not releasing the strap.

"I'm so sorry."

Screw fighting for composure, I fought not to kill the man standing in front of me. "For what?" I barked.

"For you having to go through this, it must be awful. No one deserves to go through this pain."

"What the hell do you know? Just leave." I gave him my best death stare, but he didn't explode.

"I'm just trying to say sorry." He shook his head, shrugging his shoulders.

"Sorry?" Grief turned into white hot rage. "Get out of my face, out of my life, and out of my city."

"Finley, calm down, Ari didn't mean to upset you." I spun around and stared at Eli, but my death stare also didn't work on him.

"I swear, Eli, if you weren't engaged to my sister, I would punch the snot out of you right now! How can you defend him? He and Tom concocted a little plan to frame Aidan for attempted murder. So you heard him say he wanted to kill you? So what. Show me a man who would not get pissed off when his wife's ex-shag doesn't get the picture that she has no intention of ever being with him again."

The way Ari had acted nullified everything he ever meant to me and erased my pity for what he had endured being held captive by Sophia. *Was he really abducted?*

"I was here when someone took a shot at him when he exited the building. It happened."

"That does not mean my husband pulled the trigger. And if he did, you would be dead." I failed to hide the smile that spread across my face. The shock in Ari's eyes made it worth forgetting my grief for a moment.

I turned to Eli. "I will see you tomorrow at my usual time. I will rather wait outside the police station than be here."

"Please don't leave." Ari stepped in front of me, blocking my exit.

"Bad move, Ari. This time I won't just slap you."

"Don't you understand it's because I care so much about you that I don't want to see you get hurt?"

"Aidan is not the one hurting me, dipshit. You're the one who reminds me of the rage I felt towards murderers and paedophiles. I haven't embraced this rage in over a year and a half, but here you are not taking no for an answer. And to top it all off, I'm one-hundred percent sure you and Tom orchestrated the entire shooting incident."

"What possible motive could we have which puts my life in danger?"

"You tell me. It's no secret – you both hate Aidan. I don't understand either of your reasons. Come on, Ari, I'm not the only woman in the world. Find someone else, move on, and for the love of guns, leave Marcel." My teeth bit into the strap and I yanked off the gloves.

"I'm sorry to break it to you, sweetheart, but I'm not leaving. Not without you."

My eyes closed, my heart rate increased, and my uncovered hands drew into fists.

"Ari, that's enough. I swear I will stand back and watch her kill you."

Ari threw his arms up, grinned like a hyena, and left.

"Eli, I can't do this anymore. What the hell is going on with him? He left two years ago, he chose to go on that mission, told me to move on, and now that I'm married he wants nothing more than me."

"I've never seen him like this and I've known him for close to eighteen years, if you count the years we spent on separate assignments. He won't listen to me, I tried talking to him. I even tried arranging dates for him with some of my students. Spending so much time with you and Lizzie is turning me into a woman."

"Phone Aidan and go for a drink like you guys used to do, or go surfing. I don't care what you do, but he needs a friend as much as I do. Kyle is not into the things you two are."

Eli grinned. "Great idea. A strip club opened next to Rip

Tide, maybe we should go there."

My eager fists finally found an outlet. Later that night, Aidan asked whether I was to blame for the bruise on Eli's shoulder.

Captain Taylor and detectives Shaw and McMann waited for me in the room now being utilised for the task force hunting Sophia. The task force comprised of the four of us; not much of a force, but it was better than hunting her by myself. We started our meeting by covering what we knew and then took turns to update each other on what we had learned since our last meeting two weeks before. I can't remember much about what they said during the meeting. I may have had a few liquid Walkers for the courage to leave the house when all I wanted to do was hide under our bed and cry.

While it was my turn to talk, Captain Taylor's mobile phone rang, and his face turned white.

"Grab your stuff. Now. I will explain on the way." He rushed towards the door without glancing back. The three of us followed, and once we were speeding towards I didn't know where, Captain Taylor spoke for the first time. "A body has been found outside Rip Tide. A note was pushed into the victim's pocket." He lit a cigarette, taking long, and deep drags of bliss.

I considered asking him to hand me the pack, but instead I asked, "What did the note say?"

"Don't know yet, the first responder saw it sticking out of the victim's front shirt pocket and left it unread."

"Why are we heading out there?" Detective Shaw asked, opening the window next to him. I breathed in the second-hand smoke as deeply as I could.

"The note is addressed to David Ezra. The description of the victim matches Logan Reid."

Detective McMann lit his own bliss.

No smoking, you haven't touched a cigarette since sneaking one at your bachelorette party. Don't do it.

I covered my nose with my hands, blocking out the smell of temptation. "Sophia saw David Ezra at Rip Tide; Logan Reid is her offering to him. If we consider everything she has done so far and what we understand to be her reason, she wants David Ezra back. In her eyes, he's the ultimate alpha male, he's stronger than death. Who wouldn't want that in their child's gene pool? If you looked at it from her point of view."

I watched buildings pass us, focusing on streams of grey and blots of colour, my longing for a child of our own suppressed.

"Could the first responder make a visual identification?"

"No, not much for visual identification." Captain Taylor took another drag and flicked his cigarette out the window. *Above the law he vowed to uphold.*

"Decomposed, or did she take her confusion and rage out on him?"

"The latter. Brace yourselves. What are the terms you used Finley? Oh yes, our submissive might not be so submissive after all."

I need nicotine.

The victim's body lay in the alley between Rip Tide and the strip club Eli had mentioned taking my husband to. The smell of decaying food and stale alcohol hid the familiar smell of a body decomposing; in the humid air, the smell lodged in my throat. Who would have guessed people eat food at a strip club? Down the alley, on the corner of the wall, our only hope protruded.

"Captain Taylor, can you get us the footage?" I raised my hand in the direction of the camera facing us. Perhaps Booty Bump's owners would be more forthcoming and we wouldn't need a warrant. The owners of Booty Bump didn't know, or perhaps they did, that the name refers to a drug which is administered anally.

"I will see what I can do." He walked to the owner who upon hearing the request first shook his head, then nodded.

Deep lacerations criss-crossed the victim's face and neck,

the rest of him obscured by his clean, blood-free clothes. *She redressed him post-mortem.* I watched as the forensic pathologist removed the note with great care. He opened it on a piece of brown paper, and after the tech had finished taking photos, he called Captain Taylor and myself over.

Captain Taylor squatted next to the letter as I peered over his shoulder. Not yet comfortable at a crime scene not created by my own hand.

David, I made a mistake. Please come back to me. I love you. S.

"It wasn't Sophia who took the shot at Ari. Why would she kill the man she wants back?" The startled expression on his face made me realise I had said it out loud. "Captain, my husband didn't take that shot."

"I know Finley, but if it wasn't Sophia, who are we looking for?"

"I have no theories to share. But you can access Aidan's military records; the man doesn't miss."

Captain Taylor pushed to his feet and towered over me. "Doctor Walker is no longer a suspect in the investigation. His alibi is solid, not that he needed it, in my opinion. Why are you bringing it up?"

"I considered Sophia a suspect and I'm trying to make sense of the violence in front of me." I couldn't admit that I had seen, and done, far worse. "May I attend the autopsy?"

"Of course. You're privy to all information related to this investigation."

"We never got around to discussing the other victims' movements on the days their diaries had those two-hour blank spaces."

"They were all in the vicinity of Doctor James' office, which is also his home address. He's sixty-eight years old, Finley, he can't be responsible for this."

"Somehow, this traces back to him or his address. I need to talk to him."

"I will send the detectives with you. Would prefer it if Ari went with you."

I shook my head and stared down the alley. "Captain, as you are aware, the situation is complicated."

"Yes, it is, but this victim brings the total to six, not counting the one survivor. These murders must take precedent over personal issues."

Vendettas would have been a more accurate description.

"Fine, Ari can meet me there, but either detective Shaw or detective McMann has to accompany me."

"I will ask detective McMann to call Doctor James now and set up a meeting, might do him good to learn how you conduct an interview."

It's better than having him see how I interrogate.

Detective McMann and I arrived at Doctor James' house minutes before our scheduled time; he was still in the 'doing everything by the book' ignorant new detective stage. I made a mental note to do the driving in future.

Ari waited for us on the kerb, pushing his mobile phone into his pants pocket as soon as we pulled up, the same hyena grin on his face as earlier that morning. I strode past him without acknowledging his presence.

Doctor James was taller than I had imagined him. Despite his age, he had an air of wit and sophistication about him. Ari took the liberty of making introductions. "Doctor James, this is Finley Williams. Finley, Doctor James."

I held my hand out to the older man and corrected Ari. "Finley Williams-Walker."

A knowing look played across Doctor James' face, but as quickly as it appeared, he regained control.

"Doctor James, the information I'm about to share with you is privileged as it hasn't been released to the media. Over the past two years, seven men were abducted, and thus far we have only found six bodies. Ari, or as you know him, David Ezra, is the only survivor."

The doctor gestured for us to sit in his living room. "Seven abductions? Why hasn't this been made public?" He shook his head, repositioning his glasses as he, too, took a seat.

"Because of the positions the victims held in their professional capacities and as citizens of this city, the police thought it best to withhold the information from the public. Doctor James, we believe the men might have been clients of yours. Do you prefer patients or clients?" I watched his response. He offered me nothing.

"Clients. Why do you think they are my clients?"

"You're a busy man, Doctor, so I will cut to the chase." He smiled at the subtle compliment. "David Ezra was your client. The other six men's mobile phones were all tracked to within a kilometre radius from your home. More of interest to me is that they all had two hours left blank in their weekly schedules." I didn't mention that the information had previously gone missing.

"Men such as the ones whose deaths we are investigating are not the type who want the world to know if they are seeking professional help. Doctor, we can get a warrant, but I, we, would appreciate your cooperation with this investigation. I realise you won't hand over their files, but do you mind confirming whether the following men were in fact your clients?"

"Of course I will help in any way I can, ethically."

I leaned forward in my seat and listed the victims' names. "Doctor, these men were murdered, and we are nowhere close to finding their killer. Your full cooperation will be appreciated. If in fact these men were your clients, we will do our utmost to keep your name out of the media."

"Mrs Williams-Walker, at my age, you don't care about bad publicity anymore. I take on certain clients because I love what I do. You have the same fire I had at your age." *I hadn't even showed him a glimpse of my fire.*

Doctor James confirmed all the men were his clients and agreed to allow me to review their files, as long as it remained on his property. Ari objected, and I reminded him David Ezra was in danger; curiosity my motive not concern for his safety.

"You can both leave. Detective McMann, I will call you

when I'm done, if you don't mind giving me a ride back to the station?" They both left.

Doctor James made coffee and retrieved the files from his office, placing the stack on the dining room table.

I rolled the mug between my hands. "Doctor, would you mind telling me if the men came to see you for similar reasons?"

He smiled. "Please call me Jimmy, all my colleagues do."

"Thank you, Jimmy." I returned his smile.

"They all had difficulty establishing and maintaining intimate relationships. Either they worked too many hours a day and didn't have time to meet women, or they worried the women they met were only interested in their social standing and money."

I could read through David Ezra's file later to learn his motive. "Did any of them mention they were interested in the BDSM lifestyle?"

"Why do you ask?" Question for a question.

"Jimmy, I wouldn't if it wasn't relevant to the case."

"None they shared with me. It became clear through our sessions that they *all* wanted a strong, successful partner in life, not just someone to cook, clean, and warm their beds. I don't know how all of this leads back to me."

"Do you have a receptionist or someone else working with you?" I had seen no indication of another person in the house.

"No. My wife scheduled my appointments and took care of the accounts. At the time of her passing, I had a thriving practise and employed a young gentleman to help me with the administration. It didn't work out, so I had to let him go."

"I'm sorry for your loss."

"And I'm sorry for yours." He saw the bewilderment in my eyes. "You carry it. People like you and me, we feel other people's emotions, I suspect it's the reason we chose the careers we did. Do you want to talk about it?"

"Thank you, but no. I'm here in an official capacity." I have never been one to talk to anyone about my problems, let alone a complete stranger. Nothing a bucket full of spent rounds at the shooting range couldn't heal in my past. Now the only thing I needed was to be in the same room as Aidan.

"The offer stands, Finley. When you're ready, my door is open."

Empaths don't do so well when they are on the receiving end. "Thank you very much for your kind offer, but I need to focus on finding this killer before she abducts, and kill, again." I swallowed the remaining sip of coffee to indicate I was done with the discussion of my not-going-to-happen therapy sessions.

"Do you think she will come after David Ezra, sorry, Ari?" He raised an empty mug to his mouth. The man had a tin throat, he drank his coffee the moment he placed the tray on the table.

"Yes, I believe she will."

"Why him?" *Good question.*

"He survived. David Ezra is, therefore, the ultimate of the alpha males who have been killed. If she wants the best genes for her child, then he would be it." I lifted my eyes to find concern in his. "What's wrong, Doctor James?"

"You care for him, don't you? And call me Jimmy."

"I trust the subject of our past may have come up in his sessions with you."

"It did. He described you and what you had shared in great detail, it was the only times he smiled. You meant, perhaps still do, the world to him. I'm worried about his feelings towards you, and this goes against everything we are taught as counsellors, but it's my duty as a human to warn you, his obsession with you might not be based on love."

The doctor confirmed what both Aidan and I suspected. "I'm aware of Ari's feelings, he has been very vocal even though I keep reminding him that I'm married."

Doctor James leaned forward in his chair. "Finley, I will be blunt, but you will read all of this in his file. Your marriage is not a closed door for him, he sees it as a challenge, and even though he came to see me as David Ezra, I know it was the real him who spoke to me. He will go beyond what any reasonable person would to get you back. His knowledge of Doctor Walker rivals what he knows about you."

Nausea crept out of once familiar places. "Thank you for your candidness, I appreciate it. I'm sure Ari's past came up in your sessions. The man is extremely capable in covert operations, and I'm keeping an eye on him. He won't destroy what I fight for every day."

"That is how my wife and I viewed our marriage; it is something to be fought for. When you meet the one person in this world who understands you at your core, the light and the dark, you must do everything to protect it and never forget how precious that connection is." *I won't.*

"As I've mentioned, the killer we are looking for is a woman."

"Why do you suspect the killer is a woman?" He removed his glasses, wiping the lenses with his tie.

"This is not to leave this room."

"Never."

"The men are abducted from their homes; she keeps them for a period of six months before she kills them and then moves on to the next victim. They are raped during their captivity, but she wines and dines them first, Ari described it as a date. I suspect she's trying to conceive, but for some reason is unable to, or perhaps carry to term. The only exceptions to the six-month intervals have been Leo Wayne and Eric Parker."

"That doesn't surprise me." His words did me.

"Why are you not surprised?"

"Leo Wayne had a vasectomy after his first marriage ended; he had two children with his first wife and wanted no more. Eric Parker might have been gay. He never said it out loud, but I had a feeling he would have acknowledged it once he realised I would not judge him. Eric's parents where strict and had this vision for his life. Him being gay did not fit in their picture."

"Tell me about the man who used to work for you."

"I do not see the relevance." Questions formed in his eyes.

"This is a serial murder investigation, sometimes the smallest thing breaks the case wide open."

"Simon only worked here for three months. I decided not to employ him on a full-time basis, and as he was still on probation, I asked him to leave. He can't be responsible for this, he's a gentle soul. And this was over three and a half years ago."

"Why did you ask him to leave?"

"He asked one of my clients on a date. It's unprofessional, regardless of sexual orientation, and I won't allow it."

"Who was the client?"

He frowned. "If my memory doesn't fail me, Griffin Stark."

"Jimmy, Griffin Stark is the first victim. I need an address or any information you have on this Simon. I'm sorry but I need to take these files to the police station."

Doctor James gave me the address he had for Simon, last name Alexander, and allowed me to take the files.

Captain Taylor came to fetch me; I spoke the entire way back to the police station. Only once did I stop to phone detective Shaw to ask for a background check on Simon Alexander and the residential address Doctor James had given me.

Fifteen

By the time Captain Taylor and I walked into our cubicle of an office, Detective Shaw was ready to share what he had learned about Simon Alexander.

"He doesn't exist. Well, not anymore. Until three and a half years ago, there are bank records and the likes for him, but after Doctor James fired him, na-da. He withdrew all the money in his two bank accounts and vanished." Detective Shaw sat back and locked his fingers behind his head, letting out an exasperated sigh.

"How much money are we talking about?" I took my chair.

"Rough estimate, a couple of million."

"A couple being how much exactly?" My leg jumped. I hate indirect answers.

"I estimate around three million."

"How did Simon, a personal assistant, get hold of so much money?"

"He inherited it. His mother died when he was young, and his father died about a year before Simon ceased to exist. No siblings."

"Would it be possible for us to see the will?"

Captain Taylor turned to me. "We can't without a warrant, and at this point we don't have enough to get one. Why do you want it?"

"Why wait a full year to cash out and vanish? It wasn't because he got fired for hitting on a client. I believe Griffin Stark plays a far bigger role in this than we think. It's my opinion that he was the trigger."

Griffin Stark had been an astonishing man. Had we met under different circumstances I would have been more than interested in pursuing a romantic relationship with him, despite the fact that I prefer my men dominant and dangerous outside of the corporate world.

I asked the other three members of our rag-tag task force to leave me to review the files. Doctor James had requested that I keep the information private and only disclose what is crucial to the investigation. The two detectives had to track down Simon Alexander. No one disappears without a trace unless someone helps them.

As always, I left Ari's file for last.

I phoned Aidan and told him I would be home late, but promised to make it up to him.

The victims all shared the same agony of not finding the right mate. I wiped my eyes as I read through the notes Doctor James had made. For the time being I focused on the job at hand, forgetting his warning about Ari.

The files held no answers as to who had abducted them, but I wondered if Sophia had knowledge of the things these men had disclosed during their sessions. It would explain how she knew what to say and how to say it. Ari had told me how she boasted about her degrees and her upbringing, selling herself as a thoroughbred racehorse. Who wouldn't want their DNA to mix with someone of the same breeding and social standing?

David Ezra's file mocked me as I took longer than needed to review the other six files. I made another cup of coffee. Unopened, it lay in front of me, and as much as I wanted to open it, I couldn't bring myself to do it. Could it not wait for the following day? *No!*

I read and reread every single note, over-analysing every word, sentence, full stop, and exclamation mark. Without a doubt what Ari had been through could be described as nothing short of hell, the dreams he still had and the powerlessness he had felt the year he spent undercover. Not a speck of the man I had once loved remained in the person in that file. Yet the notes stated Ari had fallen deeply in love with me, or perhaps, the idea of me. *Why can't you let me go?*

He had told Doctor James in great detail what drew him to

me when we had first met, and the shock at discovering I had met someone by the time he returned. However, he needed to be in my life. *Needed.*

I left the station close to midnight and headed home, but instead ended up in front of Lizzie's house. Ari still lived there. *Why?*

As I reversed out of the driveway, he pulled up next to me. He didn't know the things Doctor James had written about him, the words I recognised as obsessive.

Warnings.

On instinct I reached for my SIG. I have never backed down from a fight, least of all now when it affected Aidan. Ari meandered around my SUV and tapped on the passenger window; I let it down, instinct still in place.

"There is no need for that, Finley." Alcohol filled my nostrils as his eyes flicked to my gun-holding hand.

"Need for what?"

"I can see your hand on your gun." Instinct released its grip, no point in denying it.

"We need to talk." What I would say, I didn't know.

"I take it you have read the file."

I unlocked the doors, and he climbed in, bringing more alcohol fumes with him.

"You've been drinking, we can discuss this when you're sober."

"Tomorrow might never come."

I looked at the digital clock, tomorrow did, and I told him so. He laughed.

"What happened to the man I fell in love with? Or did he never exist?"

"I haven't known who I am in more years than I care to remember." *Alcohol acting as truth serum or forking his tongue?*

"Why don't you find out who you are and start over?"

"I told you before, I can't leave you. Not again."

"Why Ari? Why are you so *obsessed* with me?" A word underlined multiple times in his file.

"I have spent the greater part of my life being whoever I needed to be to get the job done. Doing whatever I had to do, and ensured my team always won. Then I met you and yes, I was undercover at the time, as you know, but with you I remembered who Gabriel is. He was still in here." He pressed his hands to his chest.

"So, your real name is Gabriel?"

"Yes, not even Eli knows. The man who touched you, kissed you and made love to you, that was Gabriel, not Ari. Gabriel fell in love with you. How did everything get so messed up?"

I didn't have an answer for whoever sat in the passenger seat. Not a single word coming from his mouth I believed. Much like we listen to politicians.

"I should've never taken the assignment, told them I wanted out, and stayed with you. Fought to reclaim who I haven't been since I was eighteen years old."

"It's never too late, Gabriel, you can still get out."

"Say it again. Please. Say my name again." The light from the porch illuminated wet streaks on his face.

"No. You know what will happen if I do."

A broken man or a pathological liar turned to face me. "What?"

"You will try to kiss me, and I will dislocate your jaw with my fist. I can see you're hurt, and the Finley who loved you a long time ago might want to help you, but that version of me no longer exists. I'm sorry you're hurting, but you can get out now. You *need* to get out." I played his game.

"It's not that easy, you have no idea what's going on."

"Tell me and I can get someone to help you. I can't be the person who saves you."

"Leave with me." He reached for my hand, but I jerked it out of his reach.

"No." I would rather substitute spaghetti with barbwire and consume it.

His fingers traced my face, avoiding my lips. "I'm sorry, Ley. If you remember anything from this conversation, remember this, Gabriel loves you more than Aidan ever can."

I doubted he would remember anything from our conversation once he was sober. Ari, or Gabriel, tried to kiss my forehead. I jerked back so fast I slammed the back of my head against the window.

Ari, Gabriel, whoever he is, got out, walking with uncontrolled strides towards the front door.

Aidan lay awake when I got into bed. He pulled me into his arms, and I told him everything Ari, or Gabriel, had said. Even the contents of Doctor James' file on David Ezra I shared with him. He listened, and after I finished, left our bed to make a phone call on the balcony. I couldn't hear who he spoke to as he had closed the door behind him. Aidan had told me to trust him to take care of it. I did.

There is only one sound more irritating than the sound of your alarm clock and that's the ringing of your mobile phone a good hour before the time you set it. Aidan handed me my phone with my morning coffee. How can you not love a man who brings your morning coffee with only a towel covering his not modest modesty?

I answered without glancing at my mobile phone's screen, not caring who the thief of my sleep was. My eyes remained on the man in front of me, savouring every detail which made him my Aidan. "Walker." I greeted the thief. Aidan's smile reached his eyes and he pressed his mouth to mine.

"Sophia placed an advertisement in this morning's paper." *Does anyone still say hello or ask how you are on a rainy morning?*

I took my coffee, walked to the sliding door, and stared at water pounding water on the other side of our wall.

"Can this wait until I get to the office?"

"I'm aware you only left here around midnight, Finley, but no, this can't wait." *Why would Detective Shaw know my comings and goings?*

Aidan pulled me into his arms as I threw my mobile phone

on the bed. "Don't forget we have an appointment with Doctor Brown this afternoon at 1600 hours."

"Crap. I need to shave."

"Doctors don't look at that, my love."

"I'm talking about my legs, but thank you for answering a question I and a billion other women have had for years." I cupped his face and brought his mouth to mine. No starting any day without my morning kiss.

The other members of the task force were already seated when I rushed into our office. Captain Taylor handed me a coffee before I took my seat.

"Good morning all. How are you today? The weather is a bit of a surprise, is it not?" A gleeful smile found itself onto my face.

"We know you had a late night and expected a snarky comment."

I hate when people anticipate my mood. "Anything more you wish to add before I get started?"

All three men shook their heads.

"Detectives, one of you must look into properties around the estuary which were purchased with cash. Several organised crime syndicates purchase properties with cash around there but dig until you find something. Sophia is comfortable there, it's her territory. See if her parents or a relative owned property there or if they perhaps weekend or holidayed there. Whoever does not look into this, please go back to Rip Tide and see if anyone remembers or knows her. Yes, you did this exercise, but the staff work on rotation and maybe someone remembers something."

My eyes fell on the sombre man to my left. "Captain, isn't it perhaps time we made these killings public? Share a photo of her on the evening news and in the newspapers. Someone knows her, she didn't just go to Rip Tide because of boredom. She's not a VIP member, she bought access for the night. Sophia, without a doubt, hunted that night only to find David

Ezra alive and flirting with another woman. That brings me to the advertisement. We need to talk to Ari. He knows how to word it so it sounds like David Ezra. The longer she focuses on finding him, the better."

I drank two headache tablets with the last of my coffee and continued. "I have an appointment this afternoon with the fertility specialist at Marcel General to discuss possible reasons for her inability to conceive or perhaps carry a child to term." It was not a complete lie. Aidan had proposed I discuss my suspicions with Doctor Brown during my consultation.

"I need copies of everything you found on Simon Alexander. He's connected to this, I just don't know how yet. Before my meeting with Doctor Brown I will visit Doctor James again, I need to ask him a few more questions." Not all about the case.

Captain Taylor nodded and said he would phone Ari and ask him to come in.

Ari appeared in the doorway ten minutes earlier than we expected him. "Good morning, Mrs Williams-Walker, I brought you a peace offering." He held the croissant out to me. Clearly he had not been drunk enough to forget our conversation a few hours earlier.

"Thank you. I take it you needed pastries for your hangover."

"I wasn't drunk last night. Old trick, you spill some alcohol on your clothes, and the way I walked to the door was for my safety. You're the last person I want pissed off behind my back with a gun, knife, or even your bare hands."

I didn't tell him I was the least of his worries. The expert marksman I call my husband had him in his sights. I gestured for him to take a seat and as he sat, my mobile phone rang.

"Good morning, Lizzie, how are you?" We hadn't spoken much since I had lost the baby.

"Finley Duncan Williams-Walker, why have I not seen you in weeks? You're coming over for dinner tonight. I will not take no for an answer. Your husband is amazing, and I need to do something to thank him for setting up the meeting with Graham Hamilton. We are signing the agreement in the next hour." In the background I heard the familiar sound of her high heel shoes clicking over a tiled floor.

"I will talk to Aidan and get back to you. Don't you rather want to come to our home? You haven't had one of our award-winning pizzas. I'm dying to use the pizza oven again, and this weather is perfect for it." The award Aidan and I had given ourselves, but it still counts.

"It sounds like a better plan. I will bring all the ingredients and you leave the cooking to me." I'm not one to deny Lizzie her guilty pleasure. "Talk to Aidan and let me know."

"He's in theatre this morning but I'm seeing him later this afternoon and will get back to you. I need to go. Fizzie-Lizzie, I love you."

"Fin, is everything okay?" The clicking on her end stopped.

"Yes, I just miss you. You and I are both too busy at the moment."

"I think we are being adults now." I heard her smile.

"Must be it. We should convince the men to go to the lake house next weekend. I haven't been there since the wedding." It reminded me too much of the darkness I still fought to keep behind me.

"Okay, I need to go. Graham Hamilton has arrived. Your husband is a hero."

"You have no idea. Bye Liz."

There was a part of Aidan's life he chose not to discuss with me, but I knew enough to deduce he was involved in something unofficial yet somehow sanctioned by the government. If not for my own safety he would have told me, but as soon as it came up it was placed in the vault where we kept the not-to-be-discussed topics.

I forgot Ari was in the room. Or was it Gabriel staring at me? A truth no longer hidden in his eyes.

"Did Captain Taylor tell you about the advertisement Sophia placed in the Marcel Daily?" I asked him. The croissant remained untouched in front of me.

"Yes, but I haven't seen it."

"Here." I slid the newspaper towards him and kept my eyes on Ari as he read, his face expressionless.

He leaned back in his chair and returned his eyes to mine. "What does the great Finley Williams propose we do about this?"

I would have preferred cooking a six-course gourmet meal rather than answer or be in the room with him. I hate cooking and I wanted to make him bleed.

"We need to force her to come out and play. I'm a little worried about the subtle threat she made towards the woman she saw you with. Captain Taylor has already informed Sergeant Daniels about the situation, for her own safety."

"So that's her surname." He smiled a one-night stand kind of smile.

I filled the ensuing silence with the dumbest question possible. "You're not seeing her?"

"Why would I? She's not the woman who fills my dreams. She's not the woman I crave."

If we were not in a police station, I would have leapt over the table and wrapped my fingers around his throat, squeezing until his dark skin turned blue. *Come on, Aidan, make this go away.*

"What do *you* propose we do?" Changing the subject, a better option than committing murder. No matter how much I wanted to wipe the constant lust-filled longing from his face.

Ari still refused to wear shirts big enough to accommodate his bulging biceps, pecks, and shoulder muscles. The only man I had ever known with a more perfectly defined body – the one who brought me my morning coffee wearing only a towel. Aidan had his subtle ways to preoccupy my mind.

"Right now, there is only one thing I want to do. It has to wait until you beg me." His laughter filled the whole building. *Ari? Gabriel? Dead man.*

Captain Taylor and the two detectives walked in and took their seats, not without first giving me questioning looks.

"Ari, I will ask you again. What do you propose we do in

response to this advert?"

"Nothing." Defiance replaced the lust in his stare.

"I recommend you go back to Rip Tide every week for the next month. Sophia might be watching, waiting for you to return to the last place she saw you. Why not lure her into a trap?"

"Will you be on the bar every night? You can be overwatch."

Bad move referencing my husband, no matter how subtle.

"Detectives, did either of you find properties with no mortgages?" I refused to be baited by Ari.

Detective Shaw answered, "Finley, you can call us by our first names. No need for formalities once you have stood next to one another as a decomposing corpse is being dissected."

"My apologies, John." The man had a valid point.

"There were over thirty properties purchased during the time frame. We are looking into each of the buyers. It's going to take me some time. Playing Sophia's game for the time being will not be a waste of time, in my opinion." He spoke as his thumbs dabbed at the screen of his mobile phone.

"I agree we need to play her game and use David Ezra as bait, but we need to consider that she's intelligent and might expect a trap," Detective Andy McMann weighed in.

"What did you find that you haven't shared with the rest of us?" Captain Taylor stood and poured five cups of coffee.

"I found records for Simon Alexander; he holds a Master's degree in physics. His father was a physics lecturer at the University of Marcel."

I got up to pace the room. "We don't have evidence Simon and Sophia are connected. But Sophia had been very vocal about her level of education when speaking to Ari. It's plausible we might be looking for the same person."

"No way. Sophia is a woman."

I allowed the words to find structure before I answered. My hands steady on the table, my eyes steadier on Ari's. "Simon may have undergone gender reassignment surgery. You said her voice is husky."

"No. Impossible. No." He stormed out of the office.

My being relished in his shock.

Nothing but the utmost concern visible on my face.

Sixteen

Show me a woman who enjoys going to the gynaecologist and I will show you a liar. In all my years, I have only known one, and that's because she's a little, okay, very, weird. Not my sister or a close friend. I wish it was mandatory for men to be forced open and have a swab of pain thrust into them. It's something we females need to endure as part of womanhood and procreation, considering how close men come to death when they have a head cold. *Poor babies.*

As I walked down the passage towards Doctor Brown's office, I, for the first time, wondered whether Aidan's patients enjoyed going for check-ups. Or was it uncomfortable for them when such a gorgeous and distinguished man looked at their most intimate parts but saw them as nothing more than a throat, eye, or limb? Ever since I learned of his specialisation field, I have never thought of him as anything but *my* lover.

Aidan sat in the waiting room. I couldn't help but wonder why the other women found themselves there. Doctor Brown is one of the best fertility specialists in the world, and is renowned for his precision in laparoscopic surgery. Our consultation started at the exact time scheduled. I appreciate a doctor who doesn't make his patients wait – perfect first impression.

He greeted both of us by name as we took our seats across from him at his desk. In hindsight, going to one of Aidan's colleagues might not have been the wisest decision. Then again, Doctor Brown is the best in the country and only the best will do for Doctor Walker's wife.

"Finley, I believe you recently suffered a miscarriage." I nodded. "I'm going to send you for blood tests after we are done here, to check your hormone levels. Aidan, you also need to give a semen sample for analyses. Before we do your internal examination, Finley, why don't you tell me about any factors I need to be aware of."

I suspected he knew but was too polite to say out loud. "It should be in the medical records sent by the military physician who tended to me, but during my last tour I was held captive for four months, tortured, and raped daily. Almost two years ago I was abducted and tortured, you will see the scar from a stab wound I sustained next to my left ilium."

When two doctors are in the room, you try to sound intelligent by using their jargon. This had backfired on me as a teenager when I referred to my tibia as my labia. *Face-palm.*

Neither Aidan nor Doctor Brown flinched when I discussed the details of the rapes and torture. Aidan had seen what the Scarecrows had done to me, he had stitched me up and saved my life when I had flatlined. Twice.

Doctor Brown completed the internal examination, and I kept my eyes on the screen above me. Out of the corner of my eye I saw him glance at Aidan when he examined my left ovary. Later he told me that the left fallopian tube had been severed, making the right my only functioning one.

"What would be our best option, IUI or IVF?" Yes, I had consulted Doctor Google long before the appointment. I preferred it that Doctor Brown tell me instead of my husband.

"Both are options but considering your age and what your body had been through, I propose in vitro fertilisation rather than intrauterine insemination." I didn't need explanations for the acronyms which haunted my sleep.

"Aidan?" I squeezed his hand.

"I agree, IVF would be our best option."

"Okay, then IVF it is. Do you need me to call your office on the first day of my next cycle?" Both men smiled.

"Yes. Finley, please try to cut back on stress and ensure you get enough rest."

"I'm in the middle of a serial killer investigation, no way I can cut back on stress, not until we make an arrest."

"Carl, I will ensure she rests and handles the stress of the IVF process and the serial killer investigation." No point in arguing with Aidan.

As we left Doctor Brown's office, I realised I forgot to ask about our suspect. But I lived with a gynaecologist – I could ask him. "Aidan, what did you mean when you said the stress of the process?"

"Did you not listen when Carl explained what this procedure entails? All the pills and injections which have to be administered at specific times on specific days. The appointments with him, the egg retrieval process, and the day of the transfer. The week we have to wait after the transfer before you can go for a blood test, and then two days later for another blood test."

I had heard, but not listened. My body failed not only me but also the love of my life.

Aidan grabbed me as my legs gave way. "What's wrong?"

"You deserve to be a father, Aidan. I'm failing you." My hands grabbed hold of his shirt.

He led me to his office, and to my surprise, his receptionist had left early. Aidan made me sit on the couch and crouched in front of me, taking both my hands in his. "You will never fail me, my love. Do you have any idea how many patients I see who require some form of assistance to conceive? It's a miracle you're alive. To be a father is not a condition of my love for you. I love you, Finley Walker, and I'm spending the rest of my life with you. Children or no children."

I pulled his face to mine and tried one last unaided time for a baby. It was worth a shot.

Lizzie joined us for dinner, but Eli had to work. She never asked her fiancé what he did most nights of the week. Aidan left Lizzie and I to talk and went for his evening run on the beach. We had decided earlier that we would tell her about our decision.

I watched as she kneaded the dough; she refused I do

anything as she wanted me to focus on talking. Eli had told her about the baby we had lost, but I never got the chance to tell my sister in my own words. Why I didn't tell her remains a mystery. It isn't something you tell someone over the phone. Perhaps I spared her the loss of another of her family members; after all, she had identified and buried our parents.

"Lizzie, I lost our baby a few weeks ago. I'm sorry I wasn't the one to tell you. Don't ask me why, but I didn't have the words."

"Finley, do you really think I didn't know you were pregnant? Your face beamed, astronauts thought they had discovered a new sun." She wrapped her arms around me, and I cried not only for the baby we would never hold, but for the first time in my life I faced a different kind of fear. One I couldn't shoot, kill, or lock in a wine cellar.

What if IVF doesn't work? What if I never get to be a mother?

She wiped my cheeks and held me until I found my voice. "What I'm about to ask you might put you in a difficult position with Eli, but, Lizzie, I can't risk this getting back to Ari or anyone else. Aidan and I feel very strongly about our business remaining private."

"I promise whatever you tell me I will forget the second you say it." Lizzie never broke a promise to me.

"Aidan and I are going to try for a baby again. We saw a fertility specialist today and after looking at all our options, considering what my body has been through and my age, we are going for IVF."

Her face lit up. "That's wonderful, Finley. I'm so happy for you. The hormones might be rough, and I know it's a terrible thing to go through, but you're strong and Aidan loves you. As long as you two stick together there is nothing you can't overcome."

Aidan walked into the kitchen, drenched in sweat, yet Lizzie ran up to him and threw her arms around his neck. "Thank you for being the man I always prayed my sister would marry. You have no idea how much it means to me, as her sister, that you love her as she is."

They share a deep bond, at first formed over a love of medicine and healing, but over the years they came to view each other as blood. Lizzie is after all Aidan's only sister. Lizzie promised to keep the information to herself, understanding our need for privacy.

After she left, I climbed into bed and snuggled into the hollow of Aidan's arm, resting my cheek on his chest. "You're my calm." His scent had the same effect on me as a bottle of my once beloved Walker.

"You need to find a way to manage your stress with this investigation." Aidan pressed his lips to my hair.

"As long as Ari stays out of my way, I will be fine."

Aidan pulled me on top of him and whispered into my ear.

I eased back and stared down at him. "Doctor Walker, have I told you today how absolutely taken I am with you? You surprise me daily. And on top of it, I swear you're getting more handsome each day you get older."

I burst with laughter as he pushed me out of his arms, pulling me back in the same movement.

"Like your once beloved liquid Walker?"

"I have loved you my whole life, I just didn't know it until the night I met you." I cringed.

"Wow, that's the worst line yet."

"My bad. Kiss me before I think of something worse to say."

The following morning, I drove to the police station and thought about the lengths people will go to in order to have children. At least there is always the option to adopt. Not that it's a case of 'at least'. It implies that a child was unwanted by his or her biological parents or taken away from unfit parents for the child's safety. The number of children on adoption lists is staggering. I had done research while Aidan showered. Not because we considered it, but I wondered whether Sophia might consider it and needed to know what adoption entails.

Before Aidan had left for work, he listed all the reasons a woman might not conceive unaided by modern medicine. The miracle of conception, implantation, and an embryo growing from microscopic cells to a full-term baby remains in God's hands. There is only so much people can do.

"Sophia, what happened to you that you can't conceive? Why do you lack the confidence to meet a man, fall in love, get married and or try to fall pregnant? If you are who Ari perceived you to be, you should have men falling over themselves to be with you. What happened to you to turn you into a killer? Why not make use of a sperm donor? Are you considering adopting? Do you qualify to adopt as a single parent? Perhaps not, otherwise you would have considered it, or do you want a child which has half of your genetic make-up?"

The space in my helmet offered no answers. I would sell my Monster the day I received the call Aidan and I had prayed for the night before, but until the IVF cycle started, I would get as much mileage out of it as long as the weather allowed.

I placed my helmet in the corner of the office reserved for my belongings; no locker for the student-consulting-profiler. The day before I had gloated in Ari's shock and had forgotten to contact Doctor James to set up an appointment to further discuss Simon Alexander.

As I returned my phone to the desk after talking to Doctor James, Ari strode into the office. His chest pressed forward, covered by folded arms. "Sophia is not, and never has been, a man."

Denial, or would he offer proof? "I'm listening." I swung my chair to face him.

"She doesn't have an Adam's apple." He pointed to his.

"Please sit." He took the chair next to me and moved closer, into my personal space. I held my position.

Oh, Ari, Gabriel, you're an ignorant fool.

"If she started with hormone replacement therapy during puberty, it would develop in the same way for women born female. And even if she didn't, she could have gone for chondrolaryngoplasty, or if you prefer, a trach shave. Did you see a scar on her throat? But then again the scar does become less visible over time."

His olive coloured face turned anaemic. "It's impossible, there is no way in hell I was raped by a man."

"If she's a post-op transsexual, she's now anatomically a woman and always considered herself one. You mentioned once that you had the idea that another man had been where you were being kept."

"You're enjoying this, aren't you?" Anaemic turned scarlet.

"Not in the least. The only thing I will enjoy is seeing her behind bars. She's a rapist and murderer. And, Ari, we don't know for a fact that Simon is Sophia or that Sophia used to be Simon. So calm down until we find proof."

"What are you doing to find this killer? Or can't you hunt without your mask?"

I ignored his last question. "Everything with the few bits of evidence I have. Did you go to Rip Tide last night like I proposed?"

"No." Defiance streamed out of him.

"Then what more do you want me to do if no one else is playing their part in this investigation?"

"You're the profiler, Finley. Aren't you supposed to tell us where she lives, what colour car she drives, and what she has for breakfast every morning? Not to forget whatever the trigger was for her to resort to murder."

"Do you see a film crew?" My nails dug into the armrests of my chair.

"What?" Two deep grooves formed between his eyebrows.

"This is not a television series or a movie. In real life it doesn't work like that. I will let this one go, write it off as due to your current unstable emotional state. I will find her and when I do, you can bet your ass I'm going to shove it in your face." *Calm, control your cortisol levels.*

I wanted to laugh at the idea of a man shoving his manly bits in Ari's face. With an inappropriate yet hysterical mental picture, I did not expect Ari's comeback. *Tit for tat.*

"I dream about you shoving it in my face." He bit his lower lip and glared at me.

The part of me he got in his face? My fist.

As I made my way to the door, I realised someone blocked my exit. Captain Taylor leaned against the doorframe, unable to hide his smile. He nodded and stepped back for me to pass. "I expected this to happen days ago. Perfect right hook."

Seventeen

Doctor James waved as I pulled into his driveway. It never occurred to me that he no longer saw clients every day.

"Good morning, Finley, how are you today?" Old world manners.

"Good morning, Jimmy, you have an immaculate garden. Do you mind if we step inside to talk?" Parents who raised me well, tried to at least, had taught me to open with a compliment.

He led me to his office, and it was exactly how I had pictured it. Clinical yet warm and inviting. While Jimmy made coffee, I scanned his bookshelf, noticing a couple I own. A fake plant on top of the bookshelf caught my attention. *Odd place for it.*

Jimmy took his psychologist seat, and I, the spot a client would. It felt uncomfortable, not to my bum.

He finished his coffee and placed the mug on the glass table between us. "Did you review *all* the files?"

"Yes, and I spoke to him. Did he ever mention his life before?"

"Only that you had reminded him of who he once was and that he wanted to be that person twenty-four-seven. David, my apologies, Ari, made it clear he wanted to be with you. He hated not being truthful with you."

"I noted this in your session notes. He told me his real name – *if* it's his real name."

"My guess is he meant much more than his real name by opening up to you. *If* he was truthful."

My eyes lifted to the plastic plant; a tingle flared up in my palms. "I didn't set up a meeting with you to discuss him but thank you again for the indirect warning. Jimmy, how well did you know Simon Alexander? Before you answer, I need to ask something unrelated. Your house is filled with living plants, your garden is straight out of a magazine, so why do you have a fake plant on that shelf?" I pointed at the object of my curiosity.

"A gift from Simon to thank me for taking a chance on him and to show he had no ill feelings regarding my decision not to employ him on a permanent basis."

"Do you mind if I have a look at it?" Rubbing my palms against my legs did nothing to ease the tingle.

"Not at all, but do you mind telling me what has you so tense?"

"I don't know." I removed my shoes and climbed on top of a chair to reach it.

My throat closed. My heart pounded in my ears. "Do you have a box or a cloth?"

"What is it, Finley?" He walked around his desk to help me off the chair.

I glanced at the plant and placed my index finger against my mouth. Doctor James found a cardboard box, and I placed the synthetic thing inside, closing the lid. I led Jimmy into the garden and told him I needed to make a call.

The crime scene investigators arrived an hour after I placed the call to Captain Taylor. Jimmy and I waited on the veranda. I avoided his subtle questions about my emotional state by redirecting the conversation to the investigation. The day had been cooler than most, but my cheeks were flushed.

When I had spoken to Captain Taylor, I was adamant he got permission to have Eli involved in the case. We didn't have the luxury to wait for the cybercrimes unit to find time to follow up on this lead. No matter how stern I had been regarding David Ezra needing to reply to the advert placed by Sophia and for Ari to go to Rip Tide and bait her, no one gave my warnings any serious consideration. Their reluctance was a clear indication that I hunted alone.

Aidan had been adamant about lowering my stress levels; an impossible task with a serial killer on the prowl.

While I hunted her, she hunted her own prey.

I promised myself I would find Sophia before we started with the IVF cycle. *Three weeks – no pressure.*

Eli arrived and I introduced him to Doctor James. His presence was comforting.

"Doctor James, please excuse us, I need to speak to Mrs Walker?"

"When can I go back inside?" Jimmy asked me.

"Once we are done collecting evidence. If you prefer, we can have an officer take you to the police station or a place of your choosing. We will arrange for you to be brought back as soon as possible."

"That's kind of you, but I will go wait at my neighbours. This way I will be close by if you need to ask me more questions." He walked across the road and entered a house, the only one on the street with a red door. The door would have looked better painted black.

I turned to my friend and future brother-in-law. "Eli?"

"I will have a look at whatever you found and will also search both his computers. What was in the fake plant?"

"A camera. Simon, or someone else, has been watching all of Doctor James' client sessions. He knows everything about everyone who has walked through those doors. This specific camera model needs its battery replaced. How did he get in? And when did he get in? I didn't want to ask Doctor James, he's upset enough about all of this, but I have no choice."

"I will do everything I can to get you the footage, and the address where it was streamed to. Finley, what did Ari do?"

"What do you mean, what did he do? He isn't aware of this current development."

"He came to train with me earlier. His left eye is one of your best works to date." Approval spread across Eli's face.

"We are in the middle of a serial killer investigation; I'm not going to stand here and waste time discussing Ari. Please get to work, I need answers. We all do."

"Okay, but this discussion is not over." He made his way

into the house. Eli is a brilliant hacker and my best chance at locating Simon. With what I had to go on, I couldn't be sure whether Simon fell in the suspect or victim pool.

Later, when I brought it up with Doctor James, he was shocked to even consider the possibility of what Simon might have done. Or how he got access to Doctor James' house. Jimmy's routine had remained the same for most of his life. Every morning, between seven and eight, he went to the gym. Over the years, the intensity of his exercise regime had changed, and he reminded me how important it is to stay active and take care of your health. I couldn't agree more. My trigger finger enjoys a good workout.

By the time I left for the police station, Eli had found a hidden folder on Doctor James' laptop. The folder held footage from when Simon's employment had been terminated until the moment I found the non-oxygen-giving plant. Eli promised to send it all to me by the time I sat down in the unventilated room we referred to as 'task force central'.

Just like Lizzie, Eli kept his promises. I scanned through the files for the men Sophia had murdered. I had no desire to intrude on the other patients who bared their souls to their psychologist. I did, however, make notes of the men who fit the victim profiles and asked Detectives Shaw and McMann to assess their risk profiles. All the sessions for the victims I arranged in separate folders for ease of reference should I need to go back to any specific session.

My index finger hovered above the mouse. On the screen in front of me, Griffin Stark's first interview waited for my intrusion. I removed my earphones from my laptop bag, plugged it into the laptop, and placed the ear buds in my ears.

Dread spilled over me like a tidal wave; I once knew this man intimately. Ever the professional voyeur, I clicked on the play button and listened to him recall the night we had shared – it haunted him.

Griffin Stark knew my name, he had regretted being unable to pursue a relationship with me, and still spoke of it during his last session. I'm not so self-obsessed that I didn't realise it was the fantasy he craved more than me, as an actual woman. How he came to know my identity – the way I walked and laughed at the golf club where my father, Lizzie and I spent most Sunday afternoons after a round of golf. He had said my father would never have approved of me dating a man ten years my senior.

Griffin Stark had been a good judge of character. My father would never have approved, knowing full well a man that much older and as successful had no intention of having a relationship with a twenty-two-year-old student because of her fascination with the criminal mind.

Griffin could have had any woman he wanted. Why did Sophia want him after hearing how he spoke about me, as well as a number of his other lovers? The sound of a gun being cocked sounded in the back of my mind.

A hand clasped my shoulder, and my body lifted off the chair. "Aidan, what are you doing here?"

He pulled back the chair next to me and placed a brown paper bag on the table. "I brought lunch." Aidan took my face in his hands and brushed his lips against mine. "Did you hear about the fire at Marcel General this morning?"

I shook my head.

"The fire originated in a utility closest on the floor where the consultation rooms are located. I had to cancel the rest of my appointments for today while the arson investigators complete their investigation. So many firefighters walking up and down the passages, it would only scare patients, and smoke was still being extracted when I left."

"Are you okay?" I waited for his answer and pressed my lips to his.

"Are you playing voyeur?" Aidan tilted his head towards my laptop screen.

"Sort of. I found a hidden camera in Doctor James' office today. Eli located the recordings on Jimmy's computer. He's still tracking to see who accessed Doctor James' computer.

Whether it was Simon or Sophia, and I still think they are the same person, that person knows my name. Griffin Stark mentioned me by name."

Aidan pulled me into his arms, and I embraced the safety he offered, no matter how uncomfortable it was seated next to him on a separate chair. I told him about Griffin Stark's sessions and reminded him of Ari's.

"Aidan, I promise I will do everything possible to find whoever is responsible for these murders and put an end to this before we start the cycle."

"You will, but you also need to get everyone involved in this investigation to commit to helping you. You can't do this on your own, not unless you want to go off book, which I know you don't. If Simon is Sophia, and she knows your name, *you* might be in danger. Three of the men are linked to you and although your history with them has no part in this, if she makes the connection, there's no way to anticipate how she might react."

"Let's have lunch and then I will go see Captain Taylor. Maybe no one takes me seriously because I'm not a qualified profiler, yet. Aidan, I should excuse myself from the case and have the real profilers take over. What if I don't find her, or him, in time?"

He stood, positioned himself on the desk, and pulled me into his arms, rubbing his hands up and down my back. "I will not have you doubt yourself. You hunted far worse killers down on your own when we met. Were you, Mrs Walker, not the one who helped with two profiles last year? Those suspects were apprehended because of the profiles you compiled. Finley, you can do this in your sleep, if you allow yourself to think like your prey. I understand why you no longer want to embrace the darkness, but you have no choice. You can't hunt monsters if you don't allow yourself into their world."

His warm breath on my ear, the words I needed to hear the most followed.

"Remember when I told you I love you more each day?"

"I don't recall you ever saying you love me." His mischief filled my being and in that moment, I loved him even more.

"How is our other situation going?"

"We can discuss it tonight. First eat, then you crack the whip on everyone and be the woman I fell in love with in an abandoned building, not the one I met at Alias. Right now, you need to be Finley Williams-Walker. Tonight, you're only allowed to be my wife."

After Aidan left, I spoke to Captain Taylor and called an emergency meeting with the other members of the task force. Ari and Eli I also summoned. Once everyone was seated, I introduced them to Finley Williams-Walker.

"Gentlemen, thank you for meeting me. I understand our resources are limited, but I will no longer accept this as an excuse for us not to make headway in apprehending Sophia, or Simon. Every morning for the next two weeks we will meet at 0800 hours sharp. We will each take responsibility for the tasks assigned and together we will apprehend the suspect or suspects."

Ari held up his hand, and I nodded. "Why are you in such a rush all of a sudden?"

"I have been in a rush since the day I was brought in on this case. If no one else has questions, I would like to continue." No visible responses, but questions kept shooting at me from Ari's eyes.

"I started reviewing our victims' sessions with Doctor James, the same footage our killer had access to for years. During my meeting with Captain Taylor I informed him my name came up in Griffin Stark's sessions; we had been acquainted years ago through my father. Because of the sensitivity of the information the victims shared, only Captain Taylor and myself will review it. Eli, Captain Taylor and I hereby give you strict orders not to view any of the footage or share any of the content if you have seen it."

Ari grinned, I ignored the taunt in his stare. Captain Taylor tapped on the table, ever so subtle.

Time to tell them what I had seen. "I scanned through some of the other footage, specifically for the time range of seven to eight in the morning when Doctor James goes to the gym every weekday. At first Simon replaced the camera's batteries, but shortly before Griffin Stark disappeared, Sophia took over the responsibility. I had a facial comparison done. We are looking for the same person. Simon Alexander is Sophia."

I took turns focusing on the person I gave instructions to. "Eli, you need to locate the IP address from where the footage was downloaded. We need to find an address for Sophia, whether it be a work or home address. We need it now."

"John, we need answers about who bought properties around the estuary without applying for a bond. Please send me your shortlist as soon as possible."

"Andy, go to Simon's high school. Talk to his teachers and ask about his friends. Get as much background information as you can."

"Ari, two undercover officers will escort you tonight, you *will* go to Rip Tide." He shook his head; I stared until he controlled the movement.

"I'm going to..." Captain Taylor's phone rang, and he excused himself, shutting the door behind him.

"Finley, you do realise we are all capable of doing our jobs?" Offended – not a strong enough word for Detective McMann's reaction to my instructions.

"Of course I do, Andy, but this investigation has been dragging on, we now have more than enough leads to hunt her down and put an end to this. In less than three weeks, I want to leave an interrogation room with her full confession." I offered my most sincere predatory smile, hiding my maternal longing behind it.

"How do you know Griffin Stark? Rather, why did *your* name come up in *his* sessions?" Defiance radiated from Sophia's only living victim.

I fought hard to keep my adrenaline and cortisol to Aidan-approved levels. "How we knew each other is not pertinent to the investigation. The fact that Sophia knows my name might be. She might have noticed me at Rip Tide the night she saw Ari, aka David Ezra. She's highly intelligent, so we can assume she already made the connection."

"What you're saying without saying is that you and Griffin Stark had a sexual history." Ari could never not poke the dragon.

"The facts are: Griffin Stark was an acquaintance of my father and we sometimes played golf together. He mentioned to Doctor James that the only times he felt relaxed was when he played golf with friends. And spending time with their families made him yearn for his own. My name came up because of the bond my father and I shared. Something Griffin Stark had hoped to have with his own child one day. Nothing more to it. Get your head out of the gutter and focus on finding the person who held you captive." Lies never tasted so sweet.

Lowering my voice, I leaned forward, steadying myself with my hands on the table. "Do I need to remind you that you inserted yourself into this investigation to track her, but it backfired when she abducted you? Focus your energy on finding her. For her victims." A triumphant snarl echoed in my mind.

Captain Taylor returned to his seat; defeat followed him.

I asked what everyone dreaded to hear. "Who has she taken?"

"Peter Grayson. He didn't show up for work this morning and his vehicles are all accounted for at his house."

Silence filled the office, leaving no room for oxygen.

"She won't keep him long, only took him because David Ezra still lives. I believe the level of violence and frustration we saw in the manner she killed Logan Reid will be far worse this time around. Sophia has already started unravelling. We need to stop her before she kills Peter Grayson."

I dialled Doctor James' number. "Hello, Jimmy, pardon my rudeness, but was Peter Grayson a client of yours?"

"No. What's going on Finley?"

"He's missing. At this point in the investigation I can't disclose any details. Thank you very much for taking my call, I will talk to you soon." I ended the call and sat for the first time since the meeting had started. "Peter Grayson was not a client of Doctor James. Where was he last seen?"

Captain Taylor shook his head. "At Rip Tide."

My eyes cut into Ari. Darkness clawed its way up in my soul, desperate for air. "If David Ezra was there last night, Peter Grayson wouldn't have been taken as a substitute. This is the second death on your hands, Ari."

I pushed my chair back and walked out of the office straight to the shooting range.

Nothing better than emptying magazine after magazine into a paper target. Although I do prefer human targets. The sound the bullet makes upon entry is not as satisfactory when cutting through paper. Shooting always brings clarity.

Captain Taylor and Ari sat in the office when I returned. As I opened the door, the tension struck me in the face.

"What happened?" I asked.

Captain Taylor offered no answer which forced me to look to Ari.

"You were right. Not going to Rip Tide last night was a mistake. I take full responsibility for what happens to Peter Grayson."

My laughter added to the weight in the room. "Are you going to go to prison for his abduction, assault – no, let me rephrase – his torture, rape, and murder?"

"No, of course not." Ari shook his head.

"You can't possibly take responsibility for what's being done and will be done to him. Just leave, Ari. We don't need your help on this case. After all, you're her victim, and you were unsuccessful in apprehending Sophia when it was your responsibility to put an end to her." Not what I wanted to say, but we were not alone. It's wise to never make death promises in the presence of a police officer.

Captain Taylor rubbed his hands over his face. "Finley, we need to reply to Sophia. Ari can word it, as David Ezra."

I wondered how many aliases Ari, or whoever he was, had over the years, but a day would come when I would know the truth. The actual truth, and not more of his well spun lies.

"Did it help?" Ari swung his chair to face me.

"Did what help?" We all have a game level and I had reached mine. Another man had been abducted, Logan Reid had suffered a horrific death, and I had had enough of Ari and everything he had done since returning to Marcel.

"Nothing calms you like emptying your guns, and not only your SIG, you shoot your Glock as well."

"Shooting doesn't calm me. It gives me clarity." I didn't add that my calm comes from Aidan and his whispered words.

I pulled my laptop closer and started typing; both men dropped their heads to their laps, neither making a sound. "Does this sound like David Ezra?" I waited for them to put their mobile phones down. Why do people resort to looking at their phones, trying to feel connected to the world whenever they get the chance?

Dear Sophia.

I have tried to understand why you discarded me. Did our time together mean nothing to you? I would have stayed with you, because I want to be with you. Over the months we spent together I fell in love with you. I crave your touch, and I need to know I'm the only man you want.

If there is someone else in your life, let him go, but not the way you let me go. If we are to spend the rest of our lives together, I do not want to spend it on the run. You deserve everything this life has to offer, and I want to be the man who gives it to you.

I will wait for you where you saw me last, where we should have met. Come back to me. I need you.

David.

Ari kept his focus on me as I read. When I met his eyes, he said, "That's precisely what I say."

Captain Taylor glanced at me; I bit my tongue.

"Perfect. Ensure it's published in tomorrow's paper. Ari, tonight and every other night you will be at Rip Tide. Don't get side-tracked with other women, it will put her off like it did last time."

"Don't worry about me. When I'm on a mission, nothing side-tracks me. Are you coming with tonight?" he asked.

Captain Taylor collected his things and headed for the door, but before stepping out he turned to face me. "Finley will not be going with you to Rip Tide tonight or any other night. Two officers will accompany you. Come, let me introduce you to them so you can get acquainted and make it believable that you're there together as friends."

As Captain Taylor closed the door, the tension eased from my neck and shoulders. I sent David Ezra's reply to the newspaper.

For dinner, Aidan and I had a picnic next to our swimming pool. The lights from the garden and pool created a fairy-tale atmosphere for a discussion which was anything but magical.

"A patient's husband was killed by a sniper last night." Aidan poured more liquid Walker as he spoke.

"Why do you say a sniper killed him?"

"He was shot with a custom made .308 bullet from a distance of eight-hundred meters."

I intertwined our fingers and moved closer to his side. "How do you know this?"

"You're not the only one with friends in the police, my darling wife." Danger sparkled in his eyes.

"Is that a vault topic?"

Aidan pressed his lips to my forehead. "Yes. For now."

"Okay, vaulted. Where was he shot and what is the possible motive?" Sniper's never kill at random, not the military-trained ones who live by a code.

"He was shot around 1930 hours as he left the gym. As to the motive for the killing, the day before yesterday I informed his wife that she had tested HIV positive. She suspected him of having an affair and wanted to get tested for sexually transmitted diseases. I ordered the tests but didn't expect to inform her that he brought home more than just the bacon."

"If that isn't motive to kill someone then I don't know what is. How did she take it? Dumb question, I would have killed him with my bare hands."

"She vomited on my desk, the shock overwhelming. I referred her to a psychologist, never suspecting her husband would be murdered. I only expected her to file for divorce, and perhaps lay a charge of attempted murder if he was aware of his status and still had sex with her."

"This happened during the time you went jogging." I watched the faint lights of a ship on the horizon, resting my head on his round shoulder.

"Are you accusing me?" Aidan stood and pulled me to my feet. His fingers brushed through my hair and he lifted my face to his.

"Never. I'm just worried."

"Don't be, I have everything under control. You only need to focus on the Sophia investigation. You have me to take care of everything else."

"Please stop treating me like I'm a porcelain doll. I can take care of myself and I'm in this with you. I hate it when you don't share things with me, and yes you told me to trust you, and I do, but I don't want there to be any surprises, or secrets. We promised to always be honest with each other, but you need to stop keeping things from me. I can't focus on falling pregnant when I'm worried about you. I have a terrible feeling about a bunch of things, and we need to face it together."

His breath warm against my neck; dangerous and comforting words bore into me. With whispered words he answered many of the questions I had, opening the door to more.

I struggled with the idea of having a man in my life who wanted to protect me when I had been a soldier, a hunter of human predators, and almost a qualified profiler. Aidan didn't help the situation by keeping things from me no matter how much he said it was to protect me.

Trust is like a spider's web, strong but thin. It holds nothing but death for unsuspecting prey.

Did Aidan spin his own intricate web?

Eighteen

David Ezra's reply to Sophia was published the day after I submitted it. I read it in print and waited for everyone to join me for our first 0800 hours meeting; it was 0750 hours, in my book, they were all late. I took the photo someone had pushed under the door and wrote number eight above it on the evidence board. Peter Grayson smiled down at me and I prayed we would find him unharmed that same day.

I handed the men coffee as they trickled through the door, opting to do something civil instead of what I wanted to do and say. Captain Taylor had joined me as I stood watching Grayson's photo, the man's patience level the same as mine. Over the years I have known him, his demeanour towards me had changed, he had become somewhat protective. *Why?*

The meeting, just like the one the day before, was mine to lead, and I waited for the team members to give feedback. Detective McMann's excitement was visible from the moment he walked in and I asked him to wait until Eli and Ari joined us.

Ari, of course, the last to stroll through the door, even though I had noticed his SUV when I pulled into the parking lot.

The moment Ari's behind met the chair, Andy's verbal diarrhoea started. "I spoke to the teachers at Simon's old high school — well, the three that are still there. They all said he was a gifted student, but a loner. He didn't take part in any sports and only had one friend. I tracked Natalia Lee down and spoke to her over the phone. They lost contact after high school as she moved cross country with her family, but she said something interesting. She always suspected Simon was gay; he wanted to wear her clothes and asked her on more

than one occasion to do his make-up. Back then she didn't
know about transvestites. They never left Natalia's room when
he was dressed up and Simon never invited her to his house.
Before he would leave, he would scrub his face because he was
petrified of his father."

"The term is transgender, not transvestite. Please note it as
such in your report. Have either of you found a location for
Sophia yet?" I asked Eli and Detective Shaw.

Eli answered first, "The IP address is for a coffee shop
close to Alias." He didn't have to remind me of Alias' location,
it was where Aidan and I had officially met. "They don't have
surveillance cameras inside, but I will go there today to ask the
staff if they recognise her from the photo of her at Rip Tide."

Detective Shaw looked worse for wear; more years had
carved their mark into his face after this investigation had
started. "There are three homes we identified, I will head out
there after the meeting. Captain, I need back-up, who can you
spare to go with me and Andy?"

Captain Taylor agreed and said he would make officers
available.

We all turned to Ari who had stood up while Andy shared his
information and now leaned against the wall next to the small
window, one knee bent and the accompanying foot pressed
against the wall, arms crossed over his chest. "Nothing to add.
She wasn't there last night. Perhaps she will be tonight after
she reads the reply to her message. *If* she reads the newspaper."

"Captain, I want to go with to view the properties," I said.

"No. It's too dangerous." *Too dangerous?*

"If she's there, she might respond better to a woman."

"The woman her first victim spoke of?"

Point taken, but I was in no mood to have another man treat
me like a fragile doll. "She won't know who I am. If I need
to talk to her, I will introduce myself as Finley Walker, not
Williams-Walker. You asked for my help, this is me helping."

"No, Finley, you need to continue reviewing Doctor James'
sessions with the victims." His tone told me to back down, out

of curiosity more than authority.

"Agreed." The smile on Ari's face made my spine straighten; I didn't have to see it to feel it.

The call came four hours later; the detectives had located Sophia's house. No sign of Sophia or Peter Grayson. Captain Taylor summoned me as he strode past the office holstering his service pistol. We drove in silence to the address and when I saw the house, I knew the location of the room Ari had spoken of.

"I want to spend time alone in the house. Everyone must please wait outside until I'm done." Captain Taylor did not object.

The room was as Ari had described it, but the bedding and curtains were navy blue. The darkness inside the room was not caused by the decor. Sophia's longing and pain hung like a late summer fog not only in that room, but throughout the entire house. The instant I stepped through the front door, it drew me in.

Each room I absorbed, seeing her world and basic needs. Pain pulsed through me as I touched the objects in that room, through the latex gloves covering my hands. A deep longing filled me, but no anger. I realised Sophia's anger might never have come to light in this room, yet she had almost whipped Logan Reid to death. *If not in this room, where?*

I ran through the house and yelled for someone to open the garage door.

Gun raised, I stood behind the crouching officer as he broke the lock and lifted the rusty roll-up door. Screeching sounds filled my ears while the sun cooked my back. Sunlight touched blood as the door clunked into position.

I ran towards the man. Number eight on the board.

Trembling fingers slid through blood, desperate to feel his pulse. "Get an ambulance. He's alive!"

***

Peter Grayson was airlifted to Marcel General, his life dangling by a thread. Darkness called his name.

Sophia's anger became mine as I stared at my hand; Peter Grayson's blood had dried. The house itself had been spared from her wrath, but where I stood it circled me. The knout lay on a workbench next to the St. Andrew's Cross. If it was a whip, I would have expected a fedora close by. *X marks the spot.*

Her wrath begged me to dance; I whirled, taking in every blood-spattered surface. Our tango ended when nausea fought for release.

"If, when, Peter Grayson wakes up, I want to be the first person to talk to him. How did she get him?" I hoped he would survive.

"She met him the night of his disappearance at Rip Tide, witnesses saw them leave together." Captain Taylor motioned the forensics team into the garage.

"If she got him to leave with her out of his own free will, why do this to him?" I put my hand to my stomach and breathed deep, stepping out into air not thickened by the familiar copper smell.

I answered myself. "She's losing control, it's no longer about finding a mate. She's punishing men for her inability to fall pregnant, or perhaps because David Ezra survived. Captain, if we don't catch her soon, this will escalate."

"Perhaps she hasn't seen David's reply."

"I'm beginning to wonder *if* it will affect her." I pointed to the garage behind me. "This, she enjoyed. Now she kills looking at their faces. No longer hiding behind their backs with a shovel. Do you know what it takes to whip someone to the brink of death? She didn't do this in one go, she rested and came back."

"Let's head to Marcel General, there is nothing more we can do here."

"You need to set up a roadblock on the main road, she might not yet know that we found her home. Request that the forensics team search for surveillance cameras, maybe she installed some as a security measure."

If she was as intelligent as I believed her to be, she watched us from wherever she was. This meant not only did she see my face in Doctor James' office when I found the camera, but I walked around inside her home, stepped into her domain. The very room in which she kept her victims. Blinded by her pain, I never thought to look for cameras.

Before I climbed into Captain Taylor's car, I drank in the silence, the isolation, and the despair. If we didn't stop her, she would continue, and it would spiral.

Some profilers say serial killers want to get caught, but I do not share their opinion. Who wants to give up playing the god of death? Sophia had discovered a side of herself when she saw David Ezra alive. A side she might never have known existed. *What will she be capable of once she has him?*

"Captain, we shouldn't use Ari as bait. She *will* kill him. She might keep him, remind herself she wants a child, but when that fails, he will end up worse than Logan Reid and Peter Grayson."

He waited until I closed the passenger door before turning to me, his expression unreadable. "And is that not what you want?"

"No. Why would I?"

Captain Taylor turned the key in the ignition, kept his eyes on the road ahead, and his thoughts to himself.

Nineteen

Logan Reid did not die from the lashings. The cause of his death forever listed as – internal bleeding. The instrument Sophia had used to inflict enough force to rupture Logan Reid's liver was not inside the garage, the house, or the surrounding area.

Peter Grayson's body, once cleaned, showed no signs of trauma to his torso. Apart from the strips of missing flesh. The doctor who tended to him in the emergency room had ordered x-rays, and Grayson's internal organs were still intact. Extensive plastic surgery might restore his physical appearance. Could anything be done to heal his psyche? He was kept sedated for two days; his doctor agreed to contact me as soon as Peter Grayson was strong enough for visitors.

Captain Taylor decided it was time to release Sophia's photo to the media. I didn't agree with his decision. Sophia was on the run. For days, her home at the estuary crawled with police officers and the forensic investigators. Detective McMann had found the cameras.

She remained one step ahead of me.

As soon as I returned to the task force's office, I made composites of how Sophia might change her appearance. The public was on the lookout for a woman with long auburn coloured hair; I wanted the police to search for her no matter how she looked.

Whoever *they* are, they said change is as good as a holiday, but I suspected it would enrage Sophia to be forced to change her appearance. She takes great care in how she looks, and even though Simon had been a fair-skinned, red-headed man, Sophia had transformed herself into a vixen.

I finished the composites, printed them out, and put them up across the building. Sophia's altered appearance I sent to police stations across the city and neighbouring towns. I had to close the net on her.

Two days after Peter Grayson's rescue, I received the call I had been waiting for. Upon waking, he requested to speak to the police, and water. In that order. I met Detective Shaw outside Grayson's hospital room. Little remained of one of the most handsome men I had ever seen, but the strength which had made him into the most successful corporate lawyer in Marcel remained, if not stronger.

"Good morning, Mr Grayson, I'm Detective Shaw and this is Finley Williams-Walker."

I stretched out my arm and shook Grayson's hand. When I closed my eyes, I could still see his blood on my hands. No nightmares for Ari, the one responsible for what Peter Grayson had to endure.

"You're the one who found me?" Strained words jumped out of him.

I focused on his unswollen eye as he kept hold of my hand. "Yes, sir."

A bandaged hand gestured for me to take a seat. "Did you find her?"

John stepped closer. "Not yet, but the entire city is looking for her."

"Mister Grayson, what can you tell me about the woman who did this to you?" With the little strength he had, I wanted him to answer questions which could lead to her capture. My own deadline loomed.

"When I met her at the club, she was unlike any woman I have ever met. She's mesmerizing. Beautiful, sexy, and intelligent. We spoke for hours about many subjects few other women even know of." He had no reason to justify leaving with her, we all make mistakes out of loneliness, hurt, boredom, or just being horny. With my past, I will never judge anyone.

"Mister Grayson you don't have to justify leaving with her." I took hold of his hand; he smiled.

"Please, call me Peter."

"Peter, what can you tell me about her? The woman who did this to you, not the one you met."

"She was angry, kept referring to me as David. She started with my body, covered my head with some latex mask but later she took it off and then she did this." He pressed his fingers to his face, mindful of the stitches.

"Detective Shaw, would you mind giving us a moment?"

John left the room without a word, he knew why I had asked.

Again, I took Peter's hand. "Peter, when she took you to that house, did she take you to a room or directly to the garage?"

"I woke up shackled to a bed." I had seen the trolley she used to cart the men around when unconscious.

"My next question might be difficult, so if you don't want to answer, you can nod." Fire drained from his eyes. "Peter, did Sophia rape you?"

He pulled his hand out of mine and tried to turn his head towards the window, but the pain kept his eyes on mine. "No." *No?*

"Peter, did she drug you with Viagra or something similar and had *non-consensual* sex with you?" I hate that word, only using it to soften the harshness of my question.

"No, why do you ask?" He tried to shake his head, but the bandages around his neck didn't want to budge. Neither did I.

"She raped her other victims."

"What other victims?"

"Peter, you were her eighth victim, the second to survive."

I gave him a sip of water and waited for him to make sense of my words.

"Eight victims. Six dead. Two survivors?" he asked.

I nodded. "She's a serial killer." Bobble-head Finley. I prefer action figures.

"She didn't rape me. We didn't have sex either. I want to meet the other survivor."

"I can arrange it but will need to clear it with your doctor.

Did she say anything that could be of importance to this investigation?"

"No. She was angry, that much I can tell you. She kept calling me David, and I tried to remind her I'm Peter."

Ari should've been at Rip Tide. *Why wasn't he?*

"Peter, I will arrange for the psychiatrist who is seeing the other survivor to come and see you today. If you remember anything, please contact me immediately."

"You're not a detective?"

"No, I'm the consulting profiler on this case." If I had time to finish my thesis, I might have been more than just consulting. There are only so many hours in a day.

"How many more victims will it take before you apprehend her?"

A thousand wasps stung me from all sides. "I'm sorry this happened to you, Mr Grayson. I promise you we are working day and night to find her."

The door closed behind me, yet the harshness of his words still bore into me.

"And?" Detective Shaw stepped closer.

"He claims she didn't rape him, and he wants to meet David Ezra. John, he blames me for this. Peter Grayson blames me for our inability to catch this killer."

"Welcome to the big leagues, kid. This is your life now. You need to roll with the punches from now on." The punches he had to roll with in his close to thirty-year career visible on his face.

I could do with dishing out a few punches of my own and phoned Eli as I drove out of the hospital garage. Aidan was in surgery; punching Eli would have to bring calm.

Ari dropped the jump rope at his feet as I walked in and undressed me with his eyes. I scanned the building, calling out to Eli.

"He will be back any minute. If you want, we can spar until he gets here."

"No, thank you, I will warm up on the bag." As I walked past him, he reached for me. *Bad move*. "Peter Grayson wants to meet David Ezra." I yanked my arm from his grip.

"Why?" Ari touched his bare chest; my eyes stayed on his.

"You can ask him yourself when you go see him. Captain Taylor will contact you with the time."

"What's wrong?" He again reached for my arm, but I stepped back. Our dance since he returned; he reached, and I remained out of his clutches. No chance in hell we would win any kind of competition.

"Sophia's photo was released to the public. Everyone knows there is a serial killer on the loose. To top it all off, I'm the profiler who can't find her. So much for a career in this field. No thanks to you."

"This isn't on you. You aren't the only person involved in this investigation. Stop playing the lone wolf, you will only make it worse for yourself if you do."

"If you don't mind, I want to warm up before Eli gets here. And I won't discuss this with you any further." I brought my insecurities up. During the drive from the hospital, I had thought about nothing but the IVF cycle ahead of me and my fear of never giving Aidan the child he deserved. The child we both longed for.

"What's really going on? Trouble at home? Doctor Walker not taking care of all your needs?"

"No. My marriage is not up for discussion." Aidan and I had a common enemy but neither of us knew who the real enemy was. We had our suspicions but nothing concrete.

"I should've been at Rip Tide the night Peter Grayson got abducted."

"He left with her out of his own free will."

"I should've been there."

"Why weren't you? What was so important that you put off catching a killer?"

"Did you ever consider I might be busy tracking another?"

"Who?" I pulled on my boxing gloves.

"I can't tell you." His eyes told me he wanted to, but not for any good reason.

The punching bag dangled in anticipation of my pounding; I swear so did Ari's face. I turned, heading towards the end of the building, ready to release my frustration.

"Finley, you don't know what's coming. I don't want you to get hurt."

Rage trumped frustration. Jab. Cross. Hook. My fists exploded from my sides. He should've seen it coming. Ari had once trained me for war.

Ari gave as good as he took and we both released months of pent up frustration, not only with each other. My kicks for everything he didn't say but implied, and the reason for Aidan and my recent vault topics.

Ari hid something.

Whatever it was it made me more fearful than not stopping Sophia.

Sweat dripped on my chest as I pressed the mobile phone to my ear. "How is the rest of your week looking?"

"I have surgery every day and back-to-back appointments scheduled with patients. Why?"

"We should go where you almost gave me a heart attack." The corners of my mouth twisted.

"Alias, The Marcella, the lake house, Wild Bay, Vietnam, Fiji. Please don't tell me you want to make a weekend out of the very first place I made your breathing stop?"

Who wants to spend a whole weekend in a decrepit parking structure? Maybe meth-addicts who need a change of scenery or shelter. I had only one place in mind. We had to go where he had saved my life, the first time.

"Finley, I would love to stay there every day with you, but I can't. What I can do is drive out after work and will drive into the city every day. You need to be in the woods and I'm not letting you go by yourself."

"I will go home and pack for both of us; when you get off

work, meet me there. I love you, Aidan Walker."

"What's wrong?" Whatever he had been doing, the noise stopped.

"Nothing, we just need time away."

"We need something else and loads of it." Butterflies scurried inside me at the promise in his words.

"Yes, we do. I have a few other boxes in mind I want you to tick for me. Boxes no parent should leave unticked. You know which ones I'm talking about, Doctor Walker."

"I love you for so many reasons, Mrs Walker, but that dirty mouth of yours drives me crazy."

I returned my mobile phone to my backpack to find Ari standing behind me. My muscles ached but I could summon enough strength to smack the disproval from his face. I waited for him to hammer the final nail into his coffin.

"Are you leaving in the middle of the investigation?" He took his time covering his torso in another too-small shirt.

"Yes." Bored by the sight, I gathered my belongings and placed them in my backpack.

"Captain Taylor called me and asked we meet him at the hospital, Peter Grayson wants to talk to me."

"You go talk to him. Captain Taylor can fill me in later. I need to work on my thesis."

"Doesn't sound to me like you plan to work on anything in the coming days but ticking some list with Aidan."

My cortisol levels increased, so did my heart rate, and the left hemisphere of my brain became more stimulated. Perhaps it was time for anger management classes; then again, I love being angry, it fuels me.

"Do I need to remind you that had you been at Rip Tide, there would be no need for you to meet with Peter Grayson? Where were you? What was more important?"

"I'm working on something. My employer won't appreciate me discussing the details with you. If you want, I can drive through and spend the days with you ticking a few boxes. If you can hide your smile, your husband will never know."

"You ignorant fool. Underestimating Aidan Walker is the biggest mistake of your life."

I left without looking back.

Twenty

The lake house was home, from the first moment I had walked through the front door. I relished in the darkness of the surrounding woods. Every morning I went for my run, always the same route. Aidan waited for me on the deck with my good morning kiss, and coffee. We spent our nights making love and being a normal, recently married couple ticking boxes; not all of them entailed being naked. No work talk, but we spoke at length about the other situation we both saw approaching like a dark avalanche. The mechanisms started turning, Aidan fought against it, leaving me to watch without knowing what he faced. I hated every minute of being sidelined. No matter how many times I told him as much, he reminded me that I needed to focus on the IVF cycle and catching Sophia in the following two weeks. *No pressure.*

The task force still met at 0800 hours each morning, but we were no closer to finding her. The hotline set up after her face went national had not stopped ringing, but nothing came of the information. How could she not have an employer, employees, or friends? She was a ghost. Or was she Simon during the day and Sophia only at night? How would that even work?

I considered discussing the matter with Ashley but decided against it as she now had another victim who needed her unbiased and objective to aid his recovery. She remained professional in her sessions with Ari but told me more than once that he was up to something. Ashley warned me – Ari wasn't done with me, not yet.

Making him disappear would be easy, considering the current circumstances.

I knew Sophia better than anyone without meeting her. Her use of a knout intrigued me. I regretted not using it during

my torturer days. Although, the cat-o'-nine-tails gave 1.
workouts and stupendous messes to clean.

If profiling didn't work out, I could always fall back on .
career in cleaning up crime scenes. In that game I had reached
the highest level, and previous experience had proven I have
the stomach for it. That knowledge will come in handy the day
I clean up the mess Ari, Gabriel, whatever his name, leaves
behind.

Aidan might have been calling the shots, but he knew full
well that when the day comes, I will do what has to be done. I
wanted nothing more than to step up to the plate and take the
swing. Maybe I'm a team player… As long as it's part of team
Walker.

How can one have all these dark and torturous thoughts,
yet also pray for new life?

Aidan bought me a new Mercedes-AMG GLS 63, stating
it was more fitting for a mother. This of course, a half-truth.
I had stood on the porch watching him remove the tracking
device from underneath my G-Class. Aidan found one on his
G-Class, too. Both devices ended up at the bottom of the lake.
After tossing it, he had stood on the lakeshore making a phone
call out of earshot.

Doctor James became my go-to. I could have gone to my
mentor, Professor Scott, but Jimmy had answers to questions
I needed answered. Not only about the investigation. Jimmy
and I spoke on his porch. I often wondered when he would
be comfortable enough to allow patients back into his
consultation room. "Jimmy, the police made sure there are
no more cameras in your home or office. Eli has set up extra
security measures on your computer ensuring you won't be
hacked again." Cicadas tried to drown my words.

"Yes, but it is such a nice day outside."

It wasn't; the sweat rolling down my back said as much.
"None of this is your fault." His demeanour and laid-back
clothing gave it away.

"But it is, Finley. How could I not see Simon was unstable?"

"Did Simon ever talk to you about going for gender reassignment surgery?"

"No. I picked up on certain things and concluded he didn't have an easy or happy childhood. But it's not a precursor for murder." *Not always.*

"No, it's not. I need you to remember how many serial killers spend years going undetected or even considered capable of their horrendous crimes." I reached for his hand. Touch is effective for many reasons.

"What burdens are you carrying?" He placed a clammy hand on top of mine, playing my game.

"Many, *Doctor*, but I'm not here in a personal capacity. I need your opinion on why Sophia deviated from her modus operandi when she abducted Peter Grayson from Rip Tide. She didn't rape him."

Grayson had confirmed this to Ari, rather David Ezra, during their meeting. Sticking to his recollection of events even after David Ezra told him what Sophia had done to him.

"She's becoming desperate and she will get more violent with her next victim. And the next victim, and the next. The rate at which she will escalate is difficult to determine. But you know this, why are you asking for my opinion?" He didn't give me the opportunity to lie. "Ah, because you're second-guessing your abilities. It's normal. Not one killer is the same as the previous or the next. You're tasked with finding a female serial killer, which is extremely rare, even more so because she is violent and not only poisons or murders patients or people in her care. Sophia is an anomaly."

"A glitch." I covered my face with my hands. "There is a reason she spent the better part of her life as a man only to now live as a woman. Is it because her father wouldn't allow or accept his son as a daughter? Jimmy, what if Simon was never Simon but has always been Sophia?"

"I believe this is how transgender individuals view themselves."

"No, what I mean is, what if an overbearing and controlling parent created Simon? What if Sophia has always been a woman but was raised as a boy?" Again, the sound of a gun being cocked sounded in my mind. "I need to ask a detective to look into Simon Alexander's medical history. There has to be a reason she, Sophia, can't conceive."

"Perhaps her reasons are the same as yours?" His words came out of nowhere and punched my soul across the tiled floor.

"I'm not here in a personal capacity." My hand rubbing my stomach answered him. Longing for a child has the same effect as alcohol; it makes you vulnerable and stupid.

"You need to use your own experience when you interrogate her, make her view you as damaged, as she is." *That wouldn't take much effort.*

"I have no idea what I will say to her when we catch her, but I can make her feel at ease as a woman. It will take time to get a confession out of her." *Time I don't have.*

"Stop doubting yourself. No matter what you do, she must never make the connection between you and Griffin Stark. Put off asking about him for as long as you can."

"The last thing I want is my colleagues to find out about our history, it will forever change the way they look at me as a professional."

"The actions of your youth should not be held against you, but people can be narrow-minded and judgemental. Even more so in a predominantly male field. You have to be seen as one of the boys, and if they see you as a sex object you will need to work so much harder. You need to control how this information gets out."

He spared me by not including *stupid* in his first sentence.

"Finley, are you worried about your husband's reaction if this comes to light?"

"He knows. I don't keep secrets from him."

"But he keeps secrets from you?" Jimmy reached for my hand, but I pulled it out of reach.

"No, and again, I'm not here in a personal capacity."

"Are you worried about Ari's reaction?"

"He will love it and find ways to bring it up for as long as he remains in Marcel. I will request he not be allowed to view when I interrogate Sophia; everyone keeps forgetting he's one of her victims."

"See, *you* are in control."

I needed someone impartial to remind me of it. "Thank you. Will there ever be a time you don't analyse me when we meet?"

"Off the record, and completely unprofessional of me, but I analysed the woman David Ezra spoke of during his sessions. From what he said, I gathered you're a force of nature and that you're capable of doing equally good and bad things. You need to embrace what you are for the sake of hunting criminals and your own cohesion. To empathise with killers is a gift, Finley. You don't realise just how capable you are, not yet. Perhaps you did once. Stop fighting it. When Sophia sits across from you at that table, forget everything you were taught, everything you think you know about her, and listen to her, see her like no one has ever seen her. As long as she doesn't make the connection between you and Griffin Stark, you have a chance, but once she realises who you are, she will shut you out. If she doesn't try to kill you."

Those who work with the darkness of this world need regular therapy sessions. If you keep it bottled up inside, Post Traumatic Stress Disorder is in your future. I have had my fair share of dealing with it, and to an extent, still do. So does everyone else I know who has been involved in law enforcement and those who served their country. I was concerned about Detective Shaw's wellbeing. I mentioned to Captain Taylor he should be more assertive in making debriefs and regular therapy sessions mandatory. Too many cases of murder-suicide amongst police officers, and the warning signs blinked faster each day for John.

I reviewed the medical records we found for Simon Alexander and asked Detective Shaw to locate a copy of Simon's birth certificate. A few hours later he called saying he had found something. I answered his call as I sat overlooking the lake, procrastinating yet again. The thesis would finish itself, as they all do. I was in a sarcastic mood.

"Finley, Simon Alexander was not born in a hospital, home birth. The father went to register the birth, and that was it."

"No records of visiting a paediatrician or a nurse for vaccinations?"

"I found records of vaccinations but not of any visits to a paediatrician after birth. What is it you aren't telling me?" A chair squeaked in the background, the sound familiar. Someone sat in my chair.

"I believe Simon has always been Sophia, born a girl but raised as a boy. Can you dig a little more into her parents' backgrounds?"

"I will. Finley, Peter Grayson spoke to me this morning. I will send you his statement. And Ari is on his way to talk to you about their conversation."

"Please tell him it isn't necessary. I'm putting in extra hours on the case, and my thesis. I don't have time to talk to him." The grey pebbles in the driveway crushed under the weight of something heavy. I removed my SIG from the holster on my belt and walked towards the front door.

"He left about an hour ago."

"He's here. Please inform me as soon as you find something."

"Will do."

I ended the call and opened the door.

Ari shook his head at the barrel of the gun aimed at his forehead. *I'm not bluffing.*

"'I'm going to reach into the back of my SUV, not taking out a gun."

The barrel remained fixed on him; it took all my self-control not to squeeze the trigger.

"I brought you something." He closed the back door and

stepped away from his SUV holding the biggest bouquet of red roses I had ever seen. Ari needed both arms to carry it. The bouquet almost covered his face.

Fact number one – red roses are not my favourite flowers.

Fact number two – I would have preferred Ari's face covered in his own red.

He handed me the flowers, and I took it, walked through the house, out onto the jetty, and dropped it into the lake. I did remove the plastic covering; I wasn't about to litter, even in my agitated state. He stood motionless, hands at his sides, not as heroic as Superman.

As the dustbin lid slammed shut, I faced him, gun still in hand. "Leave now or I *will* shoot you." I had started my IVF injection and pill regiment the day before and I felt it my right to use the obscene amount of hormones running through my veins as an excuse for my murderous ambitions.

"I wanted to do something nice for you." Ari attempted puppy dog eyes, but looked more like a dog caught in the headlights.

I motioned towards the door with the barrel.

"When last did someone do something nice for you?"

"I think you need to schedule a follow-up examination with your neurologist. I swear Sophia killed half your brain cells when she smacked you with the shovel." *Childish much, Fin? Internal shrug. Blame the hormones.*

"You deserve someone who will bring you flowers every day."

Birds took off as my laughter roared out of the house. Ari returned his hands to his sides.

I smirked. "You think we shared something special, but you don't even know I'm not fond of flowers. They look pretty for a few days but die the second the stem is cut. Like our relationship. Just leave, whatever your name is."

"I have other ways to show you how much I love you." He started to close the distance between us.

"Take one more step towards me and I will drop you

right there. I will only say this one more time. Leave. Now."
Again, the barrel showed him the direction of the door before
resuming to stare him in the face.

My phone rang, and I answered the call with my unoccupied
hand. All Ari heard:

"Yes."

"I'm on top of it. Should be done in a few seconds."

"No. We can laugh about it later. First let me get rid of the
trash."

"I love you more."

I placed my mobile phone on the kitchen island without
taking my eyes off the man I itched to shoot.

"You have thirty seconds to get out of my house, get in
your vehicle, and leave."

"Finley, I'm not leaving without you hearing what I have
to say."

"One, two, three." Rage kept my hand steady, gun pointed
at the person who placed GPS tracking devices on both my
husband's and my vehicles. Behind every spook is a better
trained spook. The knowledge I kept to myself as Aidan had
instructed me to do.

"Peter Grayson was not raped."

"Four, five, six, seven." My face devoid of emotion, my
heartbeat calm.

"She injected him with something the moment they got
into her car, it couldn't be detected on his toxicology screen.
Lower the gun so we can talk."

"Eight, nine, ten." Several objects to shoot started running
through my mind. When I got to fifteen, something had to
get a bullet, and I was in no mood for the forensics team and
police officers in my house when I got to thirty.

It had rained the night before; my house would be full
of muddy shoe prints if someone forgot to wear booties.
Detective Shaw knew Ari came to the lake house. Who has
time to clean when you have a thesis due and a serial killer on
the loose? *Priorities.*

"Lower the gun so we can talk." He took a step closer; I shook my head.

"Eleven, twelve, thirteen, fourteen, fifteen." Bang!

The fireplace to the side of Ari's left leg took the bullet I wanted to gift him with in the face. A string of swear words in Hebrew followed. I replied in his mother tongue and reminded him what would happen when I got to thirty.

"What the hell has gotten into you, Finley? You're out of your mind."

Not a fair assumption coming from someone who had seen my real face, the one I hid under a mask when I hunted predators on the dark web.

"Sixteen, seventeen, eighteen." I could hear Aidan laugh as he sat watching the spectacle from his office. The smile was unsuccessful in conquering my face. "Nineteen, twenty."

"Okay, I will go. But remember this day when you come back to me. I will have to punish you for this little stunt, but then again you're the one who likes to wield riding crops and whips."

Muddy footprints, mess to clean. Muddy footprints, mess to clean.

"Twenty-one, twenty-two." Ari turned and walked out of my house. He pulled out of the driveway as my phone rang.

"Yes?" The smile conquered.

"You're going to dig the bullet out of the fireplace and fix the hole," Aidan said in between fits of laughter.

"Gladly, it's much less of a mess than cleaning up blood and explaining why I killed him while roses drift on the lake."

"The man is relentless, but I think you handled it like the professional I fell in love with." He spoke to the darkness inside me.

"I'm glad it happened here and not at home."

"Me too. I will bring dinner tonight, get back to working on your thesis, and don't forget I can see when you're not working." Aidan laughed again.

"Same goes for you, Doctor. Oh, and Aidan, you never gave me my good morning kiss."

"I did, but I will refresh your memory as soon as I get home. Don't forget to do this afternoon's injection at 1700 hours."

"Like I will forget to stab myself next to my belly button." I rolled my eyes at the hidden camera.

"It isn't stabbing with such a small needle, only a prick."

"You're a prick. If you're not the recipient of the needle, you have no say in how I describe it." I shook my head, staring up at the overhead chandelier.

"Prick used to be a term of endearment, so I will let it slide. Get to work, woman, and I will call it stabbing from now on. Whatever my wife wants, she gets."

"Well then Ari needs to get back here so I can shoot him in the face."

Aidan laughed, the sound calming the raging storm in my gut. "Patience, my love. I promise the day will come and you can do whatever you want."

A promise I will hold him too.

Twenty-one

At 0745 hours, I waited for the rest of the task force to join me for our morning meeting. John had sent me a text message saying he had found something of interest, and he would be in early to discuss it with me, before the rest of the team arrived.

The night before, Aidan and I had decided to return to our home. My appointments with Doctor Brown would become more frequent and Aidan didn't want me to drive the forty-five minutes between the lake house and the city twice a day. Both endearing and enraging in his love for me. Snug in each other's arms, in the intimacy created by the dark night and watchful stars, we decided to hyphen Williams Estate and Williams Manor with Walker. Our life, our world, was ours.

I kept reminding myself he wouldn't hide anything from me if not for my protection and to allow me to focus on catching a killer, and our dream of having a child. My deadline to find Sophia had passed, but as long as we arrested her before transferring the embryo or embryos, I could still manage my stress levels. Only the best stress-free, happy, and love-filled environment for baby, or babies, Walker.

John rushed into the office, and I willed myself not to hug him. With every passing day, my concern for him grew.

"Good morning." I handed him a cup of coffee, his first of the day. It always made him calm, the strong set of his jaw easing shortly after his last sip. One should never profile loved ones or colleagues, but with John, I didn't care about ethics; concern overruled everything. Much as it had for Doctor James and Ashley with me.

"Morning, Finley, thanks for the coffee. Before the others get here, we need to discuss what I found this morning. It was emailed to me last night, but I was asleep, only saw it this morning." He took a few sips of calm.

Caffeine is not calming; the mild anti-depressant I snuck into his coffee twice a day did the trick. I didn't clear it with the department psychologist, but I ensured it wouldn't counteract or have adverse reactions with any other medication he might have been taking. Having a sister who owns one of the biggest pharmaceutical companies in the country has its advantages.

"Please take a seat before you spill the coffee all over yourself." I pulled a chair out for him.

"Simon Alexander's father was accused of sexual harassment when he first started lecturing, a few years before he married his wife and Simon was born."

"Accused but not prosecuted?" The air-conditioner's hum filled the room.

"No, the plaintiff withdrew the charges."

"Of course she did, probably requested to do so by the university's board. Can you perhaps dig further back in his history?"

"I already have, he has a sealed juvenile record. And before you say anything, I have discussed it with State Prosecutor Anderson. He's reluctant to take it to a judge as our investigation does not relate to Simon Alexander senior and we don't have proof that Simon and Sophia are in fact the same person."

"I hate red tape." I pursed my lips.

John nodded, lifting the mug in his hand in my direction. "I hear you." He drank the last of his calming caffeine.

"Did you find anything in Simon's medical history?" I emptied the mug containing my decaffeinated coffee.

Decaf coffee is my nemesis, so is not being allowed any liquid Walker inside me while we were trying to get our own little Walker, or Walkers, in.

"Nothing out of the ordinary, only surgery on record is an appendix removal when he, or she, was fourteen years old."

"Can you track down the doctor who performed the surgery?"

"Done, he's incarcerated. Medical malpractice, a patient

died when he performed a routine procedure."

"Can we go talk to him?"

"We can leave right after the meeting, but I don't know what he can tell you."

Neither did I. Call it being thorough or desperate to solve the case and stop a killer. Perhaps desperate to sever the last thing linking Ari to my life. To protect my husband, and our future, from an unknown enemy.

After a rather fruitless meeting – no new leads or sightings of Sophia – I asked to talk to Captain Taylor in private. I informed him of what Ari had said to me about whips and riding crops. The only plausible explanations – either Eli leaked the information or Ari hacked into one of our computers. Captain Taylor, Eli and I were the only three people with access to the victims' sessions. I wanted to believe that he had hacked and not that Eli broke my confidence. Then again, they had known each other for close to two decades, and Ari still lived with Eli and Lizzie. A fact which grated on Liz's nerves; she had grown as irate with him as I was.

Ari spent every night with them, when he wasn't working. A deadly third tine on a two-tined fork. What the third tine's work involved, neither Lizzie nor I knew. I suggested she and Eli spend the weekend at the lake house as Aidan and I would no longer be there. Eli declined my offer, citing work responsibilities. When Liz and I had spoken two days earlier, she had invited me for a night on the town, and I told her about starting treatment. As teenagers, we often wanted to kill each other, typical sibling rivalry, but not once did we lie to each other. Liz agreed to stay with Aidan and me the coming Friday night. She needed to get out of her own home, and away from Ari.

Detective Shaw and I drove to Marcel Correctional Centre, a privately owned prison in a country where hard-working, taxpaying citizens' money went towards private companies in order to keep criminals away from society. One would think this is the government's responsibility – democracy at its best.

The correctional facility lay inland, surrounded by row upon row of pine trees and mountains. Perfect scenery for those who never see the outside world, except for one hour of overhead blue skies, or clouds, or the occasional passing bird.

The man previously referred to as 'doctor' was brought into the interview room as Detective Shaw and I waited, hoping for something which would lead to Sophia's arrest. Seems waiting was the main thing we did throughout the investigation.

The belly chain looked like a metal belt as it stood in contrast to the orange jumpsuit. The prisoner's shackles made him duck walk. His face looked more like a pig with his upturned nose, but his eyes screamed of the horrors of his current life. Prison will either make you or break you; it did the latter to the man who took a seat across the table from me. "Mister Lewis, thank you for agreeing to meet with us."

"It's Doctor Lewis."

My neck stiffened, and I reminded myself not to lunge over the desk and throttle him. The reason for him being in an orange outfit I had read during the drive from the police station. "*Mister* Lewis, your lawyer is not present, and you do not have to talk to us. We can, however, put in a good word for you when you're eligible for parole if you assist us by answering our questions."

"I will die in here long before my parole hearing." Educated and soft, he wouldn't stand a chance if a recruit made him his gang initiation. *In with blood, out with blood.*

"As I was saying, *Mister* Lewis, we believe Simon Alexander was a patient of yours. Twenty years ago, you performed an appendectomy on the then fourteen-year-old Simon." I slid a photo of a teenaged Simon into his view.

He shook his head. "I did not perform an appendectomy on this child."

"But you remember the surgery and patient?"

"Yes." He made a jerking move as he tried to push the photo away, arms restrained at his sides.

"Which is it?" My hands clenched under the steel table, but my face I kept unreadable.

"Simon wasn't a boy."

I nodded knowingly and asked him to continue.

"His, her father approached me and requested I perform a different surgery to what fell within my field. I refused, but he offered to pay me in cash, and I had just settled a medical malpractice lawsuit, so I needed the money."

"What surgery did you perform?"

"Salpingectomy." His eyes would not meet mine or that of the detective next to me.

"Unilateral or bilateral?" I asked.

His head jerked up. It has its benefits, being married to a gynaecologist who keeps me company when I can't sleep. Aidan and I love our bed-cuddle-chats. This time I had called him when I learned the word I had never heard or read before.

"Bilateral." He glanced down at the table.

"Was she aware of the surgery, when you removed both her fallopian tubes?" I added, as I doubted the man to my right understood what we were discussing.

"No, her father told her I would remove her appendix as it caused her stomach cramps and bleeding."

"How did she not realise at fourteen she was menstruating?"

He shrugged. "It was clear to me he forced her to live as a boy and not a girl. He told me her mother had died years before. I always wondered as to his real motive."

"Wondered, not worried?" His eyes wouldn't meet mine. "So instead of phoning the police or a social worker, you performed this extremely invasive surgery on an innocent young girl who had no say in the matter? You took away her ability to have children because of your own greed."

I pushed myself to my feet, and Detective Shaw placed his hand on my arm.

"*Mister* Lewis, we're done here. Don't expect us to put in a good word for you *if* you live to see your parole hearing," Detective Shaw said, before I uttered something far worse.

My hands shook uncontrollably the duration of the drive back to the police station. John remained silent. Man or monster? I didn't know which we had encountered in the interview room. My palms had not itched, but no *normal* human being can do that to a child. *What's normal?*

I left it up to Captain Taylor to decide whether he wanted to pursue charges against the once upon a time Doctor Lewis for what he had done to Sophia. When she learned the truth, she might decide to press charges. For her to hear it, we needed to catch her.

Would a serial killer press charges? Perhaps if she wanted a judge to take pity on her and lesson her sentence. Eight men abducted, six murdered, two survived, one of which would have scars regardless of reconstructive surgery. How much pity could she expect?

The other survivor? I didn't want to think about him. Nevertheless, he was still her victim.

Peter Grayson had been released from hospital and agreed to keep a low profile. He had no intention of going out of his house until the sight of him didn't scare himself. Grayson employed around-the-clock armed bodyguards. Horror such as what he had endured changes you forever. My body is riddled with scars, Aidan loves every last one because it's all part of me. Not only the physical scars, but the emotional ones which moulded me into who I am.

The Tuesday evening, Aidan returned home, and without saying a word, took my hand and led me into the garden. He pulled me into his arms and his mouth crashed onto mine. My abdomen screamed against the pain as he lifted me against him, but I didn't pull away. As he pulled away from me and we both stood trying to catch our breath, I knew something bad had happened.

Aidan often came home and made love to me without saying a word. On those days, his work got too much for him. He saw so much life and death; joy and soul-crushing sadness.

Forever we will be each other's calm and safe place. With what my body was going through, he knew better than to ravish me, as I wished he could. The twenty-one, two-centimetre follicles crushing my ovaries did not make me feel sexy. The egg retrieval was scheduled for the following day; still no progress on the Sophia case.

"Aidan, what's wrong?" His stubble tickled my fingertips.

"Saturday afternoon, a man was shot and killed with a custom made .308 bullet as he got out of his car in front of the apartment building where his mistress lives. His wife thought he was playing golf, as he does every Saturday afternoon."

Aidan rested his forehead against mine. "How could his wife suspect anything when he had loaded his golf clubs, not knowing that he left her to play a round with his mistress instead?"

"Which one is your patient, the wife or the mistress?"

"Both. Small world. The mistress is pregnant. The wife I referred to Doctor Brown a week ago." *Sick irony.*

"I'm not even going to ask how you came to hear about this shooting. It hasn't been in the news and I didn't hear about it at the station. You won't tell me, will you?"

"Not yet. I'm sorry, Fin."

"Where were you when the shooting happened?" My shoulders sagged, and I lowered myself to the grass. The preceding days, I had been sitting a lot, but not for long as the growing follicles, which would hopefully all contain viable eggs, pushed my insides into uncomfortable positions.

"At the exact time I went surfing. Too many people on the beach, none would be able to provide an alibi."

"Oh, Doctor Walker, everyone noticed you. A man as handsome as you, not even the men would have been able to keep their envious eyes from you." My teeth grated my lower lip.

"Stop doing that, I beg you. We can't do what I need to do to you right now."

"Do what?" I did it again as I got to my feet.

"Woman, I'm keeping record of all of your little taunts and I *will* collect."

"Promise?" My clothes fell at my feet.

"What is your end game here?" His hands pressed into my back and he pulled me down and onto his lap. The effect of my actions pressed against me.

"Just because I'm off limits doesn't mean you are. How about a round of Marco Polo before dinner?" I pushed out of his embrace and slid into the water. A pool when you live next to the ocean might seem impractical, but we spent more nights in that pool than I can remember. It was another of our things, had started the weekend we met.

"We can't do more than kiss, my love, remember, tomorrow is a big day for both of us."

I had forgotten the next day was the day Aidan made his contribution to our attempt of having a child.

"Kiss me then, and remember this for tomorrow." I winked, and he jumped into the pool. Not before teasing me with his own striptease. He's amazing in all he does, but seeing him strip always left me in tears. Good tears.

Twenty-two

The egg retrieval was not the most comfortable procedure in the world. Sure, I felt nothing more than a sting as Doctor Brown removed the eggs from the follicles, but the after-effects left me tired. Might have been more excitement and nervousness than any medical reason. Aidan did what the father of my child or children had to do. All we had to do now was wait until the next day to hear how many of the eggs were fertilised. With eleven eggs retrieved, we had a chance.

Before we left the recovery room, we prayed. Infertility brings you to your knees and if not for our shared faith, we might not have made it. Faith and laughter, even with everything else imploding around us.

I held onto Aidan's arm as he led me to Doctor Brown's waiting room. The fertility clinic led from his consulting rooms; Doctor Brown had no time to run across the hospital to see patients and transfer future hopefully not-patients.

With my back turned to the people in the waiting room, Aidan turned to me. Recognition flashed in his eyes. He whispered into my ear and I willed my body in place, fighting the urge to glance over my shoulder.

Aidan turned to the receptionist and told her it was imperative he speaks to Doctor Brown right now. I sent a text message to Captain Taylor.

The wall clock's tick didn't sync with my heartbeat. I kept myself outwardly calm, my back still towards the people seated behind me.

My palms itched. My stomach ached. Two worlds collided. Light and dark.

After months – Sophia and I were in the same room.

***

Sophia Blake got called in for her appointment with Doctor Brown. I watched as she and Aidan passed each other in the passage. She kept her predatory stare on him as he walked past her. Sophia leered at his back. As soon as the door to Doctor Brown's consultation room closed, I asked all the patients to leave and wait in the lobby. There were only two couples waiting their turn to see the doctor who held hope. Doctor Brown's receptionist escorted the patients out. Aidan had asked his colleague to stall with his examination of Sophia Blake as much as possible without raising her suspicions.

Ten minutes after Sophia Blake had entered the doctor's consultation room, Captain Taylor walked through the door, pulling his bulletproof vest tight over his chest. Swat officers in full protective gear followed him.

Captain Taylor walked to the closed door and rapped his knuckles against the wooden surface. "Doctor Brown, we need to talk, your wife's car was stolen earlier today at the country club." Doctor Brown's wife far away in Australia, visiting their children.

From the way Captain Taylor gripped his gun, I knew the same adrenaline coursed through both of us. Doctor Brown stepped out and closed the door behind him, walking towards us with easy strides.

Black figures stepped inaudible towards the door, screams followed. Aidan pulled me into the adjoining fertility clinic.

Sophia Blake left the hospital in handcuffs, surrounded by the SWAT team. She held her head high, a smile on her face. Detectives Shaw and McMann later told me she flirted with them while they drove her to the police station.

I spoke to Captain Taylor before he left and requested no one talks to Sophia until the following morning. The implication of her capture and the end of her quest had to sink in. I doubted she would ever view it as a reign of terror when all she wanted to do was to have a child. A desire and need I understood all too well.

To my left, our babies would grow for the first few days

of their embryonic life. Not inside my body, but still in God's hands.

Aidan stood to my right and wrapped his arm around me. One of our troubles had ended with Sophia's capture.

Our biggest nightmare still lay ahead.

The following morning, Sophia Blake found herself in the interrogation room. The guards removed her arm restraints; her feet remained shackled. She still wore the curve-defining blue dress she had the day before, her once auburn hair now black. I expected her to go darker as it's much easier to do when you don't have the luxury of going to a salon.

Through the two-way mirror I studied her, yet still didn't know how I would conduct my first legal interrogation, or the more accurate term, interview. Physical torture would be stopped, and I would never be able to continue hunting hunters legally. I had used the previous afternoon and evening to review all the information we had on her. *Get out of your head.*

I left the observation room and headed to the grocery store down the block, returning with a bag full of what I hoped to be icebreakers and trust-gainers. If only they were sold over the counter or from a shelf, labelled as such.

Captain Taylor waited for me outside the interview room with the item I had requested. I kept the item in my other hand, breathed deep, exhaled, and nodded. He opened the door. Sophia turned her head; our stares locked.

"Good morning, Sophia, my name is Lee Walker. I have brought you a few things."

Wordless, she sat while I placed the items in front of her before I returned to the adjoining room, to observe her, and give myself time to think. I couldn't resort to my tried and trusted ways to get information out of this serial offender.

"What's all this?" Captain Taylor lifted his chin towards the two-way mirror.

"I'm trying to gain her trust. She loves orange juice, she had four bottles in the fridge and two more in the dustbin.

The make-up, well, she's a woman and takes pride in her appearance. Sophia's a vegetarian, so she probably didn't touch the breakfast served this morning, I bought her fruit and a tofu wrap. Now we wait and see if she accepts my gesture." She did.

Sophia applied her make-up, ate the wrap and fruit. I adjusted the thermostat of the air-conditioning unit in the interview room and waited an hour. Time to make her uncomfortable. I couldn't torture her, but there are acceptable ways of convincing her to talk. Before I returned to the interview room, I returned the room to its previous ambient and Finley acceptable temperature.

Ari walked in and joined us in watching Sophia. His heat burned into my skin and I moved closer to the man to my left. Captain Taylor's eyes met mine; he instructed Ari to leave, they now considered him nothing more than one of the two surviving victims.

I waited five minutes, hoping Ari left Marcel for good. Detective McMann entered the observation room holding the two cappuccinos I had requested. Behind Andy, Ari stood in the passage. As I walked past him, cappuccinos in hand, he dared to touch my shoulder. If I didn't need the scolding hot beverages as props in the interview, they would have ended in his face.

"We need to talk." Ari removed his hand.

Detective McMann saw the fury consuming my face and left the door ajar.

"I'm busy, and you and I have nothing to discuss." I turned my back on him.

"Ley, we need to talk."

"Does it pertain to the case?" Captain Taylor asked from the door, making himself seem even taller and more daunting.

"With all due respect, Captain Taylor, this is between Finley and myself."

"Mrs Walker is about to conduct an interview with a serial killer. The very woman who held you captive for six months, the one who left you for dead. Whatever you need to discuss with Mrs Walker can wait, or better yet, send her an email and she can reply when she has time." Authority dripped from his words.

Why did Captain Taylor have my back and put himself in the position of being my protector? Was he Aidan's contact in the police? *Probable.*

Ari left without saying another word, but his eyes had screamed a thousand in a language I didn't understand. I watched him leave and wondered how it was possible to hate him this much after I had once been in love with him. With Ari, I, for the first time, understood the saying – there's a thin line between love and hate. A line I had no intention of ever crossing again. I could never love another man with the depth I loved Aidan. Why settle for far, far less? Our life, the mutual respect, the unconditional acceptance of each other's past, present and future, the nightly cuddle talk, and the every day laughter. All of it made me wonder if I had ever truly loved anyone before him.

Sophia turned to face me as the smell of her favourite hot beverage filled the room. I placed the cup in front of her, to her left, and placed my own to my right. She took a sip and positioned it to her right. I, too, drank.

"Sophia, as I said earlier, my name is Lee Walker. I'm a psychologist and wish to ask you a few questions. If you want your lawyer to be present, we will stop our discussion. For the record, our conversation is being recorded."

"Why were you in Doctor Brown's office?"

Fair question, but I wanted to be the one asking the questions. However, she had opened a door for me. "I'm unable to conceive and require medical assistance."

"What's wrong with you?"

"Too many things to list."

"Humour me." Sophia brought the cup to her mouth, so did I.

"I was stabbed a few years ago, resulting in one of my fallopian tubes being severed. Endometrioses, and my age doesn't help either." I shrugged and followed it with a sigh. "Why were you in Doctor Brown's office?"

"The man you were with, is he your husband?"

I had no intention of discussing my husband with a man-killer. "Are you seeking reproductive assistance?"

"Yes." She ran her fingers through her hair, I did the same.

"Do you mind telling me what's wrong with you?" I used her words.

"I don't know, Doctor Brown didn't get a chance to examine me."

"Have you never been to a gynaecologist before?"

"No."

All woman should from the age of eighteen. But the one sitting across from me had only started living as a woman a few years before, in her thirties. "Sophia, tell me about your parents."

"I don't want to talk about them."

"Fair enough, I also don't enjoy talking about mine." I lied, I will never stop missing them. "My father gave me his names and taught me all the things a father teaches a son."

"Did he allow you to dress like a girl?"

I ran my hands over the dress I had pulled out of the back of my closet, knowing she might not appreciate my normal pants and shirt attire. Favio sure would approve. "Yes, he did, but he still taught me to hunt, shoot, and work on anything and everything electrical." I kept my smile hidden, along with the constant longing. "What did your father teach you?"

"Nothing. He spent as little time with me as possible."

"Is this the reason you spent so many afternoons after school with your friend Natalia?"

Sophia's brows furrowed and her back stiffened. "How do you know about Natalia?" *I caught her off guard. Good.*

"I know a lot about you, *Simon*, including the reason you can't conceive."

"Do not call me that." She came to her full length and tripped, trying to lunge at me over the table.

I kept my eyes on her face, hands steady, my heart anything but calm.

Captain Taylor stormed in and pushed her back into the chair. He fastened the chains around her wrists to the desk. I protested as a sign of having the best intentions for our discussion. Captain Taylor left us, after I asked him to.

"My apologies, Sophia, I will not say *that* name again. Do you know why you were arrested yesterday?"

She nodded.

I collected the files from the table behind me. Through the two-way mirror I could feel Captain Taylor and the two detectives watch me. *Game face on, Finley.*

The files I kept on my lap, a last attempt to protect the victims from her, even in death. My heart clenched as I removed the photo of her first victim.

"Tell me about Griffin Stark." I slid the photo across the table. She tried to reach for it, but I would not allow her to touch the photo of a marvellous yet broken man. Broken long before I had met him, which I had learned watching his conversations with Doctor James.

Her chest rose and fell, the corners of her mouth twitched. "You never forget your first." *Your first kill or sexual encounter?* "I loved him more than I loved any of the men after him."

"If you loved him, why did you kill him?" I took out the photo of his skeletonised body and slid it across the table, positioning it next to his living face. She twisted her neck.

"Look at him. *You* did this to Griffin, a man you claim to have loved."

"He never wanted me as much as he wanted you, *Finley.*"

I steeled my face; my game was up – never even started – but I had a few more Aces up my sleeve. "Sophia, I want to play you a snippet of a song, tell me what the lyrics remind you of."

I positioned my mobile phone in the middle of the table

and played her one of my favourite heavy metal songs. As the drum tempo increased, I walked around the table. Standing behind her, I spoke loud enough for her to hear, but not loud enough for the overhead camera to pick up my words. "Didn't you just love the way he ran his fingers through your hair? How he tugged hard enough to show you what he wanted but never hurting you? Much. And as you opened your mouth in surprise, he took possession of your mouth, followed by the rest of you so fierce it left you riveting in heat for long drawn out minutes after climax. I still have to catch my breath when I remember the carnal need in his eyes. It set every part of me on fire the moment it flashed in his eyes, a split second before he pushed inside me. Did you ever allow him to show you his raw, strong, passion, or did you keep him tied up?"

In hindsight, Griffin Stark might have been a switch.

Silence filled the tiny room.

In the two-way mirror, fury flashed in her eyes; the restraints kept her in place. "You're the reason I killed him!" She thrashed, her screams bouncing off the walls.

"I loved running my tongue along the scar from his appendix removal." I forced a fake shiver to ripple through my body. Chains thrashed again, but I remained out of her grasp. I tilted my head to the right. "You should have a similar scar; your medical records show you had the same surgery when you were fourteen."

The rattling stopped and settled; I straightened my neck. "My scar does not look like his."

Well, there is nothing left of his scar now thanks to you and decomposition.

"Do you know why yours looks different?" She shook her head. "You did not have an appendectomy."

Her eyes darted across my face; I couldn't force mine to mimic the movement even if my life depended on it.

"Sophia, your father told you Doctor Lewis would remove your appendix as that caused your stomach cramps and the bleeding."

"I was menstruating."

"Yes, you were. I spoke to Doctor Lewis in person a few days ago up at Marcel Correctional Centre. He's no longer a doctor, serving a sentence for manslaughter and a few other charges which the state brought against him. So, let me rephrase: *Mister* Lewis told me your father paid him to perform a salpingectomy. The reason you can't conceive – your father paid to have both your fallopian tubes removed."

Sophia's pained, rage-filled screams filled the room. My heart broke for the *woman* in front of me.

Tears blinded me as I stepped out of the interview room. My legs failed and I sank to the floor. Silently, I cried with her. Arms enveloped me and as I lay my head against a chest. I recognised the smell. I pushed him away and scampered backwards.

Captain Taylor walked into the passage as Ari held his hand out towards me. "Did I not make myself clear earlier? Leave now or I will have you escorted out of the building. I don't care which strings you pull, I will cut them all," he barked at Ari as he helped me to my feet, wrapped an arm around my shoulder, and led me to the task force's office.

Captain Taylor helped me into a chair and handed me a bottle of water. Sophia's heartache, and seeing what her father's betrayal had done to her, broke me. I needed time to control my emotions before I could face her again. He took a seat next to me and wrote on a piece of paper under the cover of his other hand. Captain Taylor pushed the note in front of me; my head shook itself.

"How?" I asked.

"Long story for another day." He moved his chair closer to mine and almost whispered. "As long as you're here, I will keep you safe. I take it upon myself to ensure Ari doesn't come close to you again."

"Captain, what I said to Sophia," I buried my face in my hands, "I had to provoke her. Did the detectives hear?"

"No, I sent them out, but the music drowned out your

words. I can't keep the recording from her lawyer or Tom Anderson. We can still use it in court as she confessed to murdering Griffin Stark. You got that much out of her at least." He smiled and I offered my own.

"I promise I will be more reserved when I talk to her again."

"Off the record, did you have feelings for him? I never expected you to gauge her like that."

"Yes, I did. Adolescent, well, young adult crush on a much older man. Nothing more than that."

"She knew about you and his feelings for you even before she abducted him. Sophia watched his sessions with Doctor James. This is all on *her*. I don't judge you, Finley, but you need to get through to her about the others. In hindsight, I should never have sent you in to talk to her, she knew from the moment she saw you who you are. Maybe we should've removed you from the case all together." He refused to meet my eyes.

"Captain, I agree with you. But I understand pain and longing for a child more than anyone. I will use it to get through to her."

"Okay, one more chance, but if things go south, I will step in. And do me a favour, when it's just the two of us, please call me Oliver." He leaned closer and whispered, "I owe your father-in-law my life."

Sophia had composed herself by the time I returned to the interview room. She thanked me for the bottle of water I placed on the table in front of her.

"Let's start over. What do you remember about your mother?"

"She died, leaving me alone with *him*."

The sorrowful smile I offered her was sincere. "I know how it feels to lose a parent, my mother died, and I wasn't even in the country. Never got a chance to say goodbye."

The last memory I have of my mother is her tear-streaked face when I had left on my last deployment.

"Time was all I had with mine; the cancer devoured her in front of me. I was too young to understand why she didn't get better. For a while I prayed but then I gave up, why keep on asking when there are no answers?" She shrugged.

"How did your father take your mother's passing?" Someone knocked on the door and I walked out to speak to whomever interrupted the ground I was making with Sophia. The interruption was worth it. Detective Shaw had dug up more details on Simon Alexander senior.

"My apologies for the interruption. Are you hungry? I can order whatever you want for lunch. I'm in the mood for a vegetarian lasagne." Finley needs her meat, but for a full confession and perhaps answers to questions about her childhood, I could stomach one meatless lunch.

"I'm not hungry."

I almost slammed the table; hangry me isn't pretty, or tolerant. "We were talking about your father's reaction to your mother's death."

"Nothing changed, except *she* was free."

"Yet you remained living with him until his death. Why did you not move out after high school?"

"If I wanted to inherit what I was due, I had to stay."

"But you had to continue living as a man." It wasn't a question.

"Yes."

"Do you think your father raised you as a boy so he wouldn't do to you what he did to the women? Did he try to protect you from himself?"

"What women?"

"The prostitutes he brought to your house. Did you never suspect anything? No room your father didn't allow you to enter?"

"Only the garage, but I didn't want to go in there. It was filled with the strangest things, and he told me it was for his work and that one day I would understand when I, too, studied physics."

"So, you wanted to study physics and follow in his footsteps?"

"No, that's what he wanted. What he wanted, he got." Water spilled down her throat as she struggled to drink with her wrists still bound to the table.

I took a sip of my water. "If I got someone to remove your shackles, do you promise to not try and attack me again?" I bartered with a she-devil.

"Yes."

Detective Shaw came in and removed her restraints. She thanked him with a smile more predatory than sincere.

"We found a sexual assault charge filed against your father by a known prostitute. In her statement she describes how he took her back to your house and tied her up in the garage, she said it looked like a dungeon. He assaulted her; I will spare you the details." The details I kept in my sleeve.

"You believe a whore?"

"Your father had no right to do what he did to her, tying her on that x-cross thing. What do you call it?"

"St. Andrew's cross." She drank without spilling.

"Yes, the one we found in *your* garage at the estuary. Were his tools part of your inheritance?"

She offered me no answer.

"Sophia, did your father ever take you into the garage, tie you up and hurt you?"

"No."

"Do you think he raised you as a boy because he didn't want to do what he did to all those women to you, his own daughter?"

"One prostitute lays a charge and now you talk about women. My father wasn't a monster."

"The police," I distanced myself from the investigation in her mind, "found DNA of several women. Other bloodstains were too old to yield any results. And of course Logan Reid and Peter Grayson's blood."

As her eyes met mine, I noticed the switch.

"Tell me about the men you abducted." I placed a photo of

each victim in front of her, their photos in life at first.

Sophia shook her head.

"This is what I think happened. After your father died, you were finally free to be Sophia, but you feared rejection or getting involved with a man with the same, let me call it a hobby, as your father. You abducted men who you viewed as dominant alpha males, the ones who would give you the sperm you desire to have the strongest genetic offspring. But after months of not falling pregnant, you blamed the men, not realising the problem lies with you."

I placed my hands on the table and entwined my fingers. "Sophia, I understand. When the doctor told me I can't conceive, I also wanted to blame anyone but myself."

I positioned the victims' photos in death above their other photos but left David Ezra and Peter Grayson's after-Sophia-spots empty. "David Ezra you struck only once. You wanted to kill him, but something stopped you. What was it? Did someone catch you in the act, perhaps the army helicopter? You couldn't have known they had scheduled an impromptu training session that night."

Sophia remained motionless.

"Peter Grayson you would have killed had the police not found him. Do you know he also survived?"

"Peter is alive?" Crimson cascaded from her face down to her surgically enhanced chest.

"You didn't leave a note for David out of love. No, you wanted a second chance to kill him. You may have thought you wanted a child and it might have been the reason you abducted Griffin Stark, but you enjoy killing. Just as much as you enjoy *raping* them for months. Every day you played your little game with them; you got excited as the kill came closer. How am I doing so far?"

Sophia smirked but said nothing.

"I have to give you credit, placing a camera in Doctor James' office was brilliant. How were you able to hack into the men's diaries and delete their appointments with Doctor James?" Eli had explained it to me, but I needed her confession.

"Physics was my father's idea, his dream for his son. I wanted to be a computer programmer, so I taught myself to hack within the first year he gave me a laptop and installed a dial-up modem in the house."

"And this is how you made a living after his death and became Sophia?" I led the conversation without having any facts.

"Yes." *Well played, Fin.*

"Do you understand you will never see the outside world ever again?"

"After everything I went through, no judge will send me to prison, perhaps a mental institution, but not prison. I will play the victim card so hard you won't even see it coming. When I get out, I will find myself a new playmate." She leaned back in her chair, challenge in her eyes. "Perhaps the breathtaking man I saw you with in Doctor Brown's office. I will make him forget all about you. I have learned a lot since Griffin."

Not enough to make David Ezra forget about me.

I picked up each victim's photos and returned it to the folder. If only I could remove their faces from her memory. "Talking about forgetting things, you forgot our conversation is being recorded. Do you remember I mentioned it to you before we started, and you agreed to talk to me without a lawyer present?"

I stood and walked out, leaving a killer in the room. She had stopped being a woman yearning for a child a long time ago. I hadn't.

Detectives Shaw and McMann entered the room to take Sophia's formal confession. Captain Taylor escorted me to my car and congratulated me on my first interview. In years to come, I would perfect my interrogation skills.

It's true – you never forget your first.

Twenty-three

To celebrate Sophia's confession, Aidan planned a surprise for me. Now that the case was closed, he asked me to focus only on the transfer and completing my thesis. To me the case would only be closed once Sophia had been sentenced. So many things can go wrong until the judge hands down the sentence.

My surprise – a night at The Marcella, in the presidential suite where we had spent our first night and weekend together. The night we had met he had booked us a room within hours of meeting. It sounds naughtier than it was. Aidan still took my breath away as much as he did the first time I saw him, if not more so now.

We spent the night laughing in each other's arms. Aidan started opening up to me about the things he never wanted to discuss before. His reasoning, it was better for me to find out and go through the emotions before I fell pregnant. There were no emotions, apart from admiration for this remarkable man I get to call mine.

Aidan is his father's son – a force of nature. As I suspected, not all of his time in the military was spent on sanctioned missions. You can't not love a man who played in the grey – his actions saved countless lives. I reminded him of this when he questioned his own moral code. Sometimes things are not as black and white as we would prefer.

Aidan and I discussed my interview with Sophia, and I told him what I had said to her under the cover of song. He laughed and held me tighter. Not all of what I had said to her was true about Griffin Stark, and Aidan knew which parts referred to him.

All of it.

We hadn't spent a night together like that since we returned from Vietnam; safe from monsters.

Yet, the darkness closed in on us faster than either of us expected.

The day before the transfer, Lizzie invited me for lunch at her house, she had taken the day off. I wasn't in the mood for company but knew it would do me good to get out of my head, and my thesis could wait a few hours. Procrastination should be classified as a disease.

"Have you found a new managing director for Williams Pharmaceuticals?" I took a seat across from her on the patio. The warm breeze stirred my hair and kissed my skin.

"Yes, Nathan Walker is starting next week." Lizzie poured us strawberry juice, her way of helping me stay healthy and away from my beloved liquid Walker.

"Took you long enough to find someone."

"It's an important position to fill, I couldn't appoint just anyone. He's Aidan's brother, is he not?"

"Yes, we didn't want to tell you he applied for the position. We know how employees can be about nepotism."

"I don't care who he's related to, his resume speaks for itself."

It did. All four of the Walker brothers were beyond gifted. Of course, Aidan the most, in my unbiased opinion of the most beautiful, intelligent, and remarkable man in the world.

"Your staff needs to make peace with your decisions, and as you said, he's by far the best candidate for the position. Will this give you more time to focus on your personal life?"

"It should. How is it possible Eli and I are still not married?" The straps of her dress fell from her shoulders.

"You have been busy Liz, doing two people's work is hard when it involves a company as large as yours."

"Do you think they would be proud?"

"Of your youth or how Williams Pharmaceuticals has grown under your leadership?" She smiled, but her eyes told me the seriousness of her question. "Off course they would be proud, Lizzie. You have turned it into the company they always dreamed it would be." If only our parents were still alive to see that we were both finally living the lives they had always dreamed we would.

"Thanks to Aidan for setting up the meeting with Graham Hamilton. Have you noticed how connected the Walkers are? Now also to Williams Pharmaceuticals." Her lips turned red as she consumed more of the juice.

"Yes, your meeting with Graham had come from Aidan's connections. But, you appointed Nathan on your own. In this life it's not what you know but who you know." *True story.*

"Have you spoken to Uncle Tom lately? Walk with me to the kitchen, I need to put the quiche in the oven."

I followed her into the house; the tiles were a welcome cool underneath my bare feet. "No not since Captain Taylor removed him from the case. Will have to before the trial starts. Have you?"

"He misses you, Fin. I still don't understand how everything got so bad between you two."

"You do. He believes Aidan is the Marcel Sniper and had him dragged in cuffs to the police station after someone took a shot at Ari. I still don't believe someone took a shot at him." *That* case remained open.

"Talking about Ari, he has been acting stranger than usual."

"He has been acting strange since he got back to Marcel, or let me rather say since we found out he came back. I have an idea what went on the six months before he was abducted."

"I told Eli again last night it's time for Ari to move out, he has been staying with us for months. No way I'm coming back from honeymoon with him still living here."

"Have you set a new date? Liz, just tell Ari to his face."

The front door slammed shut.

"Tell me what?"

Ari wasn't supposed to be home for hours, it was the only reason I had agreed to lunch at Lizzie's. For the first time in my life I didn't have the strength to fight my sister's battle for her. Neither did I have any desire to be in the same room as him.

"We can discuss this later. If you don't mind, Fin and I are having some *family* time and we would appreciate having *my* house to ourselves," she said as I obeyed the patio's call.

Seconds later she walked out to join me. Ari left, the sound of squealing tyres filled the quiet of the afternoon.

"Finley, why did you shoot at him?"

I choked on my juice. Would have made for a hilarious death certificate: cause of death – half strawberry, half orange juice. "How do you know?" Faint red smears on the back of my hand as I wiped my mouth. Lizzie handed me a serviette.

"I overheard Ari tell Eli. Well, not overheard, they were talking in Hebrew in the living room while I prepared dinner."

"Since when do you understand Hebrew?"

"I started taking lessons when Eli and I started dating, he doesn't know yet. I wanted to surprise him on our wedding day."

In all her dating years Lizzie had never done anything to surprise the man she dated to this extent. A tada-moment wearing only lingerie had always been sufficient to keep them happy.

"That's a wonderful idea. How fluent are you?"

"Don't change the subject." No matter the look on her face, I didn't have my hand in the cookie jar.

"For the record, I shot next to him, not at him."

"Semantics."

"It's a long story, dear sister, and I promise I will tell you, but for the rest of this afternoon please can we talk about anything but Ari."

"Okay, do you want to tell me now about your history with a certain Griffin Stark?" Mischief played in her eyes as it always did when she said his name.

"Let me guess, you overheard another conversation between Eli and Ari."

"How I know doesn't matter, but I want to know *everything*. I always suspected something happened between the two of you. The way he looked at you all those afternoons at the golf club and you thinking of a million reasons not to go play with Dad and me."

"I will need vast amounts of alcohol to tell you the very long story, but the short version is, we spent time together and stuff happened." My fingers fidgeted with the grip of my SIG.

"Stop playing with your gun and tell me the long version, I'm getting you some Walker." She stood and plonked back down. "No alcohol for you, not if you're going to have my niece or nephew or two of them in your uterus tomorrow."

"I missed you. These past few months have gone by in a blur. Do you ever get the feeling we should've stayed in Vietnam?"

Lizzie stood and pressed her lips to my forehead. "Every. Single. Day."

Twenty-four

Two little Walkers were transferred five days after the egg retrieval. They were called blastocysts by day five, and Doctor Brown showed us on the sonogram where he placed them inside my uterus. Two tiny spots of light stared at Aidan and I as tears streamed down my face. He controlled his emotions, but I saw moisture in his eyes.

"I love you, Aidan Walker." I pulled at his shirt until his mouth met mine.

"Woman, you will never know how much I love you." He rubbed his lips against mine. Easing upright, he stared down at me. "Finley, you're my entire world."

"Easy on the cheesy, dude."

After Doctor Brown cleared me to go home, Aidan took me. Before we left the parking garage, we prayed that both, or at least one embryo would grow to be the child we had been praying for. He held my hand the entire drive, pressing his lips to the orca tattoo on my wrist every few minutes. We walked out of our home that morning as two and returned as four. Infertility either breaks a marriage or draws you closer; it brought a dimension to our marriage I will forever cherish.

Doctor Brown had said I can go for the first blood test a week after the transfer. The longest week of my life.

The time I used to finish my thesis. I sent it to the editor for review and proofreading before submitting it to Professor Scott. The experience and knowledge I gained working on the Sophia investigation proved invaluable. She had requested to speak to me again, but Captain Taylor had refused. However, the day David Ezra would be called to testify I wanted to be in court.

***

The day after the transfer, there was another fire at Marcel General. Aidan returned home a few hours after his initial call to inform me. Just as before, the fire had been set in the hospital's wing where the consulting rooms are located. It took the fire department a few hours to clear the floor; the damage was minimal. The amount of smoke made little sense for a contained fire, Aidan explained to me as he joined me on the balcony of our bedroom.

I placed his hand under my navel, he bent down and declared his undying love to my pelvis. If anyone had to see it, they might think we were into some pretty weird stuff.

"I spoke to the fire marshal; he said the fire had been contained to the first floor but smoke had filled the other floors."

"Smoke bombs?"

"Most likely." He pressed his mouth to the area he had been talking to.

"You know what you need to do." My fingers stroke along his scalp.

"Yes, but right now I want to be with you and our babies. Do you think we should discuss names? What about Duncan if it's a girl?"

My palm connected with the back of his head and he erupted with laughter. "If we have a little girl, we could name her Aly."

"I love it. But why Aly?"

"A combination of our names. And I did some research. ALY is an acronym for always love you."

"Easy on the cheesy, dude." He pulled me into his warmth. "Okay, if one of the babies is a girl, her name is Aly. What if we have a boy as well, or another girl or two boys?"

"We can decide on more names when we go for our first sonar and we see more than one baby. But I do like the name Ryan for a boy."

"You want to name our son after my father?"

"Don't ask me why, but I do."

"He already loves you more than he loves any of his sons, and my parents aren't big on family names. But, my love, if you want to call our son Ryan, we *will* call him Ryan."

The day of the first blood test, my stomach was in a knot, the strain on Aidan's face a reflection of my own. He made time to go with me in between rounds in the maternity ward and seeing patients. How he juggled everything, I had no idea, but he always made time for me. After I completed the mandatory form at the pathologist's office, he took it and ticked the 'rush' box. I bided my time at the hospital's restaurant, but nothing eased my stomach. As soon as Doctor Brown's receptionist phoned with the results, I told her I would phone her back; Aidan had to hear the same time I did. In between patients, he called me into his office and I made the phone call.

My hands trembled as I placed the phone on his desk, speaker on. "Good afternoon, my apologies for earlier, Aidan and I are together now. Are we pregnant?" Aidan took my hands in his and his eyes locked on mine.

"Yes."

"What?" I blurted, as Aidan's soul ignited in front of me.

"Yes, Finley, you're pregnant."

Aidan stood and pulled me into his arms.

"Please remember to go for another blood test in two days, we need to ensure your HCG count picks up," I think she said as the world spun.

"Will do, thank you." After that the receptionist said something else and ended the call.

Aidan fell to his knees and planted his mouth on my stomach. I had never seen him happier.

"Aidan, let's not tell anyone until we have heard a heartbeat or two hearts. Please."

"I believe with my whole heart nothing bad will happen during this pregnancy. You need to take it easy, take your progesterone every day, and before you know it, this child or children will be in our arms. It's imperative that you keep your stress levels down, I'm so proud of you for finishing your thesis by the deadline you set for yourself. No more taking cases with the police. For the next few months, you're a housewife."

I shook my head as I pulled him to his feet.

"Okay, I will allow you to continue with your work at Tabby Manor, but only if you keep your stress levels down. You sitting at home doing nothing is also not good. But, Finley, you need to do whatever it takes to keep your stress levels down."

"I hate it and love it when you take care of me and know better than I do about what is best for me."

"It's not only about you anymore, it's all about them now." Aidan placed his hand on my stomach and pressed his lips to mine.

Twenty-five

At our first sonogram appointment with Doctor Brown, we saw only one foetus with a strong heartbeat. The other one didn't develop; Aidan explained to me what the term 'vanishing twin' means. My heart ached for the baby we would also never hold, but we were too grateful for the one who kept growing to let the sorrow fester. Life had become lighter for us. I filled my days with Tabby Manor and reading about pregnancy and child rearing, the latter unchartered territory for me. The first few weeks of my pregnancy went by without any complication, I had no symptoms, but as soon as the veins appeared on my chest and breasts I ran to Aidan to show him. He loved every minute as much as I did.

The day after my fourteen-week check-up Captain Taylor phoned me and asked me to meet him at his office. He offered no explanation for his request. As I walked into his office and saw Tom, I realised it couldn't be good.

"Finley, please close the door behind you." I did as he asked and took a seat.

"Is this about Sophia? I can't see how another interview with her will be beneficial."

"No, it's not, the case is solid, trial starts in a week." Captain Taylor sat and I could have sworn he wanted to reach out to me. Tom remained standing next to the window. "As you are aware, there was a fire at Marcel General a few weeks ago. During the investigation, to search for the origin of the fire, the firefighters had to go through each office and clear it. In several offices they had to break through the walls to establish whether the fire had travelled through the air vents. They found a safe in Doctor Walker's office, and in the safe, a rifle, which has subsequently been linked to two recent shootings.

You must know two of Doctor Walker's patients' husbands were killed? Ballistics linked the rifle to the bullets retrieved from the victims. Finley, we found surveillance photos taken of the victims at the places where they were shot."

"Did you have a warrant to open the safe? For the rifle? Or to run it for ballistics? Why are you telling me this?" My nails dug into the arm rests of the wooden chair.

"Out of respect for you and what you mean to this department, I didn't want you to be blindsided by his arrest."

I kept my eyes on Oliver; a glimmer of hope played in his eyes.

"I want one more night with my husband. You can arrest him tomorrow, but not tonight. Station officers outside our home, I don't care. But after everything you have put me through," I stared at Tom, "you owe me that much."

I wanted to rip that office and Tom's face apart, but I kept my hands on the armrests.

"Finley, they won't allow it."

I pushed to my feet, slamming my fists onto the desk. Pain shot up to my shoulders. "You can and you *will*. One night, it's all I ask. Please, Oliver, I *beg* you." My eyes burned, but I fought to keep my composure.

"Okay, one night. Tomorrow morning, they have to arrest Aidan. But Finley, if he runs, they will issue a warrant for your arrest. Please don't force me to do something I don't want to."

"I won't. Tomorrow morning, I will leave the house early, even if it's a Saturday. I will phone you and you can send your men in as soon as I leave." I left without looking at Tom.

Aidan returned home and found me sitting on the Persian carpet in our living room. Before I met his eyes, I wiped mine. He put music on, the volume louder than usual, and asked me to dance to our song. I willed strength into my legs, and he held me up and whispered everything I needed to hear.

Even in these gut-wrenching circumstances he knew exactly what to say. He never ceases to amaze me.

We made love, slow and gentle because I wanted to savour every second of him but also aware of his child inside me. Sex during pregnancy has always been a weird concept to me, even before I fell pregnant.

Neither of us slept. I cried in his arms until only a tremble remained, long after my tears were spent. I dug my nails into my pillow. How could *our* life, after everything both of us had survived and the pull of the darkness we fought against to be together, turn to ash around us?

I hated being powerless. Anger has and always will be my go-to response; Aidan remained calm.

In the dim moonlight, I watched him. His strength reminded me of the calculated and patient killer I had met years before. If only I was able to read his mind. Was he contemplating the same vengeance he had dished out with a bullet when we met?

This time an unknown enemy reached out of the dark to rip us apart. *Why?*

The evidence against Aidan nothing short of meticulous. How could anyone but me believe in his innocence?

Daylight brought nothing but a soul-ripping pain. Never had I experienced anything so deep or raw. I struggled to breathe. Torture me, shoot me, but tearing out my heart – never had I felt anything as, as, I don't know how to explain it...how could I leave this man who I loved more than my own life? *I can't.*

Aidan found me on our balcony, pulled me into his arms, and whispered more of what I needed to hear. I closed my eyes, savouring his warmth, scent, the sound of his voice. His hand slid to my stomach as wetness dripped on my neck and rolled down my back.

He dragged me into the shower, washing me as tears and water mixed on my face, and his. I kept shaking my head and with each warm touch of his hands another piece of my heart was ripped out of me until nothing remained.

A dark, all-consuming rage filled the hole in my chest.

At the front door, Aidan cupped my face in his hands and

guided my mouth to his. Again, he whispered into my hair as I clung to him. The sound of his heartbeat I committed to memory. If I didn't leave that very second, I never would, or I'd die of dehydration.

Aidan proved stronger and pushed me out the door. His face as wet as mine.

Rage scorched through me as my screams filled my car. In my rear-view mirror – our home, our life, everything I fought the pull of the darkness for.

A helicopter flew overhead as I turned into the road at the same time our neighbours did. For the first time, they greeted me as I drove past, and I returned the gesture. A light in the darkness.

"I thought you would wait for my call," I said to Captain Taylor.

"What is the deal with the helicopter? You promised you wouldn't tip him off!" he growled.

"I didn't! Is the helicopter not yours?"

"No, Finley. There will be hell to pay for this."

You have no idea.

Twenty-six

There was only one place for me to go – the lake house. I couldn't face the world. My hand cupped my belly, and I realised I would never again be alone. Forever, Aidan will be a part of our child, and of me. For the first time, the house brought no comfort. I introduced it to the baby inside me through relentless sobs. The alarm tone on my phone sounded; the motion detection cameras picked up movement. I suspected the police would be there any minute to arrest me, even though I hadn't tipped Aidan off. It hadn't been necessary.

The door buckled under relentless hammering. I removed my SIG from the holster and peeked through the window. The car I recognised; the driver carved his own name into the top of my hit list.

I opened the door and lifted my right arm until the SIG's barrel pressed against his forehead. Black eyes met my rage.

"Ley, I need to get you out of here. Come, I will explain later."

"I'm not going anywhere with you, Gabriel." I pushed the barrel harder into his skin, he made no attempt to move.

"Please, I beg you. Aidan got away, and he left a note. He's coming after you and will take out anyone in his way, he even mentioned Lizzie by name. It's no longer safe for either of you in Marcel."

Aidan left no note, he was out of the house before I reached my car. Who wrote the note?

The wheels of Aidan's plan started spinning and now it was time for me to play my part. The words he had whispered to me the night before held all the truth my heart knew. He had proof of his innocence. Footage of the men who installed hidden cameras in our house and his office.

In front of me stood one of the two men who had framed my husband for murder. The other shared my sister's bed. In the world in which Gabriel and Eli operated, they forgot they were not the only black-ops specialists. How Ryan Walker connected into that world, Aidan hadn't had time to explain to me. He did show me the footage of the day the moving company's workers loaded our belongings into the back of the truck, how they tampered with our belongings during the drive. While we were running around unpacking, they had installed their own hidden cameras not realising our home already had state-of-the-art toys.

After the attempt on Gabriel's life, staged as Aidan and I had both known, he had installed cameras in his office, knowing what would inevitably happen.

"Aidan will never hurt me."

"Perhaps not you, but we can't be sure that he won't hurt Lizzie or Ashley or even Hope. Fin, I told you from the beginning, he's a killer. We need to go. Now."

Aidan would never hurt those closest to me, but I feared whoever orchestrated this whole set up would not stop until they had erased him from my life.

We knew who acted as the muscle but not yet the brains. Aidan would not rest until he identified the Puppet Master and put a bullet between his eyes. If I'm lucky, I will be there to witness it, if Aidan doesn't allow me to pull the trigger. We had a slight argument about this once, and had decided we would leave it up to the coin we hadn't used since we got married.

Who is the Puppet Master? That was a question Aidan will risk his life to answer. I reminded myself of what he had said and focused my attention on the target. The one standing in front of me. *Time for the biggest hunt of your life, Finley Walker.*

"Take me to Lizzie's." I lowered the gun, keeping it in my hand.

"Give me your phone first."

I did and watched him stomp it to pieces on my porch.

Ari held the car door open for me, and I felt nausea rise as

I got in. *Eye on the target.*

He loaded my luggage into his vehicle as I composed myself and did my best to keep my game face in place. This was not the time to make Ari bleed. Or Gabriel.

As he shifted the gear lever into reverse, I couldn't keep it back anymore. I pushed the door open and bile exited my body.

"Are you okay? I realise this must be scary for you to go through but, Ley, I'm here and I won't let anything happen to you or Lizzie."

"I'm pregnant, you idiot."

He turned to face me, a light in his dark eyes I had never seen before. "You're pregnant?" His teeth exposed as he asked, and his lips remained pulled back.

"Did you not hear me?"

He reached for my hand, and I let him take it. *Bait your prey.* "The baby is mine."

"What?" His abrupt statement caught me off guard. If not so nauseas, I might have used a few very unladylike words.

"I switched his sperm with mine." Gabriel sneered.

I shook my head. "You did what?"

Never before did I want to kill him as much as I did sitting there listening to him boast. I tightened my grip on the SIG still clutched in my other hand.

"I love you too much to let you go through the pain of having a child with a serial killer. You have devoted your life to hunting them down, how would you one day explain that to your child?"

"So you thought it was your right to father a child with me?"

"You're confused and perhaps even angry now, but one day you will realise I did this because I love you."

No, Gabriel, I'm not confused. Perhaps about your real name, but I warned you. "How did you know we were going for IVF?"

Lizzie would never have divulged our secret, not even to Eli.

He offered me no answer.

"Just drive." I made a mental note. For every lie I would catch him out on ,and for every day I was forced to spend away from Aidan, I would make Gabriel suffer.

Perhaps the Chinese were on to something with lingchi. A thousand cuts might not be enough.

Gabriel phoned Tom as he turned onto the main road leading to the city. For my benefit, he used the built-in Bluetooth system.

"Did you get Finley?" Tom asked.

"Yes, heading to Lizzie's right now."

"We tracked the helicopter; Aidan wasn't in it."

I kept my face devoid of any emotion; I wanted to laugh at their idiocy. *He's always ten steps ahead of you, you piece of excrement.*

"Finley, you're in danger, so is everyone connected to you. The note Aidan left was very explicit in what he intends to do. Ari, it's time to initiate operation Alphas."

How original. I stifled a yawn.

"Did you inform Eli?" Ari asked.

"No, will phone him now. I will contact you once you're settled, everything has been prepared for their arrival. Finley, sweetie, I'm sorry things have turned out this way," Tom said with his forked tongue; how forked, I didn't know. Not yet.

He ended the call and Gabriel reached for my hand, but I pulled away from him.

"What is operation Alphas? And don't you dare lie to me."

"It's an extraction plan to get you and Lizzie out of Marcel. We set it up in case Aidan avoided arrest."

"Was Captain Taylor briefed on your extraction plan?" I tried to read his face. I wanted to ask when they had masterminded their plan, but I didn't have the energy for more of his lies.

"No."

It didn't sound like he was lying. They had no reason to involve the police in their plan, whatever they were up to; it wasn't for legal reasons or my and Lizzie's protection.

I listened as he spoke to Eli in English, again for my benefit. He knew I understood Hebrew, and I wondered if they had known about Lizzie's lessons.

Twenty-seven

Lizzie stormed out of her front door as I exited Gabriel's SUV. He ran past her without as much as acknowledging her. I rushed to her and grabbed hold of her.

"Finley, what's going on? Eli said Aidan killed people, and he's on the run and he made threats against us." Her hands trembled in mine as she tried to control her breathing.

"Lizzie, you and I…" I pulled her into my arms, and as Aidan had whispered truth, hope, and a war plan to me, I did the same for her. She shook her head; her tears soaked my shoulder.

A black SUV came to a stop two houses up the street. Lizzie's phone rang. She stood so close that I heard his every word. My soul ached for him, for us. I wondered what he would do once he learned what Gabriel had done.

"Lizzie, listen to me. I'm sorry for all of this. Fin will explain everything to you. Please take care of her and our child."

Questions dried up her tears as she stared at me, my eyes still on the SUV. "Aidan, what's going on?"

"Nothing is what it seems, Lizzie, Finley will explain it to you. No matter what happens, you two stick together. Or rather I should say, you four. Sorry for telling you like this, I got the text message from the lab a few minutes ago."

"I am?"

"Yes. Congratulations. Liz, I…"

Eli and Gabriel ran out of the house, guns drawn.

"Bye, Lizzie, tell Finley and my baby I love them."

The black SUV made a U-turn and raced off. Shots filled the suburban quiet, but not a single bullet entered the armoured vehicle. *You have no idea who you're up against, you fools.*

Lizzie stared at them as they ran after the vehicle and asked me, "How did they know?"

"Your phone has been bugged, I don't know for how long." I took it from her hand and crushed it into the grass. "They are not who we thought, but Aidan has a plan. You and I need to stick together, and I promise I will tell you everything. But, Lizzie, we need to take care of each other if we are going to survive this."

"I'm pregnant, Fin." She shook her head, her body trembling. "It's impossible, I take my pill every single day."

I didn't tell her what I suspected Eli had done. Her life was about to change forever. "It isn't one-hundred percent effective. Lizzie, Ari believes my baby is his. Did you tell him we were going for IVF? Or did you tell Eli?"

"Of course not, you asked me not to, and I kept my promise. How can your baby be his?"

I said I would tell her later, when we got to wherever the destination of operation Alphas was. *Internal eye-roll*. Could they not come up with a better name? Aidan and I spent mere minutes naming our war plan – Deception.

"I can't leave Williams Pharmaceuticals. Fin, I realise this is worse for you, but this can't be happening."

I waited for the men to run past us again and back into the house before I answered her. "Don't worry about Williams Pharmaceuticals, Nathan won't let anything happen to it. I'm beginning to better understand the family I married into. I promise you, as long as they have our backs, we will be safe. For now, we need to stick together and let Aidan take care of this. I won't let him risk his life for nothing."

"What's the plan?" Her face sobered, reminding me the same blood coursed through our veins.

"Divide and conquer."

"Meaning?" She pulled her shoulders back, fire filled her eyes, burning to the same degree as mine.

"If we go with Ari and Eli, or whoever they are, Aidan has two less threats to worry about and he can figure out who is behind all of this. It's not just me being targeted through

Aidan, but you as well. Eli might tell you about a note, but Aidan didn't write it, he was out of the house before I even got in my car and he will never do anything to hurt us."

We both watched as Gabriel and Eli loaded the last of their suitcases into the back of the SUV. I led Lizzie further away from them. "Liz, we need to figure out what's going on, from our end of this. Ari has been relentless in his pursuit of me. Why didn't he want to move out of your house? Eli has been constantly working since we got back from Vietnam."

"I'm pregnant with *his* child. He listened in on my conversation with Aidan; Eli knows." She rubbed her hands over her stomach. "I'm pregnant."

I hugged her close. "That's all the more reason why they won't hurt us. During Ari's sessions with Doctor James he expressed his desire for a family of his own. I don't think it formed part of his cover as he had no idea the case he worked on was linked to Doctor James or that there would be recordings I would one day see. Lizzie, the sooner we figure this all out the sooner we can return to Marcel and continue with our lives. Raise our children here."

A door slammed; Lizzie started trembling again. I pulled her into my arms and reminded her we could get through anything as long as we had each other.

"Liz, honey, you need to pack. The sooner we leave the better. We need to go." Eli called out to us.

Before she left my side, I told her to pack her guns, even the unregistered ones I had given to her weeks before.

We passed the city limits. Darkness lay ahead of us, far darker than the storm which approached from the south. Neither a match for the destructive rage festering inside me. *Hello, old friend.*

My hand rubbed over my belly, the slight bump a reminder of life and the future.

My reason to fight.

Gabriel and whoever he worked for thought they were the

best at the deceitful games they played, but Aidan will always be ten steps ahead.

It's rather simple. Aidan had booked his sperm and my eggs in under pseudonyms the day of the egg retrieval.

Gabriel impregnated nothing.

For the time being it was best Ari, Gabriel, or whatever I decide to call him when I slice him scrotum to thyroid, continued to believe the baby was his. He would love this child and that love I will use to sweeten my revenge.

Lizzie took my other hand as she, too, rubbed her belly.

The back of the heads of the men in front of us begged for bullets, but I had promised Aidan I would play my part. His sacrifice to keep me and *our* child safe would not be in vain. *How does Tom factor into all of this?*

The day would come when those who orchestrated this would pay with their lives. One by one we will hunt them down and they will suffer a fate far worse than anyone who has ever crossed my path. As soon as we reach our destination, I will contact Aidan using the satellite phone he had left in my GLE when he first surprised me with it.

Apart, yet united, Aidan and I stepped into an unknown war. There is nothing we won't do to protect our life, Lizzie, and our child.

Time to embrace the pull of the darkness we both fought against daily.

I glanced down at the apex predator tattooed on my wrist. Time to embrace who I am. *This is war.*

I pity the fool who underestimates Aidan and Finley Walker.

Acknowledgements

To my family and friends - for their unwavering support and belief in my imagination and ambition.

My first pass readers - Annelize, Maricka, Marie, Naomi, Nicolina, Tania, and Yolanda. Thank you for loving Finley and Aidan as much as I do.

Megan Pereira, my editor. You do so much more for me than only better my writing.

Marcel Koortzen, thank you for allowing me use of your name, and also for being the last pair of eyes.

A special thank you to Dr AK de Bruin for allowing me to base Dr Carl Brown on him. Also to Dr JJ Odendaal for helping me kill off a character when whipping wouldn't be enough.

To my husband for loving me no matter how dark my thoughts, or questionable my internet search history for this specific book.

Most of all, to God. All I can offer in gratitude is my life.

All mistakes are my own.

About the author

Mariëtte Whitcomb studied Criminology and Psychology at the University of Pretoria. An avid reader of psychological thrillers and romantic suspense novels, writing allows her to pursue her childhood dream to hunt criminals, albeit fictional and born in the darkest corners of her imagination.

When Mariëtte isn't writing, she reads or spends time with her family and friends.

Visit www.mariettewhitcomb.com or find her on Facebook or Instagram.

www.ingramcontent.com/pod-product-compliance
Lightning Source LLC
Chambersburg PA
CBHW020059180626
46812CB00006B/2397